THE WOMAN WHO WORE ROSES

THE WOMAN WHO WORE ROSES

A Joe Court Novel

BY

CHRIS CULVER

ST. LOUIS, MO

Other books by Chris Culver

To Heidi, the best mother I know.*

*Sorry, Mom.

.

1

My cold-weather uniform felt stiff, and my utility belt's bulk made it impossible to get comfortable on my old cruiser's front seat no matter how I shifted my body, but at least I wasn't outside. That morning, my boss had put me on the speed trap, an unbroken stretch of straight pavement between the town of St. Augustine and I-55. On most occasions, I wouldn't have minded giving people tickets. If you were driving seventy miles an hour in a thirty-five-mph zone, you deserved a ticket. In this case, though, somebody on the St. Augustine County Council had planted a bush in front of the sign where the speed limit had dropped from fifty-five to thirty-five. Locals knew to put on their brakes, but the tourists oftentimes flew past it without slowing down. The county was lucky that no one had sued yet. Or shot at the officer with the ticket book.

I drummed my fingers on the steering wheel and watched the readout on my speed gun as an SUV approached. Crinkled and dry leaves flew behind it.

42

The moment the driver saw my cruiser, she slammed on the brakes so hard the front of her vehicle dipped. I waved and smiled at her. She gave me the surprised and somewhat fearful look I would have expected from a kid caught with his or her hand in the candy jar.

It was late fall, and the leaves were changing color,

drawing the tourists from St. Louis, Kansas City, and every place in between. At this time of year, thousands of people stayed in our bed and breakfasts, hiked the trails that crisscrossed the county, drank at our wineries overlooking the Mississippi River, and spent money on overpriced food and drinks at our restaurants. Where our Spring Fair brought in tourists and families of all social classes and ages, the tourists in the fall tended to be older and wealthier. Most were normal couples and families looking for a relaxing weekend, but others came to have their baser needs met—and the business leaders of St. Augustine County were always happy to satisfy those with coin to spend.

The next two cars rolled by at thirty-nine and then thirty-seven miles an hour. They didn't even bother tapping their brakes as they passed. I leaned back in my seat and closed my eyes, waiting for my speed gun to beep. Instead, my phone rang. I leaned to the passenger seat and looked at the screen before answering.

"Ian, hey," I said, glancing at my watch. It was a little after nine. "Go to school. You can call me tonight."

"I get the morning off because of the class I'm taking at SLU."

Ian was my half-brother. He was fifteen and smarter than anyone I knew. Even though he was a sophomore, he had tested out of every math class his high school offered. Rather than force him to sit and waste his time, his school let him take more advanced classes at St. Louis University. One day, he'd change the world. For now, he was just trying to survive four years of high school.

"How's it going?"

He grunted.

"It's multivariate calculus, so you know."

I had graduated with honors from the University of Missouri at St. Louis, so I liked to think I was bright. Ian was in a different league, though. Not that I would tell him that.

"If you're having a problem keeping up, make sure you go to your professor's office hours. They'll help you out."

"That's not the problem. I'm bored," he said. "But that's not why I'm calling. What are you doing this weekend?"

I leaned forward and aimed my speed gun at an approaching black sedan.

46

I considered putting on my lights and pulling him over, but the driver had already slowed down. I'd get the next one.

"I was hoping to work on the house," I said. "Why? You want to do something?"

"Kind of," he said. He paused. "So, you know I've got a girlfriend, right?"

"That's what I hear," I said.

He paused. "Well, we've been dating for a year, and we've been talking about spending some time alone together in a bed."

I forced myself to smile so that my tone stayed

pleasant.

"What are you asking me?"

"You've got that whole house," he said. "And you've got the house next door, too. Can we borrow one for two or three hours? We don't have much privacy at home, and we want to do this."

I reached to my coffee and drank a sip.

"Your parents don't give you a lot of privacy because you're fifteen. They're just trying to keep you safe."

"Sarah's sixteen," he said.

"That doesn't help. If you two want privacy, fool around in your car like other teenagers."

"Neither of us has a car," he said. "Sarah has a license, though. Can we borrow your Volvo? It's a station wagon, and the seats fold down, right?"

"Not going to happen. My car is sex-free."

"Sarah and I can fix that," said Ian. He paused. "You're my big sister, and this would mean a lot to me. Don't you want your only brother happy?"

I laughed. "You're not my only brother. And yeah, your happiness matters to me, but your parents don't want you doing this in their house. I plan to respect their wishes and prevent you from doing it in mine."

"You suck," he said. If his tone hadn't been light, that would have bothered me. Instead, I smiled.

"Be grateful your parents are looking after you. They love you and are trying to help you make good decisions."

"But that sucks," he said.

I cocked my head to the side. "Sometimes doing the

right thing sucks."

We settled into an easy silence before he cleared his throat.

"Have you made any progress on Mom?"

I forced myself to cough, giving myself a moment to think. Ian and I didn't know who our biological fathers were, but we shared a biological mom. Ian had loved her completely and absolutely. Erin and I, however, had had a more complicated relationship. Someone had murdered her when Ian was still very young. The police investigated, but they never closed the case. To them, Erin Court was just another victim in a city full of tragedy, but to Ian, she was perfect—or nearly so. My brother was smart and driven enough to do anything with his life, but he'd waste his talent if he let Erin's death drag him down. I couldn't let him do that.

"I'm working it in my free time," I said. "It's a tough case, though. I haven't made a lot of headway."

"Are you really working it, or are you just saying that?"

I adjusted my speed gun so that it pointed in a more easterly direction.

"It's a tough case."

"But it's not a tough question," he said. "Are you trying to find out who killed her or not?"

"I've got her file," I said. "I told you I'd look into it."

"Are you looking into it or not?" he asked. "Yes or no. Everybody tells me to act like an adult, but they treat me like a kid. I'm tired of it. I just want a simple answer.

Have you started investigating Mom's murder?"

I sighed and tilted my head to the side. "I haven't had time yet."

"Then what the hell are you doing?" he asked. "This is our mom. Somebody shot her, and the cops in St. Louis didn't do shit."

"That's not fair," I said, shaking my head. "They assigned a detective to the case, and she spent a week on it. She busted her ass, but she couldn't close it. That happens sometimes."

"Bullshit," he said. "If she worked so hard, why couldn't she find anything?"

He had every right to be mad, but Ian had a tendency to take that anger out on everyone around him. My face grew warm, and I gripped my phone tight.

"Sometimes you just don't get lucky, Ian. That happens."

"Is that what your boyfriend said, too? Or were you two too busy bumping uglies to bother doing your jobs?"

I narrowed my eyes and shook my head.

"Stop talking. You can get away with saying a lot of things because you're a kid, but that's out of line. Mathias isn't my boyfriend, and even if he was, it wouldn't matter. He's a professional. He reviewed her case and determined he couldn't solve it without new information. End of story."

Ian paused, but when he spoke, I could hear the hurt in his voice.

"She's my mom, and nobody even cared about her.

They just threw her away like garbage."

Before I could say anything, my phone buzzed. I pulled it from my ear so I could see the caller ID.

"They did their best. Trust me. I've reviewed the work. They didn't half-ass this case."

"But they didn't—"

My phone buzzed again.

"Ian, we'll have to talk later," I said, interrupting him. "I'm at work, and my dispatcher's calling. Go study."

"That's what you always tell me," he said.

"I know, and I'm sorry. I'll talk to you later."

I hung up before he could say anything else. Then I drew in a deep breath to calm myself down before answering my other call.

"This is Joe Court. What's up?"

"Hey, Joe," said Trisha Marshall, our dispatcher. "Good news. You're off the speed trap. We've got a body at the Wayfair Motel. A housekeeper found her while she was cleaning rooms. Emily Hayes is the first responder. She's there with Kevin Owens right now."

I grimaced and reached to my utility belt for a notepad on which I wrote down the time.

"What do we know so far?"

"Very little," said Trisha. "Darlene and Kevius are driving there now, but Dr. Sheridan's at a car accident out in Perry County."

"Tell Emily I'm on my way," I said, reaching to my shoulder to put on my belt. "And tell the boss he'll need somebody else for the speed trap."

"Good luck, Joe."

"Thanks, Trisha."

I hung up, scanned the road for traffic, and then pulled out. I wasn't far from the crime scene, so the drive didn't take long. The Wayfair Motel was on the edge of St. Augustine County near I-55. White paint peeled off the second-story balcony in big strips, exposing the black wrought iron beneath, while weeds grew in deep cracks in the asphalt parking lot out front. Two police cruisers had parked by the curb near the office. Officer Emily Hayes sat on one car's hood. Sergeant Bob Reitz sat beside her. Kevius and Darlene, our forensic technicians, had yet to arrive.

I nodded good morning to my colleagues. Bob stood.

"Morning, guys," I said. "You look tired, Emily. How long have you been on duty?"

She thought and then sighed. "Going on nine hours now, ma'am."

Though I tried not to grimace, I hated it when people called me ma'am. I was twenty-eight years old. If she wanted to call me anything, she could have called me Joe.

"We'll get you home as soon as we can," I said. "What have we got?"

She pulled a notepad from her utility belt.

"A body. The hotel's manager—Ryan Aziz—called us at 7:50 and said that one of his maids had discovered the body of a Caucasian female in a room they had thought was vacant."

I started to ask how a woman ended up in a vacant

room, but Bob beat me to it. I gritted my teeth but said nothing.

Bob was a good cop with a lot of experience on the job, but this was my case. Even though we were talking to a colleague, this was still an interview, and like every conversation, a good interview had a flow, a pattern of highs and lows. If I increased the pace of an interview, the person I was talking to would have less time to think about his or her answers. He'd give me his first impressions. If I forced a pause into a conversation, the person I was talking to would oftentimes try to fill that void. Sometimes he'd say things he didn't mean to say, or he'd give me details he didn't know he remembered. If Sergeant Reitz butted into the conversation, I couldn't do my job.

Emily looked at me and then to Sergeant Reitz.

"A couple checked in yesterday afternoon, but the male guest left after two hours. Mr. Aziz assumed the female guest had left, too. The maid—Portia Marlowe— knocked on the door at seven this morning, but no one answered. She opened the door, heard the shower, and left.

"Fifty minutes later, she returned to the room to apologize for intruding. No one answered her repeated knocks, so she let herself in again. The shower was still going. Fearing that a guest might have had a heart attack or another medical emergency, or that a guest had left the shower on before leaving, she walked toward the bathroom and found the door open. A young woman was in the shower with multiple gunshot wounds to her torso. Ms. Marlowe exited the room, ran to the front office, and told Mr. Aziz what she had found. He called us."

I'd have to talk to Aziz and Marlowe, but it sounded as if Emily had interviewed them well. I looked up.

"What time did you get here?" I asked.

Emily looked at her notepad. "Mr. Aziz called the office at 7:51. I arrived at 7:58. The victim was unresponsive. I turned off the shower and checked her pulse, but she was dead. I called in the body at 8:01."

Bob rubbed his chin with the tip of a pen.

"Did you touch anything inside?" he asked.

Once more, I ground my teeth together at the interruption, but Emily didn't give me a chance to say anything to my partner.

"The front door, the shower curtain, and the victim's wrist to see whether she had a pulse," she said. "I had to pull the shower curtain back to see the body. The victim had multiple injuries to her torso, but the shower had washed away the blood."

"When you felt her wrist," I said, "did the victim's arm move, or was she stiff?"

"Stiff," said Emily. "I couldn't move it."

So, rigor had set in. Unfortunately, that told me less than it might have under other circumstances. In typical conditions, the body's muscles would lock up somewhere between four and six hours after death, but a warm shower would throw that schedule off. The shower would also change the victim's internal temperature. She had been dead for at least a few hours, but Dr. Sheridan, our coroner, would have his work cut out for him to give us a better estimate than that.

I nodded and wrote a few notes. For the moment, I had what I needed, so I glanced up.

"Word is your oldest just got the lead in the high school's winter play," I said. "That true?"

Emily's shoulders relaxed, and a smile came to her mouth as she nodded.

"Yeah. Morgan will be playing Penelope Sycamore in *You Can't Take It With You*. It will be a fun show."

"Good for her," I said, smiling. Then I drew in a breath and looked to Bob. "Okay. I heard Kevin Owens was here. Where is he?"

"I sent him across the street to see whether they have surveillance video of last night."

The business across the street was a strip club called Club Serenity. St. Augustine County didn't have a lot of organized crime, but the little we had centered on Vic Conroy, the club's owner. He owned a lot of businesses around town, including the club, the Wayfair Motel, and the largest truck stop for about a hundred miles in either direction on I-55. Unfortunately, his business empire didn't stop there.

Young people—mostly girls but a few boys, too—worked as prostitutes in the enormous parking lot of his truck stop. When they turned eighteen, many of the girls became dancers in his strip club, but between shifts, a good portion of them turned tricks in the Wayfair Motel.

After they grew too old to dance, they either moved on or worked for him in the hotel or his other businesses as housekeepers or office staff. At every step of the way, Conroy earned a cut of the profits. He was a slimeball, and one day, I hoped to send him to prison for the rest of his life. It might be a while, though.

Sending someone to the club was a good idea, but he should have sent Emily. She was a better cop than Owens, and she'd be less distracted than Owens if she happened to run into a topless dancer. It was too late to worry about that now, though, so I nodded.

"When Owens gets back, I want Emily to knock on doors with him and see whether any guests heard shots last night. Bob, you're with me. You'll be my second on this case."

Emily hesitated, but then sighed. "I'll do that, but the clerk already told me they only had seven rooms rented last night, none of which were near our victim's room."

Emily had stretched crime-scene tape over the open door of a first-floor room, so I started toward it before looking over my shoulder at her.

"Then you'll have an easy morning. Good luck."

"Thanks, Joe," she said. "You, too."

Bob and I stopped outside the room, and I used my cell phone to snap pictures of the scene upon our arrival. Someone had pulled the bedspread and sheets from the bed, leaving a bare king-sized mattress on a platform in the middle of the room. A burnished brown leather overnight bag sat atop a round table by the front window. A cream-colored dress adorned with pink roses hung from a hook on the wall. I snapped pictures of everything.

"Pretty dress," said Bob.

"It is," I said, ducking so I could walk beneath the crime-scene tape stretched over the door. "Her bag's nice, too."

I walked into the room and pointed to a purse on the console beside the television.

"Find her wallet and ID," I said. "I'll check out the bathroom."

Bob nodded and got to work, so I walked to the bathroom. The victim's nude body was in the bathtub. She was my age—late twenties—and had blond hair and blue eyes. Even in death, she was beautiful.

Privacy was a right afforded the living, not the dead. As much as I hated to do it, I snapped pictures of her placement in the tub, of the bullet wounds on her chest and abdomen, and of the torn shower curtain. My pictures wouldn't make it to court, but other pictures would. A jury of her peers—male and female—would see every inch of her body and examine her as if she were an object to study rather than a human being. The man or woman who shot my victim stole her life and her dignity. I couldn't even cover her nakedness for fear of damaging the scene and destroying evidence. Nobody deserved that.

I left the bathroom and looked at Bob.

"You find her ID?"

"No," he said, shaking his head and turning toward

her purse. "I found something else interesting, though. She had cash and drugs on her."

I stepped beside him. He pulled a white envelope from her purse with gloved hands and opened it to expose a thick wad of bills.

"I didn't count them yet, but the bills are all hundreds," he said, putting the envelope beside the purse. Then he pulled out a bag full of white pills. "We've also got drugs. There's no prescription information, but I'm guessing it's oxycodone or hydrocodone. She's also got an engagement ring in her purse. It's still in the box."

He pulled out a black velvet-covered ring box and opened it. The ring had a platinum band and a single small diamond. It looked simple, tasteful, and elegant.

"You find a wedding ring, too?" I asked.

He shook his head.

"Nope. The engagement ring is pretty, though. When I asked my wife to marry me, she showed her ring to everybody. Why would our victim hide this?"

I nodded and looked around.

"It's a good question. Keep searching."

He nodded and opened drawers in the dresser and then the end table beside the bed. I went back to the bathroom area. She had folded a bra and panty set on the vanity beside the bathroom door. The undergarments were black lace and pretty. It wasn't underwear one would hide beneath a dress; this was underwear designed for a lover's gaze.

I snapped pictures and then knelt to look in the trash

can.

"I've got wrappers and three used condoms," I said.

Bob ambled toward me and nodded.

"Somebody threw a soda can in the other trash can," he said, glancing toward the bathroom and then turning away. "What are you thinking?"

"You've got eyes," I said. "We've got sexy underwear, an envelope full of cash, a beautiful victim in the Wayfair Motel, and condoms in the trash can. You know what that adds up to."

"So you think she's a prostitute."

"High end, but yeah. It's probably why she hid her engagement ring. She didn't want her client to see it," I said before pausing. "Still, if a john can afford to give a girl an envelope full of cash for the night, why would they stay here instead of somewhere much nicer? And why would she have a baggie full of opioids? Solicitation is a class-B misdemeanor. Trafficking is a major felony."

"I don't know, but if she was a prostitute, Vic Conroy might know her client's name."

I sucked in a breath through clenched teeth.

"Yeah, he probably does. Whether he'll tell us is another matter. I'll talk to him. Find out who rented the room. Our victim's killer fired a gun at least seven times. Five shots hit her, and two hit the wall behind her. Somebody should have heard that. Once you talk to the manager, work with Emily and talk to the guests. While you do that, have Officer Owens photograph every car and every license plate in the parking lot. If you can find a car that's not owned by the other guests, it might belong to our victim."

Bob wrote that down and then glanced up at me. "Anything else?"

"When Darlene McEvoy gets here, tell her I want everything in the room bagged and tagged. Sheets, towels, cups, condoms, condom wrappers, clothes, miniature bottles of shampoo, everything. Then I want every flat surface fingerprinted. And get elimination prints from the staff."

Bob wrote it down and then nodded before looking at me again.

"Even if we find our killer's prints, a defense attorney will argue he could have been in there weeks ago."

"Yep," I said.

"Then why would we bother fingerprinting everything? We're not St. Louis or Kansas City. We've got to use our resources wisely."

Evidently Sheriff Delgado had given Bob the same lecture about our tight budget and limited resources that he had given to me.

"Even if we can't use them in court, fingerprints will give us leverage in an interrogation room. At this stage, we document everything. You never know what'll come in handy later."

He looked around and tilted his head to the side.

"This is a pretty big room, Joe," he said. "It'll take hours. That's not even counting the time it will take to process everything and put it in the system."

"Your point?" I asked, raising my eyebrows.

"I just think there are better uses of our scarce resources."

"Noted," I said. "Now stop wasting both our time and do as I ask."

He straightened. I almost thought he'd salute me.

"Yes, ma'am," he said. He started toward the door, but I cleared my throat before he could get far.

"Hey, Sergeant Reitz," I said. He stopped and looked at me. "You're a good cop, and you know how to work a case. We're playing for the same team. I appreciate that you tell me when you think I'm doing something wrong, but don't get huffy when I disagree with you, and don't interrupt me during an interview again. If you can't work under those conditions, I'll send you home. Clear?"

He nodded but said nothing.

"Thank you," I said.

We both left the room. The morning sunlight was almost shockingly bright compared to the gloom inside. My chest and feet felt heavy, but my mind felt as if it had shifted into overdrive. The woman in that hotel room may have been a prostitute, and she may have dealt drugs, but she didn't deserve to die the way she did. I couldn't change the past and prevent her death, but I'd make sure the person who killed her paid for what he did.

First, though, I needed to identify her. Experience told me that was a taller order than it appeared.

2

I waited for a break in traffic and then darted across the four-lane street to Club Serenity. It was a squat, cinder-block building with exterior walls painted a dark maroon and a parking lot big enough to accommodate semitrailers. A cattle guard and fence separated the property from the public road out front. If there had been a cattle ranch nearby, that would have kept cattle from roaming around the business, but the nearest farm was at least five miles up the road, and they didn't have cows. It made little sense to me, but then Vic Conroy hadn't asked my opinion when he built the place.

Four cars and one police cruiser had parked outside, but the club wouldn't open for several hours. I stopped in the doorway. The room smelled like bleach, and eighties music played over the speakers. Three women mopped the floor at the far end of the room, so I unclipped my badge from my belt, held it up, and whistled to get their attention. They looked at once and nodded hello to me. One pointed to the hallway where Vic Conroy kept his office.

"The boss is already in," she said.

"Thanks," I said, returning my badge to my belt and walking toward the hallway. I was five months shy of my twenty-ninth birthday, young for someone with my position, but I wasn't naïve. Vic Conroy ran a big operation and probably grossed several million dollars a year. Everybody in the county knew he was a crook, but he had sniffed out every investigation we had ever run against him. Nobody was that lucky, which meant he had help from someone in our department. It was disquieting.

Along the way to Conroy's office, I passed two bathrooms and a door to the kitchen. Already someone was inside, prepping vegetables for lunch. As despicable as Conroy was, his kitchen made some of the best food in the county. It wasn't good enough to overcome the ambience and make Club Serenity a desirable spot to grab dinner after work, but it tasted far better than any food in a strip club had a right to taste.

As I neared Conroy's office, I heard men's voices and laughter. Conroy's office door was open, allowing me to see Officer Kevin Owens sitting on a brown leather chair in front of Conroy's desk. He had the remnants of a breakfast sandwich in butcher paper on his lap and a smile on his face. Conroy had something similar in front of him. He noticed me first and glanced up with a smile as he rubbed his hands together to knock off any crumbs.

"Good morning, Detective," he said. "Kevin and I were just talking about your station's renovation."

Owens crumbled the paper on his lap and stood as if I hadn't just caught him enjoying breakfast with a gangster.

"Mr. Conroy," I said, nodding a good morning. I looked to Owens and allowed a measure of sternness into my voice. "Officer Owens."

"I was just here checking out the surveillance video,"

said Owens.

"I see," I said, nodding. "You were watching the surveillance video and an English muffin happened to drop in your lap. It happens."

Owens's expression shifted from one of apprehension to confusion. Conroy leaned forward.

"Would you like a breakfast sandwich, Detective?" he asked. "You say the word, and I'll have Jeremy put something together for you. We've got some thick-cut bacon, and we just got a load of eggs from Ross Kelly Farms."

"I had Red Russian kale on my sandwich," said Owens. "It was great."

"I don't doubt that," I said, smiling at him. "Now that you've eaten breakfast, get out of here."

Owens shifted. "Am I in trouble?"

"Yep," I said. "Now get out of here. We'll talk later."

Owens looked at Conroy. The gangster nodded, and Owens left. I clenched my jaw tight and balled my hands into fists. I doubted Owens would have imperiled an investigation into Conroy on purpose, but he probably was careless enough to do it accidentally over breakfast. We'd have to watch him. That was a worry for later, though. I had other shit on my mind now.

Conroy was in his early fifties, and he had a hard, angular face and wiry muscles beneath his black Oxford shirt. The light reflected off his bald scalp like a mirror. He laced his hands together and leaned forward.

"We were just having breakfast," he said. "Everybody

eats, Joe."

I nodded. "Sure they do. You missing a dancer?"

Conroy considered me and then leaned back and crossed his arms.

"You're referencing the woman you found in my hotel."

"Yeah," I said, reaching for my phone and flipping through the photos until I found one of my victim's face. "Is she familiar?"

Conroy studied my picture but then shook his head. "She's beautiful. I would have loved to have her on staff, but she's not one of mine."

"Look again," I said. "She's a beautiful young woman who frequented your hotel. I don't believe I need to spell this out, but I will. You're a pimp, and I think she was one of your prostitutes. She was probably killed by a john, so it'd be in your best interests to cooperate with me. Your girls wouldn't like it if you stonewalled the detective investigating the death of one of their co-workers. Murder makes people jumpy. If it helps, she last wore a cream-colored dress with pink roses on it."

I held the phone toward him again. Once more, he studied the photograph. Then he leaned back.

"She's not one of mine."

"Then we've got a problem," I said. "Here's what I'm thinking. My victim was a prostitute. If she didn't work for you, she was probably from St. Louis. She came here to meet with a client at your motel. That's your turf, though, and you don't take well to independent operators working out of your business. You watched her with those surveillance cameras outside your club and waited until her client left. Then you killed her to keep your girls from getting ideas about going independent and costing you money."

He gave me a bemused smile. "You've got quite an imagination."

"That's what I'm told. Did you kill her?"

"No," he said, shaking his head. "You got a picture of her dress?"

I cocked my head to the side. "Why does her dress interest you?"

"Just trust me on this, Joe," he said, holding out his hand. "Let me see her dress. You brought it up. That means you think it's important, which means you took a picture."

I sighed and flicked through pictures until I found one.

"Have you seen that dress before?" I asked, holding the phone toward him.

He looked and then shook his head.

"No, but it's a Dolce & Gabbana," he said, shaking his head. "The watch on the counter is a Hermès."

I crossed my arms. "How do you know that?"

He shrugged. "My wife is a seamstress. She designs and sews the costumes for the girls who dance in my club. She likes clothes and has a similar dress. It set me back almost six grand. Her watch goes for about ten. Your victim wear underwear, or did she go commando?"

I took my phone out again and flipped through pictures until I found a suitable one.

"Do you know a lot about women's underwear?"

He nodded and looked at the picture.

"It's La Perla."

"And that's supposed to mean something to me?" I asked, raising my eyebrows.

He sighed. "It means her bra and panties likely set her back four hundred bucks. I've never seen your victim, she doesn't work for me, and she's not a prostitute, but based on the undergarments she chose for the occasion, I'm guessing she came to St. Augustine to make the beast with two backs with somebody special. If it were me, I'd be looking at her husband. He's probably pissed that she's sleeping around on him."

"If you don't know her, how do you know she's married?"

He smiled and blinked.

"How old are you, Joe? Twenty-nine? Thirty?"

"Twenty-eight," I said, straightening my shoulders.

"You've got a lot to learn about the world. As much as I appreciate the guests who stay at my humble motel, I'm not operating the Waldorf. The people who stay at my hotel stay there because they can't go elsewhere."

I raised my eyebrows.

"Your point?"

He leaned forward. "A woman who can afford a six-thousand-dollar dress, a ten-thousand-dollar watch, and four-hundred-dollar underwear could rent a suite at the

Ritz-Carlton in St. Louis if she wanted to stay somewhere nice. She came to my place for its discretion. She's hiding from something. A woman with resources wouldn't need to hide from an ex-husband or boyfriend. She'd have the money to deal with them herself. If she were hiding from the police, she'd put on something unremarkable.

"In that dress and in my hotel, she's hiding from her husband. The underwear tells us she's meeting a lover. That could be a girlfriend, I guess, but she's fucking somebody, and it's not the man who's footing the bill for her lifestyle."

It was conjecture, but he might have been right. I didn't plan to admit that to him, though.

"I know you don't have cameras at your motel, but did the cameras on your club or truck stop catch anything across the street?"

He leaned toward his desk and opened a laptop.

"Officer Owens asked the same thing," he said. "When did your victim die?"

"Yesterday," I said. "We're not sure when yet."

"I've got Kevin's contact information," said Conroy, glancing at me. "Do you mind if I email him the files?"

"That's fine," I said.

Conroy nodded and clicked half a dozen times at his computer before looking to me again.

"And done," he said, smiling.

"Thank you, Mr. Conroy."

"Call me Vic," he said. "And remember what I said when we last met: You ever want a job, I've got a place for you here."

"As a bouncer," I said.

"Real money's in dancing," he said, winking. "If you stay in shape, you'll have a couple of good years left."

I forced a smile to my lips and pretended that he didn't creep me out.

"Thanks again," I said, turning and leaving. I walked across the street to my cruiser and sat in the front seat to make a call. Trisha answered before the phone finished ringing once.

"Hey," I said. "It's Joe. You got a minute?"

"Sure. What's up?"

"I'm working a Jane Doe homicide at the Wayfair Motel. The victim was wearing a Dolce & Gabbana dress. It's beautiful but expensive. Where could you buy that in St. Louis?"

Trisha hesitated.

"I have no idea."

"Do me a favor and find out. I'll text you a picture. If my victim bought it in St. Louis, someone will remember her. The store might even have records. I can't do much until we ID this lady."

"Okay," said Trisha. "I can call around. If I can find anything, I'll let you know."

"Great. Thank you."

I texted her a picture and then looked toward the hotel. Our forensics van had parked out front, and Darlene McEvoy stood outside. She waved and smiled at me. I returned both and then sighed. As much as I appreciated having help, without an ID or a clue why our victim died, this would be a long day for everybody.

3

Mickey Lawson's arms and back ached. He and his colleagues had been digging long enough for the afternoon sun to burn off the morning fog. Miles from any coast, Isle Royale, a forty-five-mile-long island in the northwestern portion of Lake Superior, was the least-visited national park in the United State. To reach the island, tourists had to take a three-and-a-half-hour ferry ride from Copper Harbor, Michigan, and once they reached the park, hikers shared the trails with moose and wolves.

Even in the high season, a visitor could walk all day without seeing another person. In late fall, with the ferries shut down and the park closed for the year, Mickey might as well have been on the moon.

Though it was fifty degrees outside, the physical work had caused him to work up a sweat. He wiped salt out of his eyes and glanced at his partners. Mickey didn't know Adrian and Lukas well, but he trusted them to do their jobs. Their mutual employer would have killed them if they hadn't.

Mickey stuck his shovel deep in the ground, allowing him to lean against the handle. He was on a break. It was Adrian's turn in the hole while Lukas carried buckets full of dirt to their designated pile. The system had allowed them to work uninterrupted for several hours and get their job done while leaving plenty of time to get back to the Houghton County airport before their flights home. He drew in a breath before calling out. "The hole's up to your shoulders. That should be deep enough."

Adrian looked at him from inside the excavated area and nodded.

"Good," said Adrian, nodding and blowing out a slow breath. "I'm tired of digging. If the hole's not deep enough, we'll just break his legs and stick him in."

"Agreed," said Mickey. He helped Adrian out of the hole and waited for Lukas to return with an empty bucket. At six foot three and weighing at least two hundred and twenty pounds, Lukas had played middle linebacker for Wisconsin in college and did well for himself, but he wasn't big or fast enough to play professional ball. His size, though, made him a natural at his present job.

"We ready?" asked the former football player once he put down his bucket.

"Yeah," said Mickey. "Can you carry him yourself, or do you want help?"

Lukas looked to Adrian.

"Give me a hand?"

"Sure," said Adrian.

The two men followed the trail to the beach on which they had moored their boat. Thick, dark forest covered this part of the national park, leaving the area in a perpetual shaded gloom. Brown pine needles and the orange and red leaves of deciduous trees littered the ground. The sound of the lake lapping against the shore carried up from the beach. It was peaceful. There were no roads, track homes, or satellite dishes. This was the United States as seen by its earliest explorers. Mickey liked that.

Lukas and Adrian came back a moment later with Jeff Ellis, their unfortunate former colleague, slung over Lukas's shoulder. Jeff had been part of their organization's distribution chain until he took money that wasn't his. It was a stupid move. Jeff sold prescription drugs to housewives in Glencoe and Winnetka, two very wealthy Chicago suburbs, so he had never worried about being mugged or harassed by rival dealers, and he didn't have to worry about where he'd get his next shipment. He just had to sell the pills provided to him. If he had done his job, he would have had more money than he could spend.

Then, Mickey noticed irregularities in the payments Jeff passed back to him. At first, Jeff had claimed a long-term client had little cash on hand for her regular delivery and promised to pay him back. That happened sometimes, so Mickey let it go. Then it happened again with a different client. After that, Jeff stopped showing up to appointed meetings, and he refused to return Mickey's calls. In better circumstances, Mickey would have just shot him and moved on. Jeff, though, owed his partners almost twenty thousand dollars. That was harder to forgive.

"Is he awake?" asked Mickey.

"Sedated, but yeah," said Lukas, kneeling and shrugging his shoulders so the dope dealer fell to the ground. Jeff's eyes opened and shut like a child who had stayed up past his bedtime. Mickey knelt beside him and slapped him around until his eyes stayed open for a prolonged period.

"Where's my money?" he asked.

"What money?"

Mickey lowered his chin. "You stole from us. I don't care whether you took the pills yourself or whether you stole the money from your clients. Either way, you fucked up. We've got to spend resources to fix your mistake, and we don't enjoy doing that. Where's my money?"

Jeff closed his eyes and looked almost like he was falling asleep. Mickey looked to Adrian.

"You got the stun gun?"

Adrian nodded and pulled a wicked-looking black plastic device from his rear pocket. It had a flashlight at one end and a pair of spiked barbs at the other. A sticker and barcode from the equipment room labeled it the property of the Chicago Police Department.

"This guy sleep with your old lady or something?" asked Adrian, handing the device over. "Punishment seems a little over the top. We could have just shot him and dumped him in the lake to save ourselves the trouble."

"This is coming down from on high. The boss wants this guy to hurt," said Mickey, flicking the switch. The stun gun crackled to life. A blue spark, like a miniature bolt of lightning, formed between the two metal electrodes. The air smelled like ozone, and the charge passed through Mickey's arm and into his elbow despite the insulated grip. He touched it to Jeff's chest. The drug dealer's eyes flew open, and he convulsed on the ground. Lukas laughed just a little.

"I wish the department would let us use these in interrogations," he said. "It'd make my job a lot more fun."

"You're an asshole," said Adrian, snickering.

"Don't I know it?" said Lukas.

Mickey ignored his two partners and focused on the drug dealer. Jeff's eyes shot to each of the three men standing near him. Tears flowed down his cheeks.

"Let me go."

Mickey shook his head. "You stole from the wrong people. If we let you go, it'd set a precedent we can't afford. You're an independent businessman. I'm sure you understand how important it is to set the right tone with your employees."

"I didn't do anything."

Mickey held the stun gun to the drug dealer's chin. Jeff flinched and held his breath, but Mickey didn't turn the device on.

"We both know what you did," he said. He looked to Lukas. "Can you put him in the hole, please?"

"Head up or down?"

Mickey looked to Jeff. "What do you think?"

Jeff trembled. A dark patch had grown on his pants over his crotch where he had pissed himself.

"Let me go."

"Can't do that," he said. He looked to Lukas. "Head

up and facing the east. He can watch the sun rise before he dies."

Jeff tried to kick and fight, but he wore restraints on both his legs and hands. He couldn't even lift his arms. Lukas dropped him into the hole feet first. Jeff was taller than Adrian, so his shoulders would still be out, but that was fine. He had nowhere to go. As soon as Mickey threw in the first shovelful of dirt, Jeff screamed and begged. Mickey tapped him on the back of the head with the flat of his shovel to get his attention.

"You keep screaming, I'll gag you," he said.

"Please let me go."

"He's got a one-track mind, doesn't he?" asked Adrian.

Mickey looked to Lukas. "Get the duct tape and a sock. I'm tired of hearing him."

"Good idea," said Lukas. The big man left, and Mickey and Adrian continued filling in the hole. By the time Lukas returned, they were halfway done. Mickey shoved the sock in Jeff's mouth, covered it with tape, and then wound more tape around his head twice. He could breathe, but he couldn't scream. Not that it would have mattered. They were eighteen miles from shore.

Once they finished, Jeff had dirt up to his armpits. He struggled, but he couldn't move. His bosses wanted it this way. They needed an example of what happened to those who tried to cheat their employers. Mickey snapped half a dozen pictures with a burner cell phone and then emailed them to a second burner phone in his boss's office.

"We're out of here, guys," he said, slipping his phone into his pocket. "We should still be able to make our flight back home."

"Have fun, buddy," said Lukas, looking to Jeff. "And if you get thirsty, just tilt your head back when it rains. Maybe some water'll seep behind the tape."

That didn't seem to bolster the drug dealer's spirits. They left him there and walked back to the beach where they had docked the boat they rented in Copper Harbor, Michigan. The ride back was pleasant but cold. About halfway to the marina, Mickey put his burner cell phone and two big rocks in a Ziploc bag. He tossed the bag along with their shovels and other equipment overboard into Lake Superior. The tools had fulfilled their purpose and would only draw attention now.

They reached the marina a little over two hours after leaving the park. Mickey used his actual cell phone to request a car that would take them to the airport. Then he noticed a series of text messages from his mom. He looked at his partners and held up his phone.

"This is important," he said. "Give me a minute."

The two men nodded, and Mickey walked down the dock for some privacy. His mom answered her phone before it finished ringing once.

"Mom," he said. "I'm way out in the middle of nowhere and didn't have cell reception until a few minutes ago. I got your texts. What's going on?"

"It's your sister. I can't get in touch with her."

Mickey brought a hand to his hip and raised an eyebrow.

"Did you call Carl?"

"He said he hasn't seen her for almost two weeks."

Mickey sighed and nodded. Tessa and Carl may have loved each other at one point, but their marriage had long ago dissolved into a business relationship.

"I'm in Michigan. I can't do anything, Mom."

"Tessa cares about you," she said, almost pleading. "The last time we talked, Tessa and I had a fight. Her mind's been in the clouds lately, and she takes days to answer my calls. She didn't used to do that. When I asked her what was going on, she blew me off. Something's going on with her. I'm worried she's using again."

That was a problem for multiple reasons. Mickey nodded and ran a hand across his face as he thought.

"I'll see whether I can get in touch with her. If she won't talk to me, I'll see her in person."

"Thank you, honey. I knew I could count on you. You're a good brother."

"Sure," said Mickey. "She's my sister. I've got to watch out for her. Listen, though, I've got to go. I'll talk to you later."

He told his mom he loved her and then called his sister. Her phone went to voicemail.

"Tessa, it's Mickey. Mom's worried about you. I'm working now, but if I don't hear from you by the time I reach Chicago, I'm coming down to see you."

He hung up and slipped his phone into his pocket

before joining his partners on the other end of the dock. "Everything okay?" asked Adrian. Mickey nodded. "I hope so. One of our couriers has gone missing. I think I'll be going to St. Louis to find her."

4

After interviewing Vic Conroy at Club Serenity, I walked back to the Wayfair Motel and interviewed the manager. He didn't know my victim's name, although he had seen her before. The man who rented the room claimed his name was Benjamin Franklin and paid the bill in cash. When I asked for a copy of the hotel-goer's ID, the manager produced a sheet of paper with a black square in the middle.

"Sorry. This is the best we've got," he said. "It's not the best copy machine in the world."

I nodded. "Does Benjamin Franklin stay here a lot?"

He typed at his computer and then nodded.

"He has a history at the hotel."

"How about George Washington and Thomas Jefferson? They stay here, too?"

The manager's eyes narrowed as he considered me.

"What are you implying?"

I leaned forward to look him in the eye. "I'm just wondering why you rented a room to a dead president, why you allowed that dead president to pay for it in cash, and then why you didn't bother taking a decent copy of his ID. Have you heard the term 'accomplice liability' before?"

He seemed to think for a moment. Then he crossed his arms.

"I bet my lawyer has."

I nodded and pushed away from the front desk. "That's true. Ask him about it and then call me."

"Is there anything else I can do for you, Detective?"

"Yeah, but you work for a criminal. You won't help me," I said. "If I can give you some advice, though, be careful. Men and women who work for Vic Conroy die young."

He began to say something, but I left the office before he could finish. Dr. Sheridan, the coroner whom St. Augustine County shared with several surrounding counties, stood outside his van near the victim's room. He nodded to me and snapped on a pair of gloves.

"Hey, Joe," he said. "How's life treating you?"

"The hotel manager's a dick, I caught one of my officers eating with a gangster instead of interviewing him, and my little brother wants to borrow my house this weekend so he can lose his virginity in peace."

Dr. Sheridan nodded and tilted his head to the side.

"Sounds like the house thing would be a good cause at least."

I grunted and looked at the room.

"Have you checked out my victim yet?"

"Yep," he said, nodding. "Come in. I'll walk you through things so far."

The two of us walked into the hotel room and found Darlene McEvoy dusting a tabletop for prints. I nodded hello to her.

"You find anything yet?"

"Lots of prints," she said. "It'll take us a while to

process everything. As per your request, we've bagged the sheets, towels, and toiletry items in the bathroom. We've also bagged the condoms from the trash can near the bathroom and the soda can from the trash can near the front door. We'll run DNA on the condoms and see what we can find. The soda might have prints on it, so we it's possible we could ID your perp right away."

I grunted. "I never get that lucky."

The corners of her lips turned upward in a tight smile as she continued to work. Dr. Sheridan and I walked to the bathroom. The victim was still in the tub, although someone had turned her onto her side.

"Water was off when you arrived, wasn't it?" he asked.

I nodded. "The first responder turned it off. She thought it was washing away evidence."

"It may have been," he said. "I wish she hadn't, though. I checked the victim's liver temperature when I got here. It was 101.8. Without knowing the temperature of the water she was in, I can't use her temperature to figure out her time of death. I'm guessing she died at least fourteen hours ago based on her lividity."

That made her time of death before ten in the evening yesterday.

"How sure are you about that?" I asked.

He tilted his head to the side and considered. "Not very. If you want a range, I'd say she died somewhere between ten and eighteen hours ago. The water makes things tough to figure."

I tried to keep the grimace from my face. "You can't narrow that down?"

"I don't know what temperature the shower water was, and I don't know whether the temperature stayed constant the entire time she was in the shower. Given the circumstances, you should appreciate an eight-hour window."

I stepped back.

"I was asking a question, not offering a critique."

For a split second, Sheridan's expression hardened, but then his shoulders dropped. He sighed and raised his eyebrows.

"Sorry. I'm tired. I picked up three suspected overdoses in the past twenty-four hours, so I've been getting calls from inconsolable family members all night. That's on top of the family of four I picked up in Perry County two days ago. That one's a murder-suicide. Husband got laid off and killed his wife and kids... It's been a rough few days."

"It sounds like it," I said, nodding.

"Yeah," he said, breathing in. He sighed. "Let's talk about your victim. She has no visible birthmarks, tattoos, or other recognizable body modifications. She has three one-inch scars in her hypogastric and right iliac regions. It looks like she had laparoscopic surgery, probably to remove her appendix. If that's the case, she could have had it at any major hospital in the United States. I can't see any other signs of surgery."

"And none of that will allow us to identify her."

He nodded.

"I can't give you an official cause of death until I cut her open, but she has five gunshot wounds to her chest. I'll get to her when I can, but at the moment, I've got so many bodies, I've had to rent morgue space at a funeral home in Perry County."

"Just do your best, Doc," I said. "That'll be enough. I'll be out of town tomorrow, but call me if you need me."

He nodded and straightened. Then he gave me a strained smile.

"Tomorrow's the big day, huh?"

I hadn't realized news of my upcoming meeting had spread far and wide, but I nodded.

"Yeah. I'm not looking forward to it. How'd you hear about it?"

"You're the only famous detective in this part of the state. People talk," he said. "I won't wish you luck because you don't need it. You'll do well."

"Thank you. I appreciate that."

He nodded and then returned to work. I walked back to the office, where I was greeted by Mr. Aziz, the manager, who was triumphantly holding up his phone.

"I looked up accomplice liability," he said. "To prove that I was responsible for the conduct of the person who murdered that woman, you'd need to prove that I aided or agreed to aid the killer in the planning or committing of the murder."

I raised my eyebrows. "That sounds about right."

"I rented a hotel room," he said, smiling. "They come here to screw behind their spouses' backs. I didn't know he planned to kill her. You can't charge me with shit."

I considered him and then nodded. "You're well read and articulate for the manager of a cheap motel."

"Thank you," he said, winking. "You're not ugly for a cop."

I looked down at the counter. "When I spoke to you before, you said Benjamin Franklin came to the desk alone. Then you said *they* came here to get away from *their* spouses. You're holding back on me."

"I was speaking in generalities," he said. "Men *like him* come here to escape their wives. I hadn't seen him before."

"I see," I said, nodding. "If you change your mind, you know where to find me. Also, I need to talk to the staff."

"They're busy."

I nodded as if I understood. "Tell you what, then. How about I just shut the entire hotel down? I'm not sure what happened to my victim. It looks as if she died in the shower, but maybe someone shot her in the parking lot and she crawled into the shower. Maybe someone shot her in the office. You can clean up blood spatter if you know what you're doing. She could have died anywhere on this property. As evasive as your answers are, maybe I should take a more aggressive and expansive posture here. What do you think? Should I consider the entire building a crime scene and obstruct your business more than I already am, or do you want to cooperate and minimize the intrusion?"

He licked his lips. "You can talk to them while they work. We've all got shit to do. This place doesn't shut down just because one of our guests offed another."

"That'll be fine."

He pulled a walkie-talkie from beneath the desk and told the staff I planned to talk to them. Then, I went from room to room talking to the housekeeping and maintenance staff members. Several of them had seen my victim before, but none knew her name.

Occasionally she came to the hotel alone, but usually she came with a man. Everyone described him as having brown hair and being in his early thirties. He was fit and somewhere around six feet all. Sometimes he and his partner arrived together in a single car. Other times, they took separate vehicles. Nobody remembered much about the cars. Interviewing them hadn't been a waste of time, but it was pretty close.

We sealed the room at about four in the afternoon. Theoretically, we could go back in at a later time and collect any evidence we had missed, but for all intents and purposes, we had finished with it. Unfortunately, that meant I had spent hours on a murder and was no closer to identifying my victim than I had been when I had started. That was frustrating.

I left the motel and drove to my station. The St. Augustine County Sheriff's Department worked out of an old Masonic temple the county had purchased when the

Masons left town. The building was gorgeous, but the roof and windows leaked, the basement almost always smelled moldy, and the heating and air system struggled to keep the building comfortable on even mild days. To remedy that, the County Council had issued bonds and hired a major commercial contractor from St. Louis for a top-to-bottom renovation. In six to nine months, we'd have a comfortable, modern police station. Until then, we had the second floor of a noisy, cramped construction zone.

I parked and went upstairs to the storage room that had become my office for the duration of the construction. There, I filled out paperwork for the next two hours before driving home.

When he heard my car drive in, Roy, my dog, came bounding from the backyard. Roy was half Labrador, half Chesapeake Bay retriever and weighed about a hundred and ten pounds. He was lazy but loyal. We hadn't lived together long, but we had become fast friends. Seeing him made the weight of the day leave my shoulders just a little.

"Want to go for a walk, hon?"

At the mere mention of the word *walk*, he almost jumped. If a dog could grin, he did. I changed into comfortable clothes, walked the dog, and then made dinner. Before going to bed that night, I had a couple of drinks to calm my nerves.

I would have preferred to stay in St. Augustine to work my case, but I had a prior engagement I couldn't cancel. Tomorrow morning, I would drive to Terre Haute,

Indiana, where I'd meet an FBI agent who would escort me to the United States Penitentiary outside town. There, I would start negotiations with a serial murderer who, for some reason, refused to talk to anybody but me.

Already, my hands trembled, and I felt sick to my stomach.

5

Roy and I left the house the next morning at a little after six. I didn't know how long the Bureau would keep me, and I didn't want to put Roy in a kennel overnight, so I dropped him off at my parents' house in Kirkwood, an inner-ring suburb of St. Louis. Then I drove about three hours to Terre Haute, Indiana.

Since I didn't know the town well, I used the GPS on my phone to lead me to a Denny's, where I planned to meet Special Agent Bryan Costa. He was already inside when I arrived, sitting at a table with a woman I didn't recognize. She was in her mid-forties and had blond hair with dark roots, a rounded face, and faint wrinkles around her mouth and at the corners of her narrow green eyes. Her expression was ugly, but she was pretty.

I walked toward the table and smiled at them both. Agent Costa stood when he saw me and held out his hand.

"Good to see you, Joe," he said, shaking my hand. "You're early."

"You are, too," I said. I smiled at the woman, but she didn't return the look. Then I focused on Agent Costa. "And it's good to see you, too, Bryan."

The woman stood.

"Special Agent Philippa Cornwell," she said, holding out her hand. "You must be Detective Court."

"It's nice to meet you, Agent Cornwell," I said,

shaking her hand.

"Agent Costa and I just ordered brunch. Have a seat, and we'll get started."

She sat and pulled files from her briefcase. Agent Costa looked to me and then raised a hand toward a young woman talking to people at another table. She nodded and smiled at him.

"You should order something to eat," he said. "There's no food at the prison."

"Sure," I said, sitting and browsing the menu. I ordered a ham and egg sandwich with hash browns and coffee and then laced my fingers together on the table while Agent Cornwell looked through her files.

"Philippa is from DC," said Costa. "She's with our Behavioral Analysis Unit. They work on the grisly stuff."

"That sounds exciting," I said, looking to her and smiling. Her lips were thin and straight. Her eyes looked cold. I didn't know what I had done to piss her off, but she closed her eyes and drew in a slow breath.

"Contrary to what you see on television, it's not that exciting," she said. "And that's by design. We are a support unit that provides our extensive expertise and research in behavioral analysis to active investigative units. We don't work cases, but we study them so we can learn how aberrant criminals think. Our goal is to provide expertise and research that allows law enforcement across the country to intervene with at-risk individuals before they commit crimes."

"I see," I said, sitting straighter and nodding. I forced myself to smile. "It's important work."

"It is," she said. "I've read about your work with Glenn Saunders."

Saunders was a serial murderer who had worked in Missouri and several surrounding states. I had killed him and prevented him from hurting anyone else, but he had still killed well over a dozen people before we caught him. It was the hardest case I had ever worked, and, though I was glad to have stopped him, I wished I had never even heard of him.

"I see," I said, nodding.

"You were sloppy, reckless, and erratic," she said. "If you had known what you were doing, you could have arrested Saunders well before he killed all those people."

I forced the smile to stay on my lips even as heat began to build in my chest and neck.

"You're entitled to your opinion," I said, looking to Agent Costa. "You have anything to add?"

Costa sighed and looked to his partner. "Detective Court is here at the request of Director Koch. If you have a problem with Detective Court's involvement, you can take it up with the deputy director."

Cornwell stiffened but said nothing. If I had to guess, she had already talked to Koch about it and been overruled. Maybe it was juvenile, but I liked knowing she had already been rebuked.

"I'm glad we got that out of the way," I said. "Let's talk about this case. What do we want out of this?"

Cornwell slid a manila envelope across the table toward me. I opened the first page to a booking sheet filled out by a detective in Little Rock, Arkansas, upon the arrest of Peter Brunelle.

"I assume you've at least skimmed the file," said Cornwell. "In case you haven't, the man who's asked to speak to you is Peter Brunelle. He's a fifty-four-year-old former stonemason from Hope, Arkansas. In May 2006, he walked into the Southwest Division headquarters of the Little Rock, Arkansas, Police Department on Baseline Road with a cooler."

I had already read the file, so I knew what was coming next. Still, it seemed important to Agent Cornwell that she got to say this, so I said nothing.

"Mr. Brunelle asked to speak to the watch commander. When asked why he needed to speak to the watch commander, Mr. Brunelle opened the cooler and showed the receptionist the heads of three young women."

Cornwell paused and watched me. I didn't know what she expected me to do, so I nodded.

"Okay," I said. "Go on."

She looked back at her notes. "Officers placed Mr. Brunelle under arrest and began an investigation. Within a day, officers in Hope, Arkansas, raided Mr. Brunelle's home and found nothing. Cadaver dogs scoured his property. They found the remains of two of Mr. Brunelle's dogs—both of which had died of natural causes—buried on the property but no human remains.

"When questioned, Mr. Brunelle admitted murdering the women, but he refused to cooperate with the investigation or identify his victims. What does that tell you?"

I raised my eyebrows, unsure whether she wanted me to say anything. When I said nothing, she exhaled out of her nose and looked down at her notes again. She looked satisfied to have shut me up. I didn't appreciate that.

"He wanted something from the police," I said. "That he refused to talk about the heads tells me he hadn't received what he wanted yet, or he wanted to drag the process out. We don't have enough information to speak to his psychological state beyond that. Did you ever identify the victims?"

"Two of them," said Costa. "One was a prostitute from Memphis. The second was a runaway from Houston. We don't know who his third victim was, and he refused to say."

I nodded. "So he chooses victims who are unlikely to be reported missing, and if he killed these three and got away with it, he's probably killed more. Serial murders don't just quit, do they?"

Cornwell shrugged. "Sometimes they do. I've interviewed people who describe killing the same way a nymphomaniac might describe losing her virginity. For people like that, killing fulfills a need rooted in their psychological makeup. They don't stop.

"For others, killing is a fun way to spend a Saturday night, but after a while, the thrill fades. Sometimes they just stop and go on with their lives. About four years ago, we learned about a deceased hospice nurse in

Massachusetts who murdered fourteen of her patients over a five-year period. She was bored at work, so she started killing people and made it look like natural causes. Since she killed hospice patients, nobody investigated. She only stopped because killing people stopped being thrilling. We learned about the case because her husband read her diaries after she died."

I didn't know whether she was trying to impress me or disturb me. Either way, stories didn't bother me, even when they described horrific things.

"It's a wide and varied world we live in," I said. "So is this what you do at the BAU?"

She nodded. "We ask the why questions. Why do these killers kill? What makes them tick? What do they think about? Who are they? By studying violent felons, we hope that we can create generalizable profiles that will help law enforcement officials apprehend men and women like Mr. Brunelle."

She reached to her briefcase and pulled out a stapled stack of papers.

"This is a template for a behavioral interview. I'd like you to go through it with Mr. Brunelle when we get to the prison. It's thorough, but we don't have to answer everything on the first trip."

I flipped through the form. It had twenty or thirty pages of questions. Some focused on his mindset when he chose his victims, while others focused on his childhood and adolescent experiences. Cornwell was right: It was thorough. It was also invasive. I couldn't imagine sitting down with anyone, let alone a serial murderer, and going through it question by question. It'd take forever, but more than that, I didn't want to learn about his masturbatory fantasies or whether he had a loving, stable relationship with his mother.

"I'll do what I can," I said.

Cornwell leaned forward and raised an eyebrow, but before she could say anything, Agent Costa cut in.

"I'd like you to focus on the unknown victim," he said. "Brunelle's asked you to come and visit him. Let's take the opportunity to ID this young woman. Her family deserves it. I'd also like you to ask about other victims. We might learn something."

"I can do that," I said, nodding. "What does Brunelle get for cooperating? A room with a view? Better food? What?"

Costa looked to Cornwell. She leaned forward.

"It doesn't matter what he wants," she said. "He knows he's not getting out, and we can work with just about anything else. If he wants chicken fingers or pizza, we'll bring him chicken fingers or pizza. If he wants more time on the exercise yard, we'll work it out with the warden."

The waitress came with my coffee and a glass of water. She said our food would be out in a minute. Once she left, I focused on Cornwell.

"You're underestimating him," I said. "That's dangerous."

"Really?" she asked, a smile forming on her lips. "Tell

me where I'm wrong, Detective. Use your extensive experience with these sorts of murderers, but remember that for him to get out of prison, he would either need to escape from a facility no one has ever escaped from or to receive a presidential pardon."

"I know he's not getting out, but a deputy director of the FBI asked me to meet you two in a Denny's four hours from my house. I'm here right now instead of working a homicide I picked up yesterday. Brunelle's behind bars, but he's manipulating events outside them. If he can get us to have brunch here, what do you think he can persuade his fan club to do on his behalf? What about his pen pals? Surely he's got some."

"Okay, fine," she said, nodding and leaning forward. "Let's assume Brunelle is some kind of criminal mastermind and that he's engineered this whole thing so we'll meet in this Denny's right now. Let's assume he's got some master plan, and we're all pawns in his great game. So what? The prison's staff monitors his phone calls, they read his mail, and they run background checks on his visitors. He's only allowed to see his family and his lawyer. His family's never showed up, and his lawyer doesn't return his calls. This guy is a total loser. He may have been some kind of pit bull outside prison, but now he's neutered."

Agent Cornwell had a lot of experience at this, and she seemed confident. Still, I couldn't ignore the nagging voice in my head that told me this was stupid. I cocked my head to the side.

"I hear what you're saying, but I'm uncomfortable with this," I said. "A serial murderer shouldn't be able to summon me on a whim."

Costa smiled.

"If you felt comfortable going into a federal prison, I'd question your sanity, Detective," he said, looking up as our waitress walked to the table with our food. "Let's eat and drink. Breakfast is on Uncle Sam."

"Sure," I said, nodding. Despite Costa's confidence, I couldn't shake the feeling that we were going about this wrong. Agent Cornwell, though, assured me that they had this entirely under control. If the old saying was true and pride truly did go before a fall, we were in trouble because she had confidence and arrogance to spare.

6

The prison occupied well over a thousand acres of what would have been prime farmland. A row of trees ran alongside the road that led to the prison gate, but otherwise, the landscape was devoid of plants behind which an inmate could hide. The men and women who designed the facility knew what they were doing.

A Federal Bureau of Prisons pickup truck met us at the front gate. The massive complex housed a medium-security prison, a maximum-security prison, a minimum-security prison camp, and federal death row. Thousands of men, many of whom had spent a majority of their lives behind those bars, called the property home. Parts of it almost looked like a boarding school.

We squeezed into the visitor's parking lot outside the maximum-security penitentiary. Its gray concrete walls, barbed wire, and guard towers were much more foreboding than the welcoming red brick buildings of the minimum-security prison camp.

The assistant warden met us in the lobby and led us to a clerk who took our firearms, cell phones, keys, and everything else an inmate could conceivably use as a weapon. Agent Cornwell and I had visited prisons before, so we knew the somewhat specialized rules for women. Neither of us wore underwire bras—the metal would otherwise set off the metal detector—nor had we worn perfume or anything scented that morning. We'd be fine.

A few minutes after we arrived, the warden escorted us to a secure room in which we could talk to Brunelle in peace. The men here lived in individual, soundproofed cells, so the building was deathly quiet. The only sound was the whoosh of the air conditioner.

Everyone held in that building had killed someone. Some were terrorists who had built bombs that killed dozens or even hundreds of people. Others had raped and murdered strangers. Isolation may have seemed barbaric, but an inmate isolated from the rest of humanity couldn't hurt anyone—except maybe himself. Prisons like that kept the corrections officers safe, they kept other inmates safe, and they kept the public safe. Maybe I was cruel, but I'd send a serial rapist or murderer there without hesitation if it meant preventing him from harming someone else.

Our interview room was about fifteen feet by fifteen feet. The builders had bolted a stamped metal table and benches to the concrete floor in the middle of the room. Lights buzzed overhead, and big windows overlooked an empty hallway. The ballistics glass was so thick that even if an inmate somehow unbolted the table or bench, he'd never be able to break out.

Agents Costa and Cornwell sat beside one another on a bench. I sat kitty-corner to them. Then we waited.

Two guards escorted Brunelle into the room a few minutes later. The shackles on his ankles forced him to shuffle along, while the shackles on his wrists prevented him from lifting his arms above his waist. I had seen pictures of him before he went to prison, and in those pictures, he had the enormous, muscular forearms and trim torso of a man who worked with heavy stones for a living. Now, his belly protruded in his coveralls, and his face had gone soft and round. A prison barber had buzzed his hair close to his scalp, and he had at least a day's worth of hair on his chin.

The guards escorted him to a corner seat at the table and removed his restraints. He could have reached out to grab me, but two burly men would have pulled him off. The guards let him stretch for a moment before they shackled him to a thick, metal loop welded onto the table.

"We'll be outside if you need us," said a guard. "There's a panic button on the west wall and a second button on the east wall. Our policy requires us to lock the door, but we'll be watching if you need us."

"Thank you, Officer," said Cornwell. "We should be okay here."

The guards nodded and left. Brunelle looked at each of us and then opened his fist on the table to expose a bottle of hand sanitizer. Then he stared at the bottle and then at me.

"It puts the lotion on its skin."

I raised an eyebrow and looked to Agent Costa. The special agent looked as perplexed as I felt.

"Excuse me?" I asked, looking to Brunelle again.

"It puts the lotion on its skin."

Brunelle's voice was low. His eyes had an angry bent to them.

"It puts the lotion on its skin."

He said it slower this time. I opened my mouth to tell him no, but before I could say anything, a grin split his lips, and his stern countenance left as he laughed.

"I'm just messing with you," he said, picking up the hand sanitizer. He squirted some on his hands. "*Silence of the Lambs* was on TV last night. The commissary doesn't carry hand lotion, so this was the best I could do. You should have seen your expression, Detective. You looked like I asked you to eat a baby or something."

I forced myself to smile. "You probably don't get a lot of chances to make jokes here."

He put the hand sanitizer down. "I make jokes all the time, but nobody hears them. It's nice to have someone to talk to. My cocksucker lawyer doesn't even return my phone calls anymore."

I tilted my head to the side. "Might be because you call him a cocksucker."

He laughed hard enough that his face turned red. When he quieted, Agent Cornwell reached to her side and pulled her questionnaire from her briefcase.

"If we're done with the jokes, we've got questions for you."

He looked at her and then looked to me. "You're the only person I want to talk to. If anyone else talks to me, I'll start screaming for the guards. If that doesn't get them in here, I'll reach across the table and pretend that I'm trying to strangle somebody. The screws get a little jumpy when I do things like that."

I looked to Agent Costa. He nodded, so I focused on Brunelle again.

"All right," I said. "I'll be the only person who talks to you. Is it all right if I talk to my colleagues as well?"

He pointed to Costa.

"He can talk to you but not to me. She doesn't open her mouth again. I don't like women with bad dye jobs. If she speaks again, I'll walk out of here."

Agent Cornwell sighed but said nothing.

"That sounds fair. What do you want to talk about?"

He looked at me again. "I thought we could start with you. You're famous. CNN ran your biography you after you caught the Apostate. It was interesting."

I balled my hands into fists under the table but tried to keep the grimace from my face. It wasn't CNN's story, although they had run it at least twice. The video came from a local station in St. Louis. It was a selective biography of sorts. The clip told the world about the darkest moments of my life, but it didn't put them into context. That was none of Brunelle's business, though.

"I didn't know you had cable," I said.

He rolled his eyes. "Yeah. It keeps the hoopleheads in line."

I nodded and brought my hands to the tabletop.

"Why do you think you're in prison, Mr. Brunelle?"

He considered me and then leaned back.

"Before I answer, let me ask you a question. Do you believe in God?"

I shot my eyes to Agent Cornwell. She leaned

forward, interested in the conversation. Maybe this was on her questionnaire.

"It's a tough question to answer," I said. "I'm not a religious person."

He smiled. "But you are evasive. The question is simple: Do you believe in God? A yes or no will suffice."

"Then yes," I said. "I believe in God."

"Then you know God let Christopher Hughes rape you when you were a kid," said Brunelle. "God's omnipotent, so He had the power to stop it. If He's omniscient, too, He knows everything. He knew what Christopher Hughes had planned the night he hurt you, and yet, God let him rape you, anyway. It makes you wonder, doesn't it? If God loves you and wants what's best for you, and He's got both the power and knowledge to stop bad things from happening, why was your foster father able to drug and rape you?"

I hadn't expected a theological discussion, so I closed my eyes and gave myself a moment to think.

"I suppose that's where free will enters the discussion," I said. "God gives us free will. We're responsible for our own actions. Without free will, we'd just be puppets."

"That could be true," said Brunelle, nodding. "You suffered, though, didn't you? I bet you felt depressed, broken, hurt, betrayed, angry, and all those other things. Christopher Hughes promised to take care of you. Instead, he violated you. Why'd God let you suffer? Sure, if free will exists, men will sin, but that doesn't mean you have to suffer.

"Think about that," said Brunelle, continuing. "God has the power to wipe your memory if He wanted to. He could take away your pain. You might say your suffering strengthened you, but there are other ways He could have made you stronger. And was your newfound strength worth the suffering? You've got to ask that question, too. It's been bothering me ever since I saw that piece on you. I can't believe in a God who'd let you hurt like that."

I leaned back and crossed my arms.

"Are you interested in theology?" I asked. He nodded. "Did the women you murdered suffer?"

"Who can say?" he asked, shrugging. Then he looked to Agent Cornwell. "I bet you've thought about it a lot, though, haven't you? You work in the Behavioral Analysis Unit, and you see suffering every day. Must be hard being a good Catholic in your field."

I opened my mouth to ask him about the women he killed, but he shot his eyes to me before I could say anything.

"It's the way she moves her fingers," he said. "She's been praying the rosary ever since I started talking about God. Every time she finishes the prayer, she moves her thumbs as if she's counting her rosary beads. A lot of Catholics do that. Hare Krishnas do, too, so I guess she could be a Hare Krishna."

He looked at Agent Cornwell.

"Are you a member of the International Society for Krishna Consciousness, Agent Cornwell?"

Cornwell folded her hands together but said nothing. Brunelle smiled so that laugh lines formed at the corners of his eyes.

"Definitely Catholic," he said. "The Hare Krishnas smile more often."

"Why did you ask us here?" I asked.

He looked from Cornwell to me. "Boredom. I needed a change of scenery, and you're the best-looking view I've had in a long time."

"In that case, we're done," I said, standing. The FBI agents followed my lead and stood. "I'm not interested in entertaining you."

As we walked toward the door, Brunelle called out.

"You're not going anywhere."

I ignored him and knocked on the heavy metal. A guard on the outside opened the door within seconds. I stepped into the hallway.

"Wait, wait," Brunelle called. "Before you go, I want to tell you something."

"Make it quick," I said, crossing my arms.

"Where are we?" he asked.

"Prison," I said.

"But what town? What state?" he asked.

I closed my eyes, growing annoyed. "You're a couple of miles south of Terre Haute, Indiana. You know that, though."

He said *Terre Haute* over and over before his eyes brightened.

"There's a town south of here called Oaktown. I

buried a girl in the cemetery there. The coffin was about six feet down. I don't remember whose grave it was, but I buried a girl in a thick, black trash bag about three feet down on top of the coffin."

I considered, wondering why he was telling us this.

"When did you do this?" I asked.

"August 4, 1989. It was hot as hell. You dig that girl up and show me a picture of her, and I'll tell you a lot more."

"We'll take that under advisement," I said. I turned and started walking down the hall toward the main entrance. The guards stayed near the interrogation room. Agents Cornwell and Costa walked two steps behind me. Once we were far enough away that we had some privacy, I stopped and turned to them.

"Your interview style leaves a lot to be desired," said Cornwell. "You didn't ask any of my questions."

I ignored her and looked to Costa. "What do you think, Bryan?"

He tilted his head to the side and sighed.

"I think we need to go to Oaktown."

"Me, too," I said. "Let's get some shovels."

7

Mickey Lyons knocked on his sister's door and waited for an answer that never came. Tessa lived on the nineteenth floor of a high-rise building in St. Louis's Central West End. It was an upscale, fun part of town. In some ways, it reminded him of Lincoln Park in Chicago. Mickey looked up and down the hallway to make sure he was alone before reaching into his pocket for his phone and dialing his sister's number. As before, it went straight to voicemail.

"Tessa, this is your brother," he said. "I'm at your door. I don't want to let myself in without your permission, but I will. Call me right now."

He hung up and then waited, hoping his phone would buzz or that Tessa's door would open. None of that happened, so he slipped his phone into his pocket and thumbed through his keys until he found Tessa's. Before opening the door, he knocked again and waited for about thirty seconds. Then he sighed and unlocked the deadbolt.

Tessa lived in a gorgeous apartment. It had two floors, almost three thousand square feet, and an unencumbered view of Forest Park. Lightly stained hardwood floors ran from the door to the two-story living room and down a short hallway to the three bedrooms on this floor.

"Tessa?" he called. As expected, she didn't answer.

The front hallway was neat. A large pile of mail sat on a table beside the door. He leafed through it but found nothing interesting. Then he walked down the hall to the kitchen and living room.

Tessa's home was a gallery for her work. She had a bachelor of fine arts degree in painting and drawing from the School of the Art Institute in Chicago and had enough talent to make it as an artist. Mickey had even purchased two paintings from her for his own house. He wished she had followed up on her dreams and continued painting. Instead, she'd married Carl Armstrong.

Carl wasn't a bad man, but he was old-fashioned. He was very wealthy and believed a woman's place was to run her husband's household. In Carl's case, running the household had been a full-time job. For a while, she had seemed happy. But then she wasn't. Mickey didn't pry into his sister's life, so he didn't know the details. He loved her, though, and wanted the best for her. He hoped she was okay.

Mickey moved through the kitchen, checking Tessa's usual spots—the flour canister, inside the coffee pot, behind the fridge—for drugs or cash. As was true for many creative people, Tessa's gifts came with a self-destructive curse. On her happy days, she could light up a room with her smile. She made her friends and family feel important just by being with her. On her bad days, she was a destructive force of nature who left nothing standing in her path.

After searching the kitchen, he went to her master

bedroom and searched through her drawers and closet. Her luggage was still on the top shelf of her closet, so she hadn't packed a bag for a vacation, and her drawers were still full of clothes. The room was neat, and her jewelry collection looked intact. The engagement ring Carl had given her was still in its box in a drawer on her dresser. If she had been using drugs again, she would have sold it already. Even secondhand, she'd get twenty or thirty thousand dollars for the diamond. That could have bought enough cocaine to keep her high for months.

The bathroom had prescription pill containers, but the drugs had all been prescribed to her. Nothing in there concerned him. In fact, nothing in the apartment bothered him. It looked like she was doing okay.

That worried him.

He left the apartment with his gut in knots and his throat tight. As he rode the elevator downstairs, he wondered whether he should have visited more often. Maybe he would have seen signs that Tessa was having a rough time, or maybe she would have felt comfortable asking him for help. Looking back, involving her in his business had been a mistake. He should have been a better brother.

Mickey walked to his car and then searched his phone for an address he had hoped he'd never see again. His GPS told him to go north on Euclid Avenue and then west on Delmar Boulevard. He put the phone on the seat beside him and looked over his shoulder before pulling into traffic.

When Tessa left Carl, she hadn't known what her finances would look like. Mickey had given her a job as a courier in his organization, a buffer between those men and women who worked the streets to sell their product and the men who reaped the profits and ensured the business ran smoothly. Once a week, she visited thirty-four different nursing homes strewn across central Missouri and picked up pills—opioids—from the staff.

Depending on the variety and potency of the pill, Tessa paid anywhere from five to ten dollars a pill. She then drove to Chicago, where Mickey's organization pooled Tessa's pills with those of other couriers. They then sold those same pills to rich housewives for three to five times what they had paid. For her work, Tessa earned four thousand dollars a week. It wasn't the life Mickey had hoped his sister would have, but it kept her afloat and out of trouble. Still, she deserved better.

When he reached Delmar—a busy commercial strip with some great bars and a few good restaurants—he drove west until he reached Union Boulevard. Then he drove north for a few blocks. Trees and historic homes still lined the streets, just as they had near Tessa's building, but the cars that had parked on the curb weren't as nice here. Some homes had broken windows, while other houses looked abandoned.

He drove until he found a three-story, limestone-clad home that was a little nicer than those around it. The front yard was tiny, but healthy red mums in colorful pots decorated the front porch. Mickey parked out front, checked to ensure that his firearm had a full magazine, and then chambered a round before stepping out of his vehicle.

Some kids sitting on the front stoop of the house up the street stopped and watched him before whispering amongst themselves and running. They didn't know him, but they recognized he was a cop. He ignored them and took the walkway to the front steps but stopped as a young woman pulled open the front door. She was twenty or twenty-five, and she had the tight, toned body of an athlete. She smiled at him.

"Hey, good looking," she said. "See anything you like?"

"I do, but I'm not here to flirt," he said, winking. "Is your grandmother in?"

She straightened. "How do you know my grandma?"

"Lucia's an old friend," he said, reaching for his wallet. He flipped it open to show her the badge. She sucked in a breath. "Tell her Detective Lyons is outside and would like to talk to her."

Her face grew wan, and she nodded and shut the door. Mickey waited about five minutes before an older version of the young woman who had come to the door earlier stepped onto the porch. She smiled at him.

"Detective Lyons," she said, nodding. "You scared my granddaughter."

He put his hands in his pockets and looked at the concrete. "That wasn't my intent."

"She said you were cute," she said. "You touch her,

I'll cut your balls off."

Mickey laughed. "I wouldn't dream of touching her without your permission."

"I'm sure," said Lucia. "Come on up. Have a seat on the porch. It's a little chilly outside, but if you'd like some iced tea, I can have Isabella bring us some out."

Mickey walked up the steps and sat on a folding chair. The older woman sat on the porch swing. Her feet barely touched the ground.

"As much as I'd like to see Isabella again, I can't stay long," he said. "I was hoping to talk to you about my sister."

"I thought you might," said Lucia. "It's been a while since Tessa's come around."

"You sure about that?" asked Mickey.

Lucia smiled despite the menace in his voice.

"I know who my clients are, honey, and I know who's off limits. Our business relationship is too important for me to jeopardize by selling to your sister. And speaking of business, I need a resupply. My girls are running low."

"Talk to Rodrigo about that," said Mickey. "When did you see Tessa last?"

Lucia thought for a minute. "A month ago, maybe. She came over for coffee. She's such a sweet girl. I've still got that painting she made me in my bedroom. I wish she came around more often. Isabella could use an example like Tessa in her life."

Mickey leaned forward to rest his elbows on his knees.

"She's missing. My mom's been trying to get in touch with her, but Tessa hasn't returned her calls. I went by her apartment, but she's not there."

Lucia patted him on the shoulder. "Honey, I don't think you need to worry about her. She's not using again. She's in love."

Mickey glanced up and furrowed his brow, confused. "She's back with Carl?"

Lucia snorted. "Not with that asshole. She met a young man while on one of your errands. She showed me his picture last time she was here. He's handsome as all get out. If I had to guess, she's down there with him. If she's not answering her phone, it's because the two of them want privacy."

Mickey nodded. Even if Lucia was right, Tessa still should have answered her phone or texted him back. He was her employer, after all.

"You know anything about this guy other than that he's handsome?"

"He lives in St. Augustine," she said. "It's a small town south of here. He recites her poetry."

"And she's into that?"

Lucia winked. "Every woman's into that."

Mickey stood. "Thank you. I mean it. And call Rodrigo about your resupply issues. If he doesn't re-up you quickly, call me. I'll put the fear of God into him and get him off his lazy ass."

"You're a good one, Mickey. Don't let anybody tell you differently," she said, winking. "I'll see you later."

He nodded to her and then looked up toward the house. Isabella, Lucia's granddaughter, stood in the door. She waved and bit her lower lip.

"Bye," she said.

"See you later, honey," he said.

"No, you won't," said Lucia, giving him a dirty look before looking at her granddaughter. "Get back inside. You want to meet a man, go to church. You don't meet men on the porch. This isn't a singles bar."

Mickey smiled as he walked back to his car, but his good humor didn't last long. As he sat in the front seat, he called up the GPS app on his phone and set it to St. Augustine, Missouri. It was an hour away. Tessa had better be there, and she had better have a good reason for not answering their mother's phone calls.

He called Tessa's cell once more to tell her he was heading south to St. Augustine and would appreciate it if she called him back. Then he threw his phone to the seat beside him and drove.

8

The landscape outside the prison was flat and dull with farms and fields as far as I could see. We took US-41 south and drove past a lot of nothing, but once we hit Oaktown, we pulled off US-41 and onto Old 41.

The road ran parallel to the main highway, and, as the name implied, it was old. My Volvo bounced and shuddered over the patched asphalt. From all I could see, Oaktown was a quaint farm community. There was an RV park and a little restaurant that advertised its hot coffee and delicious farm-fresh burgers. I couldn't tell whether it was open because nobody had parked outside and the windows all had shutters over them.

The cemetery was on the outskirts of town, and, if I had to guess, it held a couple thousand graves. Cattle from the farm next door perfumed the area with their pungent aroma. Oak trees, some withered and old, some healthy, dotted the landscape. We parked on a gravel road that ran through the graveyard and got out of our cars. Fields lay to the south, and a copse of trees lay to the west. A dense row of trees to the east served as a windbreak and property marker that demarcated the graveyard from the neighborhood beyond. Someone partial to rural landscapes would have found it pretty, but I thought it looked spartan.

"Should we just start looking at the gravestones for a date around August 4, 1989?" I asked.

"Or we could go to a bar and start drinking," said Agent Cornwell. "Terre Haute's a college town. Since we're wasting our time, we might as well have fun."

"Why do you think this is a waste of time?" I asked.

"Brunelle's a liar," she said, looking to Agent Costa. "What's the probability that he killed and buried somebody fifty miles from the prison where he'd end up?"

"Low, but not impossible," said Costa.

"And it depends on how many people he killed," I said. "You kill and bury enough people around the country, you won't be too far from a gravesite wherever you are."

"Is that a joke, Detective Court?" asked Cornwell.

"No, and it's something to think about," I said. "Your psychological profile on Brunelle was thin. At the time of his arrest, he had little family, and his neighbors said he kept to himself. That's all you've got. Now he told us to come here. As best I can tell, that's the first time he's talked to you since his arrest. Don't you think we should figure out why he's talking now and what he wants?"

Cornwell pressed her lips into a thin line and shifted her stance as if she were starting a race. Then she crossed her arms.

"Detective Court, you don't know the first thing about the world you're stepping into," she said. "I've chased serial murderers for fifteen years and have assisted in the arrests of nineteen killers. Those nineteen men have killed well over a hundred people between them. I've interviewed dozens more serial murderers. You don't get to tell me how to do my job."

She looked to Agent Costa. He said nothing.

"I'm not telling you how to do your job," I said, speaking slowly and feeling the heat rise in my face despite the late fall temperature. "Brunelle told us he buried a body here. Maybe he lied, maybe he didn't. If he lied to us, we won't have to talk to him again, but if he's telling us the truth, we'll have gained a new source of information about his methods and about him. That's worth investigating."

Cornwell glared but didn't respond for a few seconds. Then she threw up her hands.

"Fine. We'll look at the graves. I'll get the ones across the street. You and Agent Costa divide this side however want."

She didn't give us a chance to acknowledge her orders before she turned and crossed Old 41. Agent Costa and I divided our side of the cemetery in half and started looking at dates. With three people searching, it took little time to find what we needed. About a dozen people had died in 1989, but only one had been buried around August 4, the date Brunelle said he buried his victim.

"I've got something," said Agent Costa. "Eleanor King. Born December 3, 1912. Died July 27, 1989."

I did the math in my head. She died eight days before Brunelle buried his victim, so the earth over her grave would have been fresh still. Even if they had put sod over the broken ground, it wouldn't have grown into the surrounding grass yet. He could have moved it, dug a hole, dumped a body, and covered Ms. King's grave again with no one noticing.

I knelt down and felt the soft grass over the grave. Though Ms. King's grave was unadorned, someone had placed flowers on several of the graves nearby.

"Before we do anything else, we need to talk to the local police and let them know what's going on," I said, standing and thinking. "We also need to find Ms. King's family and tell them we need to dig near her grave."

Agent Cornwell sighed. "The Bureau has jurisdiction here. You don't, Detective. I'll talk to the family. If they're uninterested in letting us dig on their grandmother's grave, we'll get a court order. Agent Costa, contact the local sheriff's department."

Agent Costa nodded, and I forced a smile to my face.

"That's fine. If you guys do that, I'll get shovels and a case of bottled water."

Agent Cornwell returned my fake smile with one of her own.

"I'm glad you've found something useful to do."

She turned and walked toward her SUV. I drew in a slow breath and closed my eyes as I imagined a small farmhouse from Kansas falling from the sky and crushing her. It was more satisfying than it should have been. When I opened my eyes again, I found Agent Costa walking toward me.

"Hey," I said. "Something you need?"

He stood beside me and watched as Agent Cornwell climbed into the driver's seat of her sedan. Once she shut her door and turned her car on, he tilted his head to the side.

"Philippa isn't usually this sharp with people," he said. "She's a very nice person."

"Yeah. She's a real peach."

He snickered a little and then waved as Agent Cornwell drove past. She didn't look at either of us.

"You caught a serial murderer who had evaded capture for years," he said. "She's assisted on a lot of cases, but she's never done that. She's jealous."

"I don't care how she feels about me. I'm a professional, and I'm here to do a job. If she can't handle that, it's her problem."

"And I appreciate your professionalism," he said. "Thank you for not engaging with her. I'll talk to her and tell her to tone it down." He paused. "You think this could be something?"

I softened my tone. "I don't know. If Brunelle lied to us, we'll shut him down and never visit him again. He knows that. He'll mislead us if he can, but I don't think he'd risk our relationship this early. We'll find something. It may not be a body, but it'll be something."

"You're probably right," said Costa, sighing. "I'll track down the local sheriff."

I wished him luck and then walked to my Volvo. Since I didn't know the area, I used my phone to search for stores nearby. There was a Walmart in Sullivan, a small town about twenty minutes north of Oaktown, and another Walmart in Vincennes, a larger town about twenty minutes south.

Both stores were equidistant, so I went south. I spent about an hour in Walmart and purchased tarps, shovels, trowels, gloves, bottled water, a cooler, ice, and three sandwiches in case the agents and I got hungry. Then I drove back to Oaktown. When I reached the cemetery, I found two marked police cruisers from the Knox County Sheriff's Department and Agent Costa's black SUV parked near Ms. King's grave. Agent Cornwell's sedan was nowhere to be seen.

As I got out of my car, Costa approached me.

"Hey," he said, nodding. "Philippa tracked down Ms. King's grandson to Bloomington. He's an IT manager at Indiana University. He's agreed to let us dig near his grandmother's grave as long as we don't disturb her casket. Philippa's driving over to get his signature."

"And these guys?" I asked, nodding toward the locals.

"They're here in case we need them," he said. "It might be a little while, though, so I planned to send them on their way."

"So we just sit around for a while?" I asked.

"Until we get the forms in order," he said, nodding. "You can take a nap if you want."

It was a little cool out, but it was comfortable in a jacket and sweater. I nodded, and, for the next two hours, I dozed in the front seat of my Volvo while Agent Costa read a book on his phone. The deputies left, but they said they'd be nearby if we needed them.

At half past five, Agent Cornwell returned with an order signed by Adam King, and we got to work. Things moved quickly after that.

Agent Cornwell put a tarp on the ground, and I started to dig. We didn't want to disturb the grave any more than we had to, so I kept the hole as small as I could given my tools. As soon as we finished, we'd backfill the hole, clean it up, and lay some flowers on the grave.

When I was about two feet down, I knelt and used a trowel. After another twenty minutes, I glanced up to see Agent Cornwell looking to the west. The sun had slunk low on the horizon. We had, maybe, twenty minutes of daylight left, but already it was getting harder to see what I was doing.

"Hey, Bryan, can you get in your car and turn on your headlights?" I asked.

He nodded and walked to his car, but Agent Cornwell crossed her arms, sighed, and shifted her weight.

"You're already almost three feet down, and you've found nothing. We're wasting our time."

She was probably right, but I didn't want to stop yet. A moment later, I heard the engine of Agent Costa's car turn over. Blindingly bright light flooded the area for a moment, but then it seemed to dim as my eyes adjusted. He climbed out of the car and stood beside Cornwell.

"I say we give it another half hour before we call it," he said. "That sound good to you two?"

I nodded and kept digging, but Cornwell said nothing. If she wanted to sulk like a teenager, she could sulk. I didn't move a lot of dirt with each trowel, but it added up. For almost fifteen minutes, I found nothing.

And then my trowel found some resistance.

I reached into the hole and touched rough fabric. It wasn't a tarp; it felt like tar paper, the kind a builder might wrap a house with.

"I've got something," I said. "Get a flashlight."

Costa bounded over a moment later and shined the light in the hole. It was deep enough I could just barely reach the bottom with the tip of my trowel. I cleared more dirt and found more tar paper.

"Allow me," said Costa, kneeling beside me. "My arms are longer."

I handed him the trowel and took the flashlight. By then even Agent Cornwell had knelt beside us. My heart started beating faster, and I bit my lower lip. With every trowel of dirt Agent Costa moved, my stomach tightened. My arms and back ached. The night air had grown cold, but sweat still formed on my brow.

"Shit," said Costa, pulling his arm back. "I think I tore the fabric."

I shined the light where his trowel had once been. The tar paper had a big enough rip that we could see inside. All of us went silent, and the world seemed to stop moving. My chest felt tight, and a prickling sensation began to pass over my scalp as I covered my mouth with a gloved hand. We were looking at a skull. Delicate tufts of hair remained on the scalp, but the skin and flesh had long since decomposed.

"Brunelle wasn't lying," I said. "We've got a body."

9

I stepped back from the hole. Agents Costa and Brunelle did likewise. No one spoke. Then Costa took off his gloves and tossed them to the ground on the tarp. He rubbed his face and sighed.

"We need to get those Knox County deputies here," he said. "We also need lights and a generator."

"You know anyone at the Indianapolis field office?" asked Cornwell.

Costa gave her a blank stare and then narrowed his eyes.

"Special Agent in Charge is Fran Something-or-other," he said. "I've only met her once."

"We need to call her," said Cornwell. "We'll need a forensic anthropologist, too. Cadaver dogs would be useless here with so many bodies underground, so we need to bring in ground-penetrating radar and see whether Brunelle buried anyone else nearby."

Costa nodded. "I agree. We've got work to do." He paused and looked at me. "You're welcome to stay and observe, Joe, but we can't use you here. You're out of your jurisdiction."

I nodded. Brunelle had left me with a lot of questions, but I had enough experience with serial murderers already to know I didn't want the answers. This was the FBI's case. I wanted no part of it.

"I've got a murder to work in St. Augustine," I said.

"I should head home anyway."

Costa held out his hand for me to shake. He had a firm grip and a rough, calloused hand.

"I appreciate you coming," he said. "You've been a big help. If you need reimbursement for anything, send an invoice to my office in St. Louis. We'll take care of you."

"Sure," I said, looking toward Agent Cornwell and the hole in the ground. "Good luck here."

He grunted. "Thanks. We need it."

I nodded and walked to my car. According to the GPS on my phone, St. Augustine was about four hours away, but I'd have to stop and pick up Roy at my parents' house. That'd add another hour to the trip, which meant I wouldn't get home until at least twelve. Maybe I could stay at mom and dad's place for the night.

Before leaving, I called Sergeant Bob Reitz. His phone rang twice before he answered.

"Joe, hey," he said. "I just sat down to dinner. What's up?"

"If you're just sitting, I won't keep you long. I'm in Indiana, but I'll be on my way home soon. Did you ID the woman we pulled from the Wayfair Motel yet?"

He sighed. "I tried, but I haven't had a lot of luck. I interviewed the staff at the motel again, but they didn't have much to add. Vic Conroy met me at the door of Club Serenity and told me neither he nor his employees were interested in talking to me. His truck stop was a bust, too. Since I struck out there, I showed her picture to everybody in Able's Diner. Two of the waitresses had seen her before, but they didn't know her name. I also tried other restaurants around town, but I got the same response.

"I also talked to Darlene at the crime lab. Her prints weren't in the system anywhere."

I nodded and thought for a moment. "Since we're striking out in St. Augustine, let's try something new. She had a lot of cash in an envelope, right?"

"Two thousand dollars in crisp, new hundred-dollar bills," said Bob. "They had sequential serial numbers. I had to write them all down to catalog them."

"That's good," I said. "If our victim withdrew two grand from the bank, there'll be a record of it somewhere. Call the Federal Reserve Bank in St. Louis and give them the serial numbers. The Federal Reserve should have a record of which bank they shipped those bills to. Go to that bank and ask about large cash withdrawals."

He paused, presumably to write that down. Then he cleared his throat.

"That's a good idea," he said. "Anything else you need me to do?"

"Use your judgment and do what you can," I said. "I'll be in tomorrow as soon as I can."

He said he'd start making calls as soon as he could. I wished him luck and then hung up and focused on the road ahead of me.

The drive to Kirkwood was easy. The roads were empty, and I sang along to a Lady Gaga album my sister had persuaded me to buy a week or two ago. I wasn't a great singer, and I didn't know all the words, but it was for my ears only, and it was fun. I reached my parents' house at a quarter to eleven. Mom was awake, and she insisted that I stay for the night. I was too tired to argue. She went to bed after giving me a hug in the living room, but Dad, Roy, and I stayed up and watched part of *The Late Show*.

Afterwards, Roy and I went up to my old room. I hadn't slept there in years, and as I stood at the threshold, old memories came flooding back to me. My room was on the very end of the second-floor hallway. My parents were at the other end of the house. Dylan and Audrey, my siblings, had rooms between us.

My door had a deadbolt. When Doug and Julia took me in, I was broken. I thought I had everything in my life under control, but I didn't. Not even close. My adoptive parents were the kindest, most generous people I had ever met, but I didn't know it then. When I moved in with them, I was a sixteen-year-old rape victim who had cried herself to sleep every night while clutching a baseball bat for protection in case somebody tried to hurt me.

I didn't know it, but Doug and Julia took shifts outside my room in case I needed somebody to talk to. Dad would sit and read a paperback with his back pressed to the wall. My mom would doze with a pillow on the floor. When they saw me at breakfast the next morning and asked me how I had slept, I'd lie and say everything was fine. All along, though, they knew I wasn't fine. They knew I needed help, but they also knew I had to ask for it.

So they had stayed outside my room, just in case I

reached out to them. Night after night, I lied to their faces and pushed them away, and night after night, they stayed to protect me. I had thought I was alone in the world, but I hadn't been alone since the day I met them. They loved me before I knew what it meant to love someone. Meeting Doug and Julia had been the best thing to happen to me. I could never thank them enough for choosing to become my mom and dad.

As I stood in that doorway and saw the deadbolt on my door, I couldn't help but think of everything they had done for me. I reached to my dog and petted his head.

"This is the first home I ever had," I whispered. He looked up at me and gave me a doggy grin. "Please don't pee on the floor."

I changed into pajamas from the overnight bag I had brought from St. Augustine and then crashed on my bed. I shut the door for privacy, but I didn't lock the deadbolt or put on the chain. Life had thrown a lot my way when I was young, but now I had a family and friends, a house, a dog, and a job. My world wasn't perfect, but it was good.

As I closed my eyes that night, I thanked God, the universe, or whoever else was listening for giving me the things I had. It was the least I could do.

Roy woke me up at about six the next morning with a wet nose on my cheek. I rolled over, stroked his back, and then swung my legs off the bed. He had to pee, so I let him into the backyard and inadvertently woke up my mom. She made coffee, and then the two of us sat and talked. Audrey, my little sister, was in Chicago at college, while Dylan, my little brother, was finishing his senior year of high school. He hoped to go to the University of Missouri, but he had also applied to Waterford College in St. Augustine. Dylan was a bit of a wild child, but it'd be fun to have him closer.

At seven, Mom and I took Roy for a walk around the neighborhood. By the time we got back, Dad had already made pancakes and eggs. We ate together and lingered a bit over coffee, but I had work in St. Augustine.

I drove home at about ten, and when I got to town, I dropped Roy off at home and went into work a little after eleven. Between the construction workers downstairs and the working police station on the second floor, the building was a hive of activity. Somebody must have told Bob Reitz that I had come in because he came by my office before I could sign in to check my email.

"Tessa Armstrong," he said. "The Federal Reserve delivered those bills to a credit union in the Central West End in St. Louis. I drove up this morning and showed her picture around. A teller recognized her right away because she loved Mrs. Armstrong's dress."

"Good work," I said, leaning back. "What do we know about her?"

"Clean record. According to her driver's license, she lives in Ladue, Missouri, with her husband, Carl Armstrong. Mr. Armstrong is the managing director of Armstrong Wealth Management. According to their website, they've got about two hundred employees and help wealthy families with estate planning and with investment advice. They're based in downtown St. Louis."

I nodded and considered the news.

"Did you notify Mr. Armstrong about his wife?"

Bob shook his head. "No, but I called the St. Louis County Police Department and asked whether Mr. Armstrong had filed a missing-persons report on Tessa."

I raised my eyebrows. "And did he?"

"Nope," said Bob, shaking his head. "If my wife withdrew money from the bank and then disappeared for three days, I think I'd call the police."

I nodded and brought a hand to my mouth as I thought.

"Looks like we've got a suspect," I said.

Bob nodded.

"What do you want to do?"

I stood and looked at him. His uniform was crisp and clean, but we needed something different for the job ahead of us.

"Go home and change into a button-down shirt and jacket," I said. "Then we're going to St. Louis to see whether Mr. Armstrong can answer our questions."

10

Mickey sipped his coffee and stared out the window at the little town. St. Augustine had turned out to be quaint. The town had a historic district with bars and restaurants that were far more upscale than he would have expected from rural Missouri, and the rolling hills, forests, and bluffs overlooking the Mississippi River were beautiful. Had it been closer to Chicago, he could have seen himself taking a date there for a long weekend.

He ate the last bit of his pecan roll—the coffee shop's specialty, so someone had told him—and wiped his hands clean on a napkin. The headquarters of the St. Augustine County Sheriff's Department wasn't far. He had thought about going there to ask about his sister but had decided against it in case she had gotten herself in trouble. Her boyfriend would be his best source of information. Mickey planned to track him down, but he had work first.

He flipped through a list of names, addresses, and phone numbers on his phone. Though she lived in St. Louis, Tessa's territory covered most of east-central Missouri. At last count, she had contacts at over thirty nursing homes. She visited some of those contacts weekly to pick up product and drop off payment, but others she visited once a month. Tessa may not have been perfect, but she was a good worker. Not only that, she knew many of the men and women who supplied her with opioids depended on the money she paid them. She wouldn't have disappeared without making some arrangement first unless she couldn't help it.

"Can I warm you up?"

Mickey looked up to see a woman with a coffee carafe standing near him. She had thick brunette hair, a pretty smile, and a nice body.

"There's nothing I'd like more, but I have to get going," he said, returning the smile. "But thank you. And thank you for the recommendation on the pecan roll. It was excellent."

"I'm glad to hear that," she said. She tilted her head to the side. "I'm Sheryl. Come back later. I'll show you around town."

His smile broadened. They could have fun together, but he had work to do.

"I wish I could, but I've got meetings all day," he said. "Rain check?"

"Definitely," she said, winking as he tossed his trash away and exited the shop. Outside, it was about fifty degrees, cool but not yet cold. He climbed into his truck and put the address of a local nursing home into the GPS on his phone. The roads rolled across the hilly landscape. In high school, with a teenager's terrible judgment, Mickey would have gotten in a lot of trouble on roads like that. He was lucky he had grown up outside Chicago without access to a car.

The nursing home was called Hidden Hills. He asked for Belinda Wells at the front desk and then sat in the reception area to wait. An older woman watched *Jeopardy!* and knit from the couch opposite him. She smiled but said nothing. Ms. Wells came out a few minutes later and held her hand toward him.

"I'm Belinda," she said. "Do I know you?"

"We've got a friend in common," he said, glancing at the nurse behind the reception desk. He pulled out his wallet and showed her his badge. "I'm Detective Mickey Lyons. Can we talk for a minute in private? You're not in any trouble."

Belinda straightened and nodded. The receptionist pretended that she hadn't seen them. Belinda led him through the hallways and then outside to a picnic table in a small courtyard area. She lit up a cigarette and stared at him.

"What can I do for you, Detective?"

"What can you tell me about Tessa Armstrong?"

She drew in a quick breath before swallowing. Then she brought her cigarette to her lips and drew in.

"I've never heard the name. Sorry."

"I see," said Mickey. "Are you sure? Tessa is twenty-nine and has blond hair and blue eyes. She's very pretty."

She shrugged and took another draw on her cigarette.

"Not ringing any bells," she said. She raised her eyebrows. "Sorry, Detective."

"Are you sure you don't know her?" he asked. "I think you'd remember her. You sell her painkillers that you steal from your patients. Best I can tell, you've been doing it for about a year now."

She lowered her hand with the cigarette and held her breath as her eyes traveled up and down his torso.

"I don't know what you're talking about," she said. "And I think it's time for you to leave. If you need to talk to me again, I'll give you the name of my attorney."

He nodded and reached to his wallet for a business card. "Okay. Enjoy your cigarette. If you change your mind, call me. My cell number is on the card."

He put it on the table in front of her and left, hoping that Tessa had trained all of her partners this well. He drove to the workplace of the next name on his list and found a male nurse who also shut him down as soon as Mickey mentioned Tessa's name. The third name on his list was much the same. The fourth name on his list had the day off, so, instead of meeting her at work, Mickey drove to her house.

Maddie Dawson lived in a ranch-style home on a big lot several miles outside of the town of St. Augustine. There was a basketball hoop in the driveway and a pair of rocking chairs on the front porch. A wind chime jingled somewhere nearby, but he couldn't see it.

Mickey knocked on the glass and wood front door. Within moments, a heavyset woman in her mid-thirties opened. She wore jeans and a green turtleneck sweater that showcased her ample chest. Her curly blond hair tumbled across her shoulders and blew in the slight fall breeze. Mickey smiled at her and held up his badge.

"Ms. Dawson?" he asked. She nodded and looked from his badge to him.

"Yeah?" she asked. He slipped his wallet back into his pocket.

"I'm Detective Mickey Lyons," he said. "So I can be sure I'm talking to the right person, do you work at Willow Bend Living Center as a nurse?"

She locked her eyes on him, nodded, and stepped back to conceal herself with the door. Mickey readied himself to put his foot in the jamb in case she tried to slam the door shut.

"Yeah. Why?"

"I was hoping to ask you some questions," he said. "Is the name Tessa Armstrong familiar?"

For a second, she didn't react. Then she looked down, and her shoulders drooped.

"How do you know her?" asked Mickey.

She wouldn't look at him, so Mickey reached to her face and gently lifted her chin.

"I'm talking to you, miss," he said, smiling. "How'd you know Tessa Armstrong?"

"I've heard the name," she said, twisting her head away from his grip. He lowered his hands.

"I hear she bought drugs from women like you."

"It's time for you to go," she said. Mickey shook his head.

"If I searched your house right now, what would I find?" he asked. "And don't lie to me."

"I'm pretty sure you need a warrant to search my house," she said.

He lowered his chin.

"You think I'd drive all the way out here without a warrant?" he asked. "Do you think I'm stupid?"

She said nothing.

"Do you think I'm stupid?" he asked again.

For another moment, she said nothing. Then she closed her eyes.

"No. You're not stupid. What do you want?"

"You sold Tessa opioids that you stole from your patients. I've already talked to your boss at Willow Bend, so don't lie to me."

She rubbed her eyes but said nothing.

"Did you sell her drugs?" he asked. "Yes or no. Tell me."

She sighed and then put her hands on her hips.

"Yeah. I sold her drugs. What do you want?" she asked. "If you've already talked to my boss, you've got the evidence you need to arrest me."

He reached to the leather clip on his belt that held his department-issued handcuffs.

"Put your hands flat on the wall behind you. I'll pat you down for weapons."

She slowly did as he asked. Despite her bravado, she trembled as he ran his hands across her frame. Her pockets were empty, and she had no weapons anywhere.

"Hold your hands together in front of you so I can cuff you."

She held up her hands. Her first sob came as he ratcheted the cuffs on her wrists.

"I can't go to prison. I'll die there. I know I will."

"Everybody says that, but very few people end up dying," he said, putting a hand on her elbow and guiding her toward his truck. He put the tailgate down to give her somewhere to sit. "How long have you been buying drugs from Tessa?"

She hesitated but then licked her lips. None of the other men and women he had spoken to made it this far. They had all shut him down immediately. He needed to know how far he could push her before she really broke.

"About a year," she said. "I know important things. I've got recordings."

A pit began to grow in Mickey's gut. He swore under his breath, but he tried to keep his face neutral.

"Tell me about these recordings."

"I taped our conversations," she said. "When she'd come, I'd put my phone down on the table, but I had the video camera going. I've got a bunch of videos of Tessa buying pills from me. I've even got a video of her talking about her boss. Some dude in Chicago. I think he was her brother or cousin or something. I can tell you about her boyfriend, too. Towards the end, I think he was calling the shots."

Mickey nodded and felt his guts twist. His body tensed.

"Okay. Tell me about the boyfriend."

She shrugged. "Let me go and I will."

Mickey shook his head. "Doesn't work like that, honey. Tessa's partners were dangerous people. If I let you go, you're dead. If you testify against them, we'll protect you. We might even be able to give you some money. How's that sound?"

"Sounds like I'd be earning that paycheck," she said. "If they're dangerous and all."

"Tell me about the boyfriend."

She lowered her chin. "I think I'd need to talk to a lawyer first."

He nodded as if that made sense. "That sounds like a good idea. Hop in the truck. I'll take you to our station."

"Will Tessa's partners kill me if they found out I talked to you?" she asked.

"Do you have Tessa on video talking about buying drugs?"

She nodded. "That and more. I pretended to be her friend. I think she needed a friend. She seemed lonely."

A chill passed through him. He nodded anyway.

"Then yeah, they'll kill you. I won't let that happen. Hop in the truck. We'll go for a ride."

She got in the passenger side and pulled the door shut. If she were under arrest, he would have cuffed her with her hands behind her back, but he had other plans for her. Mickey turned on the car and backed onto the street. He didn't know St. Augustine well, but he had noted several locations on a map on his cell phone just in case he needed an isolated location to question somebody.

He drove for about ten minutes before reaching a forested section of the road. Then he slowed and turned onto a gravel road that cut through the woods.

"Are you sure we're going to your station?" asked

Maddie.

Mickey glanced at her. "Tessa's people have cops on their payroll. I'm taking you to a safe house. We'll make arrangements for you there."

"Fuck," she said, her voice almost a whisper. Mickey drove for maybe half a mile on that gravel road before slowing to a stop.

"Step out of the truck," he said.

She looked around. "There's nothing here."

He smiled. "The safe house is a cabin. It doesn't have a driveway, and it doesn't appear on any map. That's how you know it's safe."

"Okay," she said. She hesitated and then reached to the truck's door latch. As she stepped out, so did he. "Where now?"

"Just wait a minute," he said. "I've got to get something."

She nodded, and he reached into the bed of his pickup for a nylon rope he had purchased. He held it up.

"In case you get lost," he said. She gave him a confused look but didn't move as he walked toward her. He tied a half hitch knot around the chain on her handcuffs and then pulled her toward the rear of the truck.

"What are you doing?" she asked. He ignored her and tied the other end of the rope to his truck's hitch. "What the fuck are you doing?"

"Just stay there, honey," he said. "I've got to call my partner, and I need some privacy. The rope'll keep you from wandering off."

She furrowed her brow but said nothing. He climbed into the driver's seat, put the truck in gear, and then stepped on the gas hard. The rope jerked her off her feet. Then he just kept driving. She screamed at first, but nobody could hear her. After about a hundred yards, he slowed the truck to a stop and climbed out. She had gashes and abrasions across her face. The gravel had ripped big holes in her clothes.

"Tell me about Tessa's boyfriend," he said.

She sobbed. The noise might have bothered him in other circumstances, but this woman had already tried to turn on his sister. That didn't garner much sympathy from him.

"Tell me about her boyfriend or I will get in my truck and drag you until you've got nothing left but bones. Then I'll let the coyotes eat you."

He didn't know whether there were coyotes in this part of the world, but her eyes popped open wide, and she sobbed harder.

"He's a high school teacher," she said. "She's in love with him. I don't know his name."

"Thank you."

He reached to the holster behind him. She must have seen what he was doing because she brought her hands up to her face as if that would shield her. As he squeezed the trigger, the sound of the gunshot rebounded against the nearby trees and reminded him of fireworks when he was a boy. Maddie lay on the ground, no longer screaming.

Mickey holstered his firearm and took out his phone. His boss answered on the second ring.

"It's Mickey. We've got a problem in Missouri. One of our couriers has disappeared. It's my sister. I'm worried her boyfriend hurt her. Her network may be compromised."

The other end went silent for a moment.

"I'm sorry about your sister. She's a good worker. I hope she's okay. If she's not, find the fucker who hurt her and repay the favor."

"I will," he said. "If Tessa's dead, there's nowhere on Earth this guy can hide."

11

When Bob and I reached the parking lot, I noticed that he was following me to Old Brown, the cruiser the department kept on reserve for me when I was on duty. I stopped beside the driver's door but didn't open it yet.

"Where are you going?" I asked.

He hesitated.

"St. Louis."

I shook my head. "We'll take two cars so we can split up once we get there."

"I don't know," he said, his back straight. "Sheriff Delgado was clear about the need to save money. He'd be pissed if we waste the gas."

"We're working a homicide," I said. "Money's important, but it doesn't factor into our investigation."

"Still," he said, nodding and reaching to the passenger side door handle, "I'd feel more comfortable taking one car. I don't know the city well, and I hate parallel parking. Consider it a favor."

I lowered my chin and sighed as I opened my door.

"If you insist."

So we drove north on clear roads. Armstrong Wealth Management had an eight-story brick building on Washington Avenue in downtown St. Louis. There wasn't a lot of parking nearby, so we parked a couple of blocks away on the street. The first floor held a coffee shop beside an upscale restaurant. A banner strewn across the top floor of the low-rise building next door advertised its luxurious loft apartments.

Bob and I walked into the building's lobby beside the restaurant and took an elevator upstairs to Armstrong Wealth Management's main reception area on the second floor. The room was airy and had big picture windows overlooking Washington Avenue. Thick wooden beams crisscrossed the ceiling. A man sat on a comfortable-looking suede sofa near the windows, while a couple a few years younger than me but wearing much nicer clothing sat together on a loveseat near the elevators.

The moment Bob and I stepped inside, a woman in a navy pantsuit appeared from a back hallway. She wore a headset and carried an iPad.

"Good morning," she said, smiling. "I'm Cora, and I'm an associate here at Armstrong. What can I help you with?"

I unclipped my badge from my belt and showed it to her.

"I'm Detective Court of the St. Augustine County Sheriff's Department. With me is Sergeant Bob Reitz. We need to talk to Carl Armstrong."

She straightened and raised an eyebrow.

"Okay," she said. "Can I ask what this is about?"

"It's a personal matter for Mr. Armstrong," I said.

She nodded, turned, and touched a button on her headset before speaking in a low whisper. When she finished, she turned toward us again, smiling once more.

"Have a seat, and we'll be right with you," she said.

"Is there anything I can get you while you wait? Coffee? Soda? Cucumber water?"

"We're fine," I said. "Thank you."

She nodded and walked away. Bob looked around the room.

"Nice place," he said, looking at me. I nodded my agreement. Then he tilted his head. "How do you suppose they make cucumber water? You think they just cut it and squeeze it into a cup?"

I couldn't tell whether he was being serious, so I blinked a few times and drew in a breath.

"I think they just slice a cucumber and put the slices in a pitcher with water," I said. He grunted.

"Where I'm from, that's called water with cucumber in it."

I nodded, not knowing what else to say. Bob and I stayed put in the reception area for about ten minutes before a man in a navy pinstripe suit and a light blue shirt and tie came from the elevator to greet us.

"Good morning, officers," he said, his hand outstretched as he walked towards us. Bob and I both shook his hand before he gestured toward the elevator. "Let's go upstairs. We'll talk in private."

Both the young couple and the man near the windows cast us sidelong glances.

"Are you Mr. Armstrong?" I asked.

He hesitated and then shook his head.

"I'm Bart Harrison. I'm one of the general counsels here at Armstrong Wealth. I'll relay whatever message you have for Mr. Armstrong to him personally."

"I appreciate that, but I'm not here to talk to a lawyer," I said. "This is a personal matter between us and Mr. Armstrong."

He considered us and then stepped closer and lowered his voice.

"Carl is meeting with an important client," he said. "I'm afraid he's booked."

"His wife is dead," I said. "It's kind of important."

Mr. Harrison's face paled, and his eyes went distant. Then he brought a hand to his mouth.

"Tessa or Daphne?"

"He's got two wives?" I asked, lowering my chin.

"Tessa is his current wife, and Daphne is his ex," he said. His eyes opened wide. "The kids are okay, aren't they?"

"Tessa's dead. And there were no children involved."

He closed his eyes and breathed a relieved sigh.

"I'm sorry about Tessa, but I'm glad the kids and Daphne are okay."

I nodded. "Can we talk to him now?"

"Yes, of course," said Harrison. "I'll take you to his office and then get him from his meeting. I'm sure he'll talk to you right away."

"Thank you," I said, my voice flat and annoyed. We took the elevator to the eighth floor. Mr. Armstrong had a corner office overlooking the street. Though it had big windows and a decent view of St. Louis, the room was humbler than I had expected from a man with his name on every sign in the building. No receptionist or assistant greeted us outside.

Bob and I sat on the two chairs in front of Mr. Armstrong's desk, while Mr. Harrison stood post near the window and sent text messages. Within about five minutes, a man in his early fifties walked into the room. He was heavy, but his tailored navy suit masked his bulk. Gel or mousse slicked his thick, gray hair back. His brown tortoiseshell glasses magnified his green eyes.

"Officers," he said, nodding to me and Bob before looking to Mr. Harrison. "Morning, Bart."

Armstrong sat behind his desk and leaned back.

"Did Cora offer you a drink downstairs?"

I nodded and leaned forward.

"Yes, and we declined. We're here to talk about your wife. I'm very sorry to tell you this, but we found Tessa Armstrong's body two days ago in a hotel in St. Augustine."

"I assume she didn't die of natural causes," he said, raising his eyebrows but barely reacting otherwise.

"No, sir," said Bob. "Someone murdered her."

"And you two are the investigating officers," he said, considering us before raising his eyebrows. "What was she doing in St. Augustine?"

I glanced at Bob. He gave me an uncomfortable smile.

"Witnesses spotted her in the motel with a still unknown Caucasian male," I said. "We found condoms in one of the trash cans."

He nodded. "At least you'll have his DNA."

"We believe so," I said, nodding. I paused. "Your reaction to Ms. Armstrong's death is more understated than I had expected."

"Are you accusing me of something?"

"No," I said, shaking my head. "Just making an observation."

He considered me before shrugging.

"I care about Tessa, but she and I haven't been together for some time," he said, sighing and looking over his shoulder toward Mr. Harrison. "Bart, go find Melissa and ask her to print off Tessa's list for me."

Harrison nodded and left. Mr. Armstrong leaned forward.

"I suppose you have questions to ask me. Before you start, though, know that I did not kill her and did not wish ill upon her, despite the failure of our marriage. If you tell me when she died, I'll give you my alibi."

I narrowed my eyes. "You don't' seem surprised that she's dead."

He shrugged. "I don't mean to be indelicate, but my wife was a tramp. Three years ago, she miscarried another man's child. After that, our marriage was a business arrangement. I gave her an allowance and allowed her to live her life as she saw fit. As long as her payment made it to her account, she didn't interfere with my life. It was cheaper than divorcing her."

I smiled. "It'd be even cheaper just to kill her."

He raised an eyebrow and shook his head.

"I can always make more money, but I'm fifty-seven years old. If I'm lucky, I'll have twenty healthy years left. I don't plan to squander the rest of my life rotting in prison or fearing that the police will knock down my door at any moment. My romantic feelings for Tessa waned some time ago, but I didn't kill her, and I don't know who did."

I leaned forward. "When did you last see her?"

"Two weeks ago," said Carl. "She and I had lunch in the Tenderloin Room at the Chase Park Plaza Hotel."

"Did you have lunch together often?" I asked.

He turned his gaze to me. "Once a month when she was out of money."

"Did she mention anything about a boyfriend over lunch?" I asked. He chuckled and shook his head.

"We didn't live with each other, but we were still married. We didn't talk about our love lives."

Before I could ask anything else, Mr. Harrison returned with papers still warm from the printer. He handed me one set and Bob a second set. There were fourteen names, addresses, phone numbers, and email addresses in two neat columns. I furrowed my brow.

"And these people are?" I asked.

"Every lover my wife has taken in the past three years," said Armstrong. "After she miscarried her boyfriend's child, I hired a private investigator to follow her around and ensure that she stayed away from any trouble that could fall back on me. She's struggled with drugs in the past, although I believe she's been clean for at least the past two years."

I whistled as I looked over the names.

"I'd feel jealous if my spouse had this many affairs."

"As I said, our marriage was a business arrangement," he said. "I don't condition business deals on my partner's celibacy."

"Tessa died two days ago," I said. "We're still trying to narrow the time frame down, but where were you two days ago?"

He nodded. "I worked from seven in the morning to seven at night. Then I went home."

"Was anyone with you at home?"

"Mr. Sanderson, my estate manager, saw me come in, but then he left. My housekeeper had left several hours beforehand."

"So you were alone after you came home," I said. He nodded.

"Yes. My kids stay with me on the weekends, but during the week, I spend my evenings alone."

"Every evening?" I asked. "You never have company?"

"Correct. And I've said what I needed to say," he said.

"Okay," I said, standing. Bob took the hint and stood. "Once again, I'm very sorry for your loss. We won't waste more of your day."

"Thank you," said Mr. Armstrong, sliding back from his desk and opening the center drawer. He searched for a moment and then pulled a business card out. "If you need to get in touch with me again, call my attorneys. They'll set up any future meetings."

I took the card from him and thanked him. Then Mr. Harrison escorted us out of the building. On the sidewalk, Bob looked at me.

"What do you think?"

I looked at the paper with the list of names.

"You're married, right?" I asked. Bob nodded. "If you and your wife had a falling-out, how would you react if you learned she had fourteen lovers while still married to you?"

He snickered and raised his eyebrows. "Badly. I'm not rich, though. Maybe their cucumber water mellows them out."

"Maybe it does," I said. "We'll check out the men on this list, but Armstrong's our prime suspect. Let's go. We've got work to do while we're in town."

12

Mickey Lyons knew a lot of cops. Many of them had their heads shoved so far up their asses they couldn't see opportunities right in front of their faces. Mickey understood the world, though. Drugs weren't going anywhere, and policing the drug trade was like trying to divert the Mississippi River with a bucket. Maybe you could move a little water, but the Mississippi wasn't going anywhere.

Since Mickey couldn't take every drug dealer off the street, he focused on the most violent. More important than that, he helped those who helped him. When other cops were conducting buy-busts in an area, he'd tell his nonviolent partners so they'd disappear for a while. They'd slip him some cash to thank him, and his police colleagues would clean the streets. Everybody won. The dealers who stayed out of jail treated their customers well, the violent guys rotted in a cell, and Mickey made a damn good living.

Though his sister worked in St. Augustine County, Mickey didn't know the cops here. He couldn't trust them, but he could use them. He parked near the station, checked that his badge was visible on his belt, and then started walking.

After killing the nurse, he had cut deep gouges into her legs and arms to draw out her blood. Then he dumped her body in the middle of nowhere. Her blood would draw insects and whatever predators lived out there. He didn't know who owned the property or what its owner used it for, but it was wooded and isolated. Someone would find the body eventually—probably when buzzards circled overhead—but he'd have time to get out of town before then. Since Maddie hadn't known him before he showed up at her house, no one would have any reason to look at him. He was clear.

Vans and trucks from various construction companies surrounded the police department's headquarters, while a temporary chain-link fence and opaque nylon barrier blocked off the front door. Mickey followed a sign to a side entrance. The door was open, and a hallway brought him to a set of stairs that led down to the basement and up to the second floor. He took the stairs down, figuring he had a fifty-fifty shot of ending up in the right place. That left him in a long hallway that led nowhere.

"You lost, chief?"

The voice came from one of the rooms he passed. Mickey pulled back his jacket to expose his badge before going back and sticking his head into the doorway of a cavernous room. Wire racks full of baskets stretched back like a supermarket. There was a bank vault built into the wall, and a heavyset man sat behind an old wooden desk.

"I'm Detective Mickey Lyons, Chicago PD," he said. "I was hoping to talk to somebody about my sister. She's missing."

The man nodded and reached for the phone on his

desk.

"Your sister live around here?" he asked.

"Her boyfriend does. I think she came to visit him."

The fat guy nodded, hit buttons, and then told someone named Trisha that a detective from out of town needed to see her. Then he hung up.

"Our dispatcher will meet you by the staircase," he said. "There's nothing down here."

Mickey nodded and looked around.

"This your evidence room? It's nice. How many officers do you guys have?"

The fat guy thought for a moment.

"Off the top of my head, forty-five sworn officers. We've had some retirements lately, so that may be off."

Mickey lowered his chin and nodded again.

"This is a lot of space for forty-five officers."

"It is," said the fat guy. "We're lucky. Like I said, Trisha's upstairs waiting for you."

"Thank you," said Mickey, nodding his thanks. He backtracked through the building and found a middle-aged uniformed officer waiting for him near the staircase.

"Trisha Marshall," she said, looking around. "Sorry. There should have been a sign directing you upstairs."

"I'm Mickey Lyons," he said. "And no problem. I was hoping I could talk to somebody about my sister. She lives in St. Louis, but her boyfriend apparently lives around here. I can't get in touch with her, and I'm getting worried."

Trisha nodded and started climbing the steps. He

walked beside her.

"What's your sister's name?"

"Tessa Armstrong," he said. "I don't know her boyfriend's name."

Trisha paused but then furrowed her brow.

"I'll take you right to Sheriff Delgado's office," she said. "Since you're a detective, he's the man you should see."

The pit in Mickey's stomach tightened. The dispatcher may not have said anything, but her pause told him she recognized Tessa's name. They walked through a dark second-floor hallway to an office with a nameplate outside that said *Sheriff George Delgado*. Trisha went inside first and spoke to the sheriff alone. Then the two of them emerged. Sheriff Delgado was fifty or fifty-five and had salt-and-pepper-colored hair and a craggy, pitted face. He shook Mickey's hand.

"Afternoon, Detective," said the sheriff. "I'm George Delgado. Let's have a seat inside. Trisha, can you get us some coffee?"

"I'm fine, but thank you," said Mickey. "Ms. Marshall recognized my sister's name. I'm guessing you know her, too. What's going on? Don't glad-hand me."

Delgado brought his hand to his chin. Trisha gave him a sympathetic look.

"We know your sister," said Delgado. "Let's have a seat inside. I'm sorry, but I don't have good news for you."

Mickey's throat tightened, but he didn't let his

discomfort show on his face. He nodded and followed Delgado inside. The St. Augustine County Sheriff's Department may not have had a lot of money, but they sure had space. Sheriff Delgado's office had a conference table, a comfortable seating area with two couches and a coffee table, and space for his desk and two chairs. Rugs covered the floor, demarcating the various spaces, while enormous windows overlooked the town.

The sheriff led him to the seating area and gestured to Mickey to sit on one of the couches.

"Is my sister dead?"

Delgado sat on the couch across from him and folded his hands together on his lap and nodded.

"Yeah," he said, his voice low. "A housekeeper at the Wayfair Motel found her body two days ago. Someone shot her multiple times. I'm sorry."

The pain started in his jaw, but it traveled to his neck as he gritted his teeth. His right shoulder twitched, and he balled his hands into fists on his lap.

"Do you have a suspect?"

"It's an active investigation. I appreciate that you're a detective, but we prefer to keep our investigations close to the chest—especially with family. I'm sure you understand."

It made sense, so Mickey nodded. The sheriff then spent about ten minutes asking Mickey questions about Tessa and their relationship. He had last spoken to her two weeks ago, although they had exchanged text messages five or six days ago. He didn't know her boyfriend or whether she had friends in town, and he didn't know anyone who would want to do her harm. Importantly, he was in Chicago at the presumed time of her death.

"Your sister didn't have an ID on her when we arrived at the crime scene, but we found a plastic bag containing over a hundred hydrocodone pills and an envelope containing two thousand dollars cash. Did your sister have a problem with drugs?"

She was a recovering drug addict, but opioids weren't her drug of choice. She preferred cocaine. Telling the sheriff that, though, would just give him questions Mickey would rather not answer. He nodded.

"Yeah," he said, his voice soft. He looked down at his hands. "She's been in and out of rehab, but I thought she was clean."

The sheriff sighed and nodded.

"Addiction is hard. Once you're addicted to something, you're never over it."

Mickey nodded and swallowed.

"Are drugs a problem in this county?"

Delgado shrugged and tilted his head to the side.

"Drugs are a problem everywhere."

"True," said Mickey, nodding, "but you found Tessa with a lot of pills and a lot of cash. You think she was dealing to fund a habit?"

The sheriff paused and then rubbed his chin.

"We don't know," he said. "It's possible. If a rival dealer killed her, though, he wouldn't have left the drugs and money behind."

Mickey considered for a moment and then raised his eyebrows.

"I'm a narcotics detective, so I pop street dealers daily," he said. "Street dealers—at least those hooked on their own stuff—don't have that kind of money on them. If they did, they'd use it to buy drugs."

The sheriff nodded but said nothing.

"Was my sister trafficking drugs with her boyfriend?" Mickey asked.

The sheriff leaned forward and seemed to consider his answer.

"I can't say what your sister did or didn't do. That said, St. Augustine isn't Chicago. We've got some knuckleheads who sell dope, and we've got some boneheads who take it, but our dealers are small time. You don't have to worry about your sister or her boyfriend. Ms. Armstrong had some pills on her when she died, but she wasn't some kind of drug kingpin. I'd bet my last dollar on that."

Mickey exhaled a long breath and nodded.

"I appreciate you telling me that," he said. "Tessa is special. *Was* special. She had problems, but I hope you don't judge her for those. Her husband was a shitbag. He screwed her up."

The sheriff raised his eyebrow. "Was their relationship abusive?"

Mickey shook his head. "Not physically. Emotionally, maybe. He's just a prick."

"I'll convey your observations to Detective Court. She's our lead investigator on the case. And don't worry about your sister's reputation. We keep our investigations private, and we don't judge murder victims. We'll do our best to find out what happened to her. Then we'll do our best to put her killer in prison. Murderers don't get away in St. Augustine."

A lot of officers in small police departments thought that, but very few had the resources or experience to conduct a thorough homicide investigation. Still, he nodded as if it comforted him.

"I appreciate that, Sheriff," he said, standing and reaching for his wallet for a business card. The sheriff took one and shook his hand. "I'm staying in St. Louis, but my card has my cell phone number on it. If your detective has questions or needs anything, she can call me day or night."

"I'll tell her that," said Delgado. He escorted Mickey out of the building and wished him luck. Mickey walked to his car, and once he sat in the front seat, he pulled out his phone to text his boss.

Tessa's dead.

Within moments, his boss called him back.

"I'm sorry, Mickey. Tessa was a fine young woman."

"Yeah, she was," said Mickey, his voice low. "She had a boyfriend. I think he's their primary suspect."

His boss hesitated. "You just lost your sister. You don't need to be there."

Already Mickey felt a lump growing in his throat.

"Tessa's my responsibility," he said. "I recruited her, and this is my territory. And I need the distraction."

"All right, then. What's your plan?"

Mickey followed the sidewalk toward his truck.

"I'll play it by ear. If Tessa's boyfriend killed her, he needs to die. We might have to take care of him anyway because he knows more than he should. I'll knock some sense into our supply chain down here, too. I visited one of Tessa's clients. She broke when she saw my badge and asked for a deal. She said she had recordings."

"Did you handle it?"

"Yeah," said Mickey, nodding. "She won't be a problem. If one broke, though, others might, too. I might need some help."

"I'll send you Adrian and Lukas. They're capable, and you've worked with them before. Will the locals be a problem?"

Mickey shook his head. "No. They're clueless rednecks. We'll be just fine."

As Mickey reached his car, his boss paused.

"Tessa was a good worker, and her territory brought us a lot of money. We can't afford a slowdown."

"I know," said Mickey. "We'll be back on track soon enough. I'll talk to you when I have an update."

"We're a brotherhood. We take care of our own here. Remember that. If you need anything, do not hesitate to call me."

"Thank you," said Mickey. "I'll keep you informed of my progress."

He hung up, sat down in the front seat of his car, and rubbed his eyes. Something deep inside him ached for his baby sister, but he choked it down. He didn't have time to grieve. There was too much work to do.

13

Bob and I spent the next several hours trying to track down the men on Mr. Armstrong's list. Most of the guys cooperated, but they had little to tell us. Then we met an accountant who had dated her off and on for almost a year but who wasn't comfortable dating a married woman. She refused to leave her husband for him, so that ended their relationship. I would have written off the conversation as unhelpful except that he mentioned spending time in her condo on Euclid Avenue in the city's Central West End. That was the first time we'd heard of the place.

Bob and I got the address and headed out. St. Louis's Central West End was an upscale part of town with a lot of great bars, restaurants, and shops. Outside the region, St. Louis had a lousy reputation, and to some degree, it deserved it. The city hadn't always had its current problems with crime and poverty, though. In the late nineteenth and early twentieth centuries, it had been one of the wealthiest, largest, and most cosmopolitan cities in the world. It had even hosted the World's Fair in 1904, something many people in the town still talked about as fondly as if they had attended.

The Central West End was a tree-lined remnant of that gilded era. Some of its old mansions were ten or fifteen thousand square feet, while its former hotels now held some of the nicest condos in the city. I parallel parked in front of a modern condominium complex on Euclid Avenue and called the St. Louis Metropolitan Police Department's liaison officer to let him know Bob and I were working in the area. He wished us luck and said they appreciated the call.

Restaurants, bars, and upscale shops lined the streets. Even with winter on its way, half a dozen people sipped coffee in front of the bagel shop down the street.

"I could move here," said Bob.

"Could you?" I asked. "The noise would get to me. I like the peace and quiet back home."

"There's something appealing about walking to breakfast."

I tilted my head to the side and nodded.

"That would be nice," I said. "It'd be hard to have a dog here, though."

Bob pulled open the lobby's glass front door and held it for me. The building had a marble floor and dark wood paneling on the walls and ceiling. It reminded me of an upscale hotel. I walked toward the doorman's desk and showed him my badge.

"Afternoon," I said. "I'm Detective Joe Court with the St. Augustine County Sheriff's Department. My partner is Sergeant Bob Reitz. Can you tell me which apartment Tessa Armstrong lived in?"

The doorman wore a simple navy jacket, white collared shirt, and maroon tie. He was about fifty, and the look on his face told me he had practice staring down people who requested access to his building.

"I haven't seen Ms. Armstrong for a few days. If

you'd like, I can give her a message on your behalf when she returns."

I leaned against his desk and crossed my arms.

"You haven't seen her because someone murdered her. We need to search her apartment for information related to her death. We know she lives here, but we don't know her specific address. You can tell us, or we can knock on random doors and hope we get lucky. What would you like to do?"

He blinked.

"Do you have a warrant to search her condo?"

I shook my head. "She's dead, so I don't need one. Privacy rights don't extend to the deceased."

He drew in a breath.

"I'm sorry Ms. Armstrong is dead, but I need to talk to my boss before I can give out her information."

"We're not asking for private information," I said. "We just want her address."

"Still, I can't give that out without speaking to my boss first."

"Fine," I said, sighing. "We'll figure it out on our own."

I paused when I noticed a bank of metal mailboxes, the kind I'd see in a post office, built into the far wall. Each box had a name etched onto a brass plate on the exterior. I walked over and read off the names until I came to Tessa's. Then I looked at Bob.

"She's in 1901."

"This is private property," said the doorman. "I've

asked you to leave. Unless you two have a warrant, you're trespassing."

"The homeowner's dead. As the building doorman, you don't have standing to prevent us from entering the apartment," I said, glancing at him as we walked toward the elevator. "Stay where you are. If you try to stop us, I'll arrest you for hindering prosecution. Since we're working a homicide, your act would be a felony. Sound good to you?"

He picked up his phone but said nothing. We'd have guests from the Fifth District police station soon, but that wouldn't be a problem. I knew people there. Neither Bob nor I spoke as the elevator lifted us to the nineteenth story. Tessa's floor had four apartments with hers on the southwest corner of the building, which likely gave her nice views of both Forest Park and the sunset.

Since we didn't have a key, I used the pick set I kept in my purse to pick the lock. The interior was neat and clean. A short hallway opened to a two-story living room with a spectacular view of the surrounding streets. I looked at Bob.

"You get the bedrooms and bathrooms," I said, reaching into my purse for gloves. I pulled out a pair for me and a second pair for him. "I'll get the kitchen and living room."

"Sounds good," he said, snapping on his gloves. I did likewise and started my search. The kitchen was neat, clean, and modern. Nothing looked out of place, but a thin coating of flour dusted the countertops near the stove. The table beside the front door held about two dozen envelopes from banks, credit card companies, and financial advisors, but most were junk. The living room was gorgeous but held nothing of interest to my investigation. Still, I pulled off the cushions of her sofas and looked beneath her coffee table for anything hidden.

It was just a condo, though. There were no hidden messages, no drugs, no guns, nothing that would be worth killing someone over. After striking out, I walked down a hallway. Bob was in the largest bedroom. He nodded when I stopped in the doorway.

"You find anything?" I asked.

"Nothing interesting. Bathroom had a couple of pill containers, but the drugs were all prescribed to Ms. Armstrong. She's got a lot of dresses in her closet, but no guns or cash or anything like that. I think she's an artist. There are paint supplies and an easel in a spare bedroom."

I nodded and reached into my purse for my phone.

"We'll take some pictures and go," I said, sliding my thumb across the screen. Trisha had apparently called while I was searching the kitchen. I hadn't heard. "Give me a minute."

He nodded while I dialed and walked down the hallway toward the living room.

"Trisha, hey," I said. "It's Joe. I'm in St. Louis working the Tessa Armstrong murder with Bob Reitz. What's up?"

"Any way you can come back? We've got a body."

I grimaced.

"Is the death suspicious?"

"It's a twenty-year-old girl found dead in her apartment. Could be an overdose, could be natural causes, could be something else. We need a detective on it."

"Okay," I said, sighing. "Tell Delgado I'll be on my way."

Trisha told me to drive safely. I walked back to Tessa's bedroom, where Bob was pushing shut the drawers on her end tables.

"I've got to drive home to work a suspicious death. Stick around here and talk to the neighbors and anyone else in the building who might know Tessa's boyfriend."

Bob straightened. "If you're driving back to St. Augustine, how do I get home?"

"Uber or a cab," I said. "That's why I said we should take two cars. I appreciate the sheriff's guidelines, but they don't always work in the field."

"He's not going to enjoy hearing that," said Bob.

"I'm glad I don't have to tell him," I said, looking around the room one more time. It was a nice bedroom, but the search was a bust. I looked at him again. "Good luck. I'll see you at home."

He grunted, and I hurried out of the apartment, silently preparing myself for the case that lay ahead. At twenty, my victim in St. Augustine was just a kid. I hated dead kids.

14

I hit rush hour traffic on my way out of St. Louis, which stretched a one-hour drive into an hour and a half. By the time I reached my victim's apartment in the town of St. Augustine, the sun had set, and the complex's sodium-vapor lamps cast a dull orange light over the parking lot. Almost a dozen people stood outside the yellow crime-scene tape the first responders had strewn around our victim's door.

I parked behind a marked police cruiser on the street in front of the building. A uniformed officer—I couldn't see who under the glare of the overhead lights—walked toward me as I reached for a fresh notepad and blue nitrile gloves from the evidence collection kit I kept on my cruiser's back seat. When I looked up again, I found Officer Doug Patricia standing outside my cruiser. Doug was forty or forty-five and had been a cop for about ten years. He filled in for Trisha on the dispatcher's desk some, but he stayed in the field as a patrol officer most nights. I nodded to him and opened my door. He smiled.

"Hey, Joe," he said. "I know you were working a case, so sorry to call you out."

"That's okay," I said, standing and closing my door behind me. "What have we got?"

He looked at his notepad and put the facts of his investigation so far together.

"The deceased is Jasmine Kelley. She's a twenty-year-old female Caucasian. Paramedics pronounced her deceased at 5:13 p.m. this evening. She has no obvious external injuries and no obvious cause of death. The call came in at 4:53 p.m. The caller was Cynthia Brimmer. She's a co-worker of the deceased.

"Ms. Brimmer came over after Jasmine missed her shift and didn't respond to phone calls. When Jasmine didn't answer a knock at the door, Ms. Brimmer used a key under the mat to let herself in. She found Jasmine unresponsive on the couch and called 911. Trisha dispatched paramedics. They arrived at 5:01. I arrived at 5:11."

My heart slowed, and I felt something heavy build in my gut.

"The victim was named Jasmine," I said, blinking. "Did she have red hair and big brown eyes?"

"I don't know about her eyes because they were closed, but the red hair is right. You know her?"

I brought my elbows close to my body and looked down. My arms and legs felt heavy.

"Yeah, I know her," I said. "She's a nice girl. She's a waitress at Able's Diner, but she was saving up to go to college. We've sat and talked a couple of times."

"She a friend?"

I shook my head. "An acquaintance. She was too bright to work at a diner all her life. I liked her."

Doug let me have a moment to myself before clearing his throat.

"What do you want to do?"

"Work the case," I said, glancing at him. "Any signs of forced entry?"

"Nope," he said, shaking his head. "No forced entry, and the apartment's clean. We called Dr. Sheridan's office, but they're pretty backed up. They'll be sending somebody out as soon as possible."

I nodded. "Until we learn otherwise, we'll treat it like a homicide. Have you talked to the neighbors yet?"

"Yeah. Most are students at Waterford College, so they keep odd hours. Nobody reported seeing anyone try to break into the apartment, and nobody heard anything out of the usual. The neighbor above her reported that the victim had music on yesterday evening, but it wasn't loud enough for a party."

I nodded. "You find drugs in the apartment?"

"Not on our walk-through, but we didn't open drawers or anything. You think she overdosed?"

"Unless she had medical issues we didn't know about, I'd say it's a high probability," I said. "Thanks for your work on this. Who's got the logbook?"

"Emily Hayes. She's by the front door."

I thanked him again and walked toward the apartment. The complex had a series of small, two-story buildings, each of which held four apartments. Even from the edge of the parking lot, they looked cheap. Green boxwoods ran along the base of the building and around the first-floor apartments' patios, lending them a bit of privacy. The second-story units had small balconies.

I had never been to Jasmine's apartment, but she had

a first-floor unit by the looks of things. Emily nodded to me and held out a clipboard for me to sign as I approached.

"Hey," she said. "Kevius is inside. I can call Darlene if you need her."

Kevius and Darlene were our forensic technicians. While Kevius was still young, Darlene was a veteran lab scientist with an advanced degree in organic chemistry. She was the best forensic scientist in the state and could have gotten a job anywhere, but she stuck around St. Augustine because her husband was a tenured physics professor at Waterford College. We were lucky to have her.

"I'm sure Kevius will do fine," I said, signing the log sheet. "When Dr. Sheridan gets here, send him right in."

She nodded and said she would. Then I walked into the apartment. I hadn't seen Jasmine's particular unit, but I had been inside apartments in the complex, and they all looked alike. Cream-colored paint covered the lightly textured walls, while thin beige carpet covered the floor. The living room was open to a kitchen with Formica countertops and oak cabinets.

Jasmine lay on top of a deep, heavily padded brown couch. As Doug Patricia had said, her eyes were closed. She wore a black, two-piece dress that left her midriff exposed. Even at twenty-eight, I didn't know if I could have pulled that outfit off, but Jasmine wore it well. A wooden clip pulled her hair from her face, and her makeup was impeccable. She looked ready to go dancing.

Odd considering she had died alone.

I snapped pictures of her and the room with my phone. Then I leaned closer to her. She smelled like alcohol, but there were no glasses on her coffee table or on the bar that separated her living room from the kitchen. She wasn't legally of age to drink, but maybe she went to a friend's house for drinks earlier and came home after she started feeling poorly.

I walked to her bedroom. She had a king-sized bed. The sheets and comforter were mussed, and clothes were strewn about the floor. Kevius Reid stood in her ensuite bathroom, filling out the tag on an evidence bag.

"You found something?" I asked.

"Maybe," he said, glancing up at me. "She's got four prescriptions in her name, and I'm bagging each of them in case she overdosed."

"Good thought," I said. "You find anything illegal?"

He shook his head. "Not even weed, ma'am."

"How about booze?"

He nodded. "She's got a bottle of white wine in her fridge. It's unopened. You want me to bag that, too?"

I shook my head. "No. We'll leave it for now."

He nodded, and I walked back to the kitchen. Jasmine had six frozen meals in the freezer but little fresh food in the fridge. She probably ate at work a lot. As Kevius had said, her fridge held a bottle of white wine, but I couldn't find a liquor cabinet or bar. It left me feeling a little unnerved. She had dressed to go out with friends, and she had died after drinking alcohol. Someone had been here with her.

I took a dozen pictures of the kitchen and then noticed something odd on the counter beside her toaster. It was a can of WD-40, a penetrating oil used to lubricate metal parts—among many other things. Jasmine could have used a can of WD-40 around the house, but she shouldn't have kept it around food. I picked the can up and noticed the weight. It was too heavy in the middle and too light at either end. That wasn't normal.

I sighed and gripped the middle and bottom of the can tight and twisted. The bottom unscrewed, as I had expected it to, revealing a cavity into which she had stuffed a bag of colored pills. I pulled it out, put the can down, and took pictures with my cell phone. There were about thirty round pills imprinted with stars. They looked like candy, but I suspected they were ecstasy. One of our uniformed officers should have a field test for it.

"Evening, Joe," came a voice from near the apartment's door. I glanced up to see Dr. Trevor Sheridan and his assistant, Sam, walking inside. When they saw Jasmine on the couch, they slowed. Dr. Sheridan sighed. "She's young."

"Twenty," I said. "She was a nice young woman."

He looked at me and then knelt beside her.

"You knew her?"

I nodded even though he couldn't see me. "Not well, but I had met her a few times. I found some pills in the kitchen. There's a bottle of wine in the fridge."

Sheridan nodded. "I can smell the booze on her, but

it doesn't smell like wine. Rum, maybe?"

"Maybe," I said, leaving the pills on the counter. "While you're here, I'll find her phone."

Sheridan nodded. I smiled hello to Sam and then checked out the master bedroom again. Kevius was just finishing up in the bathroom, so I asked whether he had seen her phone. He pointed to an end table beside her bed. Jasmine had an iPhone with a crack in the upper right corner of the screen. I used the power button to turn it on, but it required her thumbprint to open. We could get around that.

I carried the phone to the living room and found Dr. Sheridan in the kitchen, looking at the pills. Sam was wheeling in a stretcher from their van.

"Hey, Sam," I said. "Can you give me her thumb for a moment?"

Sam locked the wheels of his stretcher, nodded, and knelt beside Jasmine's body. He could barely move her arm, which meant rigor had already set in. It had been a while since she died. Eventually, Sam got her thumb free, and I used that to unlock her phone. It felt creepy, but it worked. I thanked him and then removed the phone's password and other security features so I could look at it later.

"She's been dead for a while," said Sam, reaching to a kit beside him for a scalpel and a thermometer with a sharp tip. He made a small incision in her side and then inserted the thermometer to get the temperature of her liver. He looked up at his boss. "She's 72.4 degrees."

Dr. Sheridan nodded. "What's the ambient temperature?"

Sam stood and checked out the digital thermostat on her wall.

"Seventy-two."

"Average body will drop about a degree and a half per hour until it reaches room temperature," said Sheridan. "Given the conditions of the room, she died between eighteen and thirty-six hours ago."

"If you can narrow that window, I'd appreciate it," I said.

"We should be able to accommodate you," said Sheridan.

I thanked him and then thought through the work I had ahead of me. The more I saw of her apartment, the more I doubted she had died alone. If I had to guess, her friends cleaned up and ran to avoid getting in trouble. Even if Jasmine had died of natural causes, I still needed to notify her family. We'd have to deal with the drugs found in her kitchen, too. I also wanted to talk to her friends.

Before doing any of that, though, I needed to walk through the apartment once more and ensure that I had seen everything I needed to see. The kitchen was clear. Kevius said he had a presumptive test for MDMA in his van, so I didn't bother touching the drugs I had found. He could handle that. Instead, I walked through her bedroom and took pictures of her bed and the clothes on the ground. The trash cans in her bedroom and bathroom were both empty.

The guest bedroom had a surprise for me. It had a simple bed and a nice makeup vanity with lights, but she had attached a camera to the top of the mirror. A cord connected the camera to a laptop computer.

"Kevius, have you checked out the second bedroom?"

Kevius came into the room and nodded.

"She's got a lot of makeup, but no drugs. The bed doesn't look like anybody's slept in it for a while. The closet's full of dresses on hangers."

"What's she filming in here?"

Kevius opened his mouth to say something, but then he shut it again. I raised my eyebrows at him.

"You know something?"

He tilted his head to the side. "The camera looks like it's pointed at the bed."

"You think she's filming porn?" I asked, my brow furrowed.

He shrugged. "Maybe not porn, but she's got some revealing outfits. Maybe she's a cam girl."

I shook my head and lowered my chin.

"What's a cam girl?"

He smiled and looked down. It looked as if he wanted to say something, but no words came out. Then he cleared his throat.

"It's like a video chat. You talk to her, and she does stuff for you and lets you watch. I've never done it, but I've seen ads for it."

I paused to process that.

"So, someone would pay her a fee, and she'd, what, dance naked in front of the camera?"

"If that's what you want," he said. "Different girls do different things."

It sounded as if he knew more about cam girls than he let on, but his personal life was his secret. I nodded again and then took pictures of the setup with my cell.

"It's something to consider," I said. I sighed. "Good luck here. I've got the dirty work now. I've got to track down our victim's family and tell them Jasmine's dead."

He nodded and gave me a sympathetic look.

"Good luck," he said.

I thanked him and nodded as I walked out of the apartment and to my car. This morning, my next-of-kin notification with Carl Armstrong had gone over better than I expected, but I doubted this one would be so easy. Tessa Armstrong's next-of-kin was a husband with whom she had an arrangement. Jasmine's next-of-kin would be a mom or a dad or a sister or a grandparent. Shortly, I would break someone's heart so badly it might never go back together again.

I hated this part of the job.

15

Since I had already unlocked Jasmine's phone, I searched through her address book until I found an entry labeled *MOM*. She had a local number. I typed it into my phone. The extension rang twice before a woman's soft voice answered. I explained who I was and asked whether she knew Jasmine. She said her name was Anna Kelley, and she confirmed that she was Jasmine's mother. She deserved a face-to-face conversation, so I got her address and told her I'd be over soon.

The Kelley family lived in a cozy two-story bungalow on a wooded lot about ten miles west of the town of St. Augustine. A baby swing hung from a tree on the front lawn, and a bright yellow Tonka truck sat in the mulch on a flower bed in front of the home's front window. I couldn't even see their nearest neighbor through the woods surrounding the house.

I parked in the driveway, but before I could open my door, two women stepped onto the porch. Like Jasmine, both women had red hair, and both were pretty. The older woman—Anna Kelley, if I'd had to guess—brought her hands to her face and cried as I walked toward her. The younger woman—a sister or cousin—put her arm around Anna's shoulder and hugged her tight.

"It's Jasmine, isn't it?" asked Anna. "She's dead. I tried calling her, but she didn't answer."

I allowed a measure of softness into my voice.

"Can we talk inside?"

The younger woman covered her mouth.

"That's it, isn't it?" she asked. "My sister's dead."

I couldn't deny it any longer, so I nodded. The two women hugged each other tighter and then fell to the steps sobbing. My knees felt weak, and skin all over my body tingled.

I sat beside them as they cried. After about ten minutes, they regained some measure of composure.

"Is there anyone you'd like me to call?" I asked. "A minister or another family member?"

They shook their heads and said no. We sat there for another couple of minutes in silence. Then Jasmine's sister looked at me.

"What happened?" she asked.

"We're still working on that," I said. "Are you Erica?"

She blinked a few times and then nodded. "Yeah. How'd you know that?"

"Jasmine mentioned you," I said. "I didn't know her well, but I came into Able's Diner at weird hours. Sometimes, I was the only customer in the building. We've talked some."

Anna, the mom, locked eyes with me. "You're that famous cop. She talked about you. She liked you."

"I'm not famous, but I liked her, too," I said, nodding. "She was bright and nice."

Somehow the silence felt heavier than it had just a moment earlier. I let them grieve for a few minutes.

"How'd it happen?" Anna asked eventually. "Was it a

car accident?"

I shook my head. "No. She died at home, we think. She didn't show up to work today, so Cynthia Brimmer—a co-worker—went to her apartment to check on her. Cynthia found her dead and called us."

They let that sink in.

"If she didn't make it to work today, she's been dead for a while," said Erica.

I nodded. "We think she died somewhere between eighteen and thirty-six hours ago."

Anna's face furrowed, and she started crying again. Erica tried to soothe her mother, but no amount of soothing would make this better.

"Was she alone?" asked Anna.

It was a tough question to answer without speculating. I looked down to the deck boards.

"It's still very early in our investigation, which means we have more questions than answers. It's possible she died of natural causes. Our coroner will look at her as soon as he can and tell us what he thinks. Until we learn otherwise, though, we'll treat the case as a murder."

Erica cocked her head to the side and furrowed her brow.

"Who would murder my sister? Everybody loved her!"

"We don't know that it was a murder," I said. "We treat it like one, though, so we don't miss anything."

She nodded, but I didn't know whether she accepted that explanation.

"Unfortunately, I have to ask you some questions," I said. "Some of them might be hard to answer, but I need you to be honest. My job is to investigate Jasmine's death. We'll do our best to find out what happened to her, and I need your help to do that. Are you okay to talk for a few minutes?"

Both women nodded.

"When did you last speak to Jasmine?"

"Yesterday," said Erica. "She wanted to show me a dress she just bought. It was cute."

"Black two-piece with a crisscrossed top?" I asked.

She nodded.

"We found her in it," I said. "What time did you talk to her?"

She wasn't sure, so she went inside for her phone to check.

"She texted me the picture at 4:07 p.m."

"Was she alone?" I asked.

Erica nodded. "She worked until two. She and her friends planned to go dancing in St. Louis."

I did the math in my head. If Jasmine had spoken to her sister at four yesterday, that narrowed our timeline considerably.

"Jasmine had a video camera in her bedroom," I said. I hesitated and looked at Anna and Erica for a negative reaction. They didn't so much as twitch. "Do you know why she'd have that?"

"She has a makeup channel on YouTube," sad Erica.

"And what does that entail?" I asked.

Erica tucked a few strands of red hair behind her ear.

"She shoots videos and tells you how to apply your makeup to get a particular look," said Erica. "It's a video blog. It's a tough market, but Jasmine was great at it. People liked her. She talked about her life and what she was doing. She didn't make much money, but if she kept going the way she was, she could have done it for a living in a year or two."

"She's also on Instagram," said Anna. "She's got almost forty thousand followers."

And that made her something of a minor internet celebrity. From my very limited brushes with fame, I knew the problems that could bring.

"Did she ever have problems with fans?"

Erica looked down. Anna sighed.

"Since she's started, she's had two stalkers," said Erica. "One was a woman named Iris Hicks. She left a lot of comments on Jasmine's videos, and Jasmine responded. Somehow, that made Iris think Jasmine was in love with her. She thought they'd run off together. She never got aggressive, though. Jasmine blocked her on social media, and that was it. The other was a guy named John Conway. He showed up at the house."

"I ran him off with a shotgun," said Anna. "I told him if I ever saw him again, I'd shoot him. He hasn't come back."

I'd look into him all the same. Anna, Erica, and I spoke for another half hour, but I learned nothing that seemed pertinent to my investigation. Before leaving, I asked whether Jasmine had any friends she might have confided in.

"Emma Hannity," said Erica. "We're not related to her, but she's our sister. Mom practically raised her."

I looked to Anna. She nodded.

"I'll call her and tell her the news about Jasmine," said Anna. "Emma and Jasmine were close. She'd know more about Jasmine's friends than I do."

Erica gave me her phone number and address.

"Okay," I said, reaching to my purse for the business cards in my wallet. I handed one to each person. "Thanks for your help. And, again, I'm sorry for your loss. I'll do everything I can to find out what happened to Jasmine. If you need anything, call me. I'm available twenty-four hours a day. I'll do what I can to keep you informed of my investigation."

Anna thanked me. Erica gave me a quick hug. I walked back to my car with my head hung low. The case shouldn't have bothered me. More than likely, Dr. Sheridan would call me in a couple of days to tell me he had found a lethal concentration of cocaine or heroin or some other drug in her system—or he'd tell me she had a previously unknown and fatal medical condition. Both would be heartbreaking for her family, but my job would be done.

Only it wouldn't be.

I couldn't find a dirty glass, but I would bet my last dollar she had been drinking alcohol when she died. Not only that, she hadn't worn that cute new dress or put on makeup to sit around the house by herself. Someone—or maybe multiple someones—had been with her when she died. Maybe they were just hanging out, or maybe they were doing illegal drugs. It didn't matter. Jasmine had a medical emergency, but instead of taking her to a hospital, her supposed friends cleaned up her kitchen and left her to die alone on her couch.

People died every day, but casual indifference to death bothered me. If Jasmine's friends watched her die and did nothing, I didn't know whether I could send them to jail, but I'd investigate them all the same. I'd also tell the world what they had done. It was the least I could do. Unfortunately, it was also the most I could do, and that sucked.

16

After my interview, I left the Kelleys' house, dropped off my cruiser at my station, and drove home in my Volvo. The sun was down, and it was getting cold. Roy was in the dog run in the backyard when I arrived. He usually jumped for joy when he saw me, but now he seemed to keep his distance a little. I petted his back anyway when he walked beside me to go inside.

"You're mad because dinner's late, aren't you?" I asked.

He didn't answer—dogs rarely spoke—but he perked up when I poured his food into his bowl. I loved Roy, but I hated coming home that late to feed him. I used to have a neighbor who took care of my dog when I was late and who kept him company during the day, but she had passed away. As much as I loved to have Roy waiting for me at home, I wondered whether this was the right environment for him. He was a great dog and a good friend, but love didn't feed him at night or keep him company during the day.

After he ate, he sauntered over to me at the kitchen table and sat down near me so I could pet him. He grinned at me the way only a big, sweet dog could.

"Are you still happy here, dude?" I asked, scratching his ear. He leaned into my hand and made a contented noise deep in his throat. "You deserve a good life."

I stopped rubbing his ear, and he opened his mouth

into a wide yawn.

"Are you as tired as me?"

Roy panted but said nothing. That was his custom. Since I hadn't played with him much that day, before heading to bed, he and I went outside. Our breaths were frosty, but he didn't seem to mind the temperature. I tossed him a ball in the backyard, and every time he retrieved it, he got a peanut butter dog treat.

When Roy moved in with me, he had just flunked out of training to become a cadaver dog. He was too lazy, my mother had said. Back then, he hadn't even wanted to retrieve a ball when I threw it—despite his breeding as a retriever. As I later discovered, though, Roy wasn't lazy. He simply didn't know how to be a dog. His breeder had brought Roy into the world for a purpose and a job. His needs as a dog didn't fit into that purpose. No one ever mistreated him, but no one played with him, either. No little boys or girls had curled up beside him, and no one had thrown him a ball to end the day. Many dogs would be fine with that life, but Roy needed companionship. I tried to give him what he needed, but sometimes I wondered if that was enough.

After about fifteen minutes in the yard, Roy's tongue hung out of his mouth. He seemed happy and tired, so we went inside. I made a peanut butter and jelly sandwich for dinner before changing into pajamas. My eyes wanted to close, but I still had Jasmine on my mind, so I turned on the news. Roy jumped onto the couch and sat beside me. I stroked the fur on his head and neck, which he seemed to like. Tessa Armstrong's death led the newscast. They didn't give many details, but a spokesman for Carl Armstrong asked for privacy.

I sighed and turned off the TV before the story finished, not wanting to see that. Then I looked to the dog.

"I'm going to bed. You can stay up."

Roy must not have been too interested in staying up because he followed me to the bedroom and then hopped to the end of the bed. He was snoring before my head touched my pillow. Unfortunately, almost the moment my eyes shut, my cell phone rang.

"What fresh hell is this?"

I grabbed the phone from my end table and answered without looking at the screen.

"Yeah?" I asked.

"Joe, sorry to call so late. I've got someone at the station who needs to see you."

I rubbed my eyes. The caller was Jason Zuckerburg, the night-shift dispatcher. Jason had been in the department for thirty-five years and had good judgment. If he thought someone needed to see me, he was probably right.

"Who is it?" I asked.

"Sheppard Altman. He's a business and finance teacher at the local high school. He says he's Tessa Armstrong's boyfriend and was with her the day she died." Jason paused and lowered his voice. "He's pretty broken up. He didn't know she was dead until he saw it on the news."

I sank into the pillow. "Shitty way to find out."

"Yeah. He might be the last person to have seen her alive."

Which meant we needed to have a conversation. I nodded and then sighed.

"Tell him I'll be there as soon as I can."

Jason said he would. Then he hung up. I sat up, and the dog cocked his head at me.

"I've got to go, dude," I said. "You want to stay inside or out?"

Roy lowered his head between his paws but didn't move from the end of the bed.

"Sleep tight, hon. I'll be back as soon as I can."

I put on some clothes, brushed my teeth, and headed out. Since the construction workers had left for the day, the parking lot outside my station had plenty of empty spots, allowing me to park near the door. Inside, the building was quiet, and the lights were dim. When I reached the conference room, I found Jason Zuckerburg behind the desk. With him, I found two men. One was Rajendra Gavani. Mr. Gavani was in his early thirties, just a little older than me, and had dark skin and hair. He was the relatively new guidance counselor at the high school. From all I had seen, he was a nice man.

I didn't recognize the second man. He wore a blue cable-knit sweater and jeans, and like Mr. Gavani, he looked to be in his early to mid-thirties. His hair, combed back and to the right, exposed a V-shaped widow's peak on his forehead. When the two men saw me, they each gave me a tight smile.

"Detective Court," said Jason. "This is Sheppard Altman and Rajendra Gavani. Gentlemen, this is Detective Court. She's the detective investigating Tessa Armstrong's murder."

Altman held out his hand, so I crossed the room and shook it. His grip felt weak, and, though he was fit, he looked as if a gust of wind could knock him over.

"I'm sorry to meet you under these circumstances, Mr. Altman," I said. "Let's go to my office. If you'd like, I can get you some coffee or tea or a soda."

"Do you mind if Rajendra comes with us?" asked Altman.

I smiled at Mr. Gavani.

"That's fine."

The three of us walked to my office, but before we sat down, Altman pointed to the hallway with his thumb.

"I need to use that restroom we passed."

I nodded.

"Okay. Take your time."

When he left the room, I sat behind my desk. Gavani took one of the two chairs in front. Gavani had helped me on a case a couple of weeks ago when he identified a young woman I had found in the home of a drug dealer. He seemed like a good guy.

"So what's going on?" I asked.

Gavani looked toward the door and sighed.

"I'm not sure," he said. "Shepp's a friend. He called at a little after ten and said the news just reported his girlfriend was dead. We live on the same street, so I jogged to his house and found him on his front stoop with his face in his hands. He said he had to talk to the police. So here we are."

I nodded and drew in a breath.

"Did you know Tessa?"

"No," he said, shaking his head. "He talked about her a lot, though. He was in love with her, and she loved him, but she had a husband. They had a complicated relationship."

I nodded.

"What can you tell me about Mr. Altman?"

Gavani tilted his head to the side. "Not much to tell. He's the best teacher we've got on the faculty. Kids love him. He also coaches the freshman boys' basketball team. The varsity and junior varsity coaches get paid, but Shepp volunteers. He's a good man."

"And even though he loved her, he never introduced you to Tessa?"

He shook his head. "She kept a low profile in town. Shepp thought her husband had hired a private investigator to follow her around. He didn't want her to get hurt."

"Mr. Armstrong did hire a private investigator," I said, nodding. "Does he have a temper?"

Gavani shot his eyes to me and then looked at the desk before nodding.

"You'll find it when you do a background check on him, so I'll just come right out and say it. The police in

Scott County arrested him last year for punching a kid's dad after a basketball game. The kid and his dad got into a fight at the end of the game. The fight got physical, and the father shoved his kid against a car while our team was getting onto their bus to go home. Shepp saw the fight and laid the guy out. It was stupid, and it set a bad example. He should have called the police, but he was just trying to protect the kid."

I nodded, and as I wrote notes, a voice called out.

"The school should have fired me."

I looked up to see Sheppard Altman standing in my doorway. He leaned against the frame and crossed his arms.

"Have a seat, Mr. Altman," I said. "Mr. Gavani was just telling me a little about you."

"Rajendra exaggerates," he said, sitting beside his friend. "Harriot Peterson's the best teacher we've got in the school by far. I'm slightly above average."

It was late, and I appreciated him coming in, but I wasn't interested in self-deprecating banter.

"I'm sorry about your girlfriend, Mr. Altman. As Officer Zuckerburg told you, I'm Detective Joe Court, and I'm the detective assigned to investigate Tessa Armstrong's death. I'm here to gather information, so I have to ask you a lot of questions, some of which are personal. Please answer them. If you want a lawyer, you can get a lawyer. If you want to leave, leave. We can even skip a question if you're unwilling to answer one, but if we skip questions, or if you leave, you'll make it a lot harder for me to solve this case. Does that make sense to you?"

He nodded.

"Good," I said. "Before we dive into this, do you own any firearms?"

He shook his head.

"No."

"Okay," I said, nodding. "The day Tessa died, she checked into the Wayfair Motel with a man who matches your description. Was it you?"

He nodded.

"Yeah."

"You have a house in town. Why'd you go to the Wayfair Motel?"

His lips curled into a tight smile.

"St. Augustine's a small town. Half a dozen of my students live within a block of my house. I didn't want them to see me with a woman. I didn't need those rumors. Plus, it was fun to go to a seedy motel."

I nodded.

"And to clarify, at this hotel, you had sexual intercourse with her?"

He narrowed his eyes.

"Why does that matter?"

"Because we found condoms in the trash can," I said. "I'd like to know whether they were yours."

He blinked a few times and then nodded.

"We had sex three times. There should be three condoms."

"Good. There were," I said. "Tessa lives in St. Louis.

Have you been to her apartment there?"

He nodded.

"Yeah. Every other weekend."

"How'd you meet her?"

A smile sprang to his lips.

"I saw her at Rise and Grind. She was drinking a cup of coffee alone. I asked whether she'd mind if I sat at the table with her. She said no, and we started talking about the book she was reading. We stayed for an hour and a half."

"And what book was that?" I asked.

"*A Long Way Gone* by Ishmael Beah. It's a memoir about a man who was swept up in Sierra Leone's civil war when he was twelve years old. It's good. You should read it."

I took some notes at my desk.

"The day Tessa died, what time did you leave the motel?"

"It was about nine-thirty. I had to go to the grocery store before it closed."

"And did you?" I asked.

He nodded.

"I barely got there in time, but yeah."

And if that was true, he might have had an alibi during the time of Tessa's death.

"Did you ever see Tessa with drugs?"

He folded his hands together and looked down. I asked again.

"Tessa had a drug problem in the past," he said. "She

was clean now, though."

"When we found her, she had two thousand dollars cash in an envelope and a lot of pills in a Ziploc bag. Does that surprise you?"

He said nothing, but he wouldn't look at me, either.

"Did you know she had drugs or that kind of money?"

He blinked a few times and then shook his head before looking at me again.

"You said I could skip questions if they made me uncomfortable. I'd like to skip that one."

I made a note of it and then nodded. We kept talking until almost midnight, but I didn't learn much new about her. I'd have to go by the grocery store and see their surveillance video to confirm he was there at the time of her death to clear him, but I doubted he had killed his girlfriend.

Before we finished, I looked at him and gave him a tight smile.

"Anything else you want to tell me?"

"I loved her," he said. "Tessa wasn't just nice. She was kind and good. She had problems, but she was a good person. I asked her to marry me, and she said yes. She planned to divorce her husband, but he was dragging his heels." He paused and swallowed. "I wanted to spend my life with her. Now, I can't."

"I'm sorry for your loss," I said.

"Yeah," he said, standing. Mr. Gavani stood beside him and put an arm over his shoulders and looked to me.

"Can I take him home, Detective?"

"Sure," I said. The two of them left, and I leaned back in my chair. Something about that conversation bothered me. As a police officer in a small county, I had worked all kinds of cases. Car accidents, murders, industrial accidents, accidental drownings—I had investigated every manner of death that existed, and I had talked to families in every stage of bereavement. Altman said and did the right things, he cried at the correct time, and he disappeared when necessary to compose himself. It was perfect.

And that was the problem.

Psychologists and psychiatrists wrote papers about the five stages of grief, but they rarely mentioned that someone grieving could experience all five stages simultaneously. They didn't talk about the unpredictability of emotion or that someone could progress and regress through all five stages of grief in one conversation—or even within one short sentence.

Watching Sheppard Altman talk about Tessa was like seeing a playwright's rendition of how someone should grieve. It was one note, one emotion. It fit the psychological model, but it didn't fit reality. Altman loved and missed Tessa, but there was more going on than he had let me see. If I had to guess, his only honest reaction to any of my questions had been the one he skipped, the one about whether he knew Tessa had drugs and money.

I didn't know where Tessa Armstrong's case was going or who killed her, but I knew now that this was more complicated than I had expected. I sighed. This job was never easy.

17

I wrote notes until well past midnight and drove home with far more questions than I'd had upon going in. Roy met me at the door when I arrived. He wagged his tail as he sniffed me and followed me back to bed.

We woke up at a little after six the next morning. It felt cool outside, so I put on a sweatshirt and pocketed a piece of beef jerky before our morning run. Roy followed me for about twenty minutes. Then I gave him his beef jerky, and he licked my hands and slowed to go home. I watched him for a moment through the woods. I loved Roy, but this wasn't working. Even though he tolerated these morning runs, he didn't like them. He was an old dog in a young dog's body. He needed a companion, someone he could sit beside and with whom he could watch the world shift from a comfortable perch on the porch. I hardly even made it home most nights, and I didn't see that changing anytime soon.

"Hey, Roy," I called. He stopped and looked at me. "I'll find you a real home. Okay, buddy?"

He cocked his head to the side and licked his nose before turning down the trail and sauntering home. I resumed my run again, but the decision weighed heavily on my heart. When I got back to the house, Roy was sitting with his hindquarters inside his doghouse and the rest of his body on the outside. He yawned when he saw me and then trotted toward me.

"You want some food?"

He almost dove into a play dive, which was his way of telling me yes. We went inside, and I gave him two scoops of dog food for breakfast before showering. As I dried afterwards, I called a friend of mine who had been injured while on the job. A woman answered on the third or fourth ring.

"Hey," I said. I paused. "This is Joe Court. I'm calling for Preston. Is this still his number?"

"Yeah. Give me a minute. He's in the shower."

Last year, Preston—we had called him Sasquatch— had been the youngest sworn officer in our department. Then, some asshole had shot him in the chest with a high-powered rifle. He survived, but he lost a lung. Now, he built custom cabinets and furniture in a workshop attached to his house. The phone bobbled, and my old colleague's voice came on.

"Joe, you can't keep calling me like this," he said, his voice serious. "You showed me your boobs once—and that was nice—but I'm in a serious relationship. It's just not going to work."

"Funny," I said. "In case you've got me on speakerphone and your girlfriend is within earshot, I did not show Preston my boobs. After he was shot, I took off my shirt and tried to use it to stanch the blood coming from his chest. For the record, I was wearing a sports bra."

He paused. "I thought you flashed me. That's what I told everybody. The whole night is a blank. My doctors said it was because of the shock of being shot."

"It was a bad night," I said. "I try not to think about it often. You're lucky you don't remember it."

"Yeah," he said. The line went quiet for a moment. "So. You wouldn't call this early just to chat. What's up?"

I looked to Roy.

"Before you left the department, you signed up for training to be a canine officer, right?"

He paused.

"Yeah. Why?"

"And to be a canine officer, you would need to live with your dog and take care of him, right? So you were in the market for a dog."

He chuckled.

"I guess I was. Then I got shot, and that plan went to shit."

"If you'd still like a dog, I've got one I'd like you to meet. He's healthy and up to date on all his shots. He flunked out of St. Louis County's cadaver dog program, but he's one of the nicest dogs I've ever met. He needs a good home, and I'm gone too often to take care of him."

"Why'd he flunk out of the cadaver dog program?"

"He was too laid back," I said. I swallowed a lump in my throat. "He's a family dog, and he deserves to be with a family who loves him and has time for him."

Sasquatch paused.

"You sound like you're close to tears."

"I'm fine," I said, straightening and forcing any emotion from my voice.

"Is this guy *your* dog?" he asked. "I know what your dogs mean to you. I don't want to take one from you."

"He is mine," I said, running a hand down Roy's back. "But he needs a better home than I can give him. If you don't want him, I'll find someone else who does."

Sasquatch paused again.

"Yeah, okay. If you're okay with it, I'd love to meet him. If he and Shelby get along, we'll see about giving him a home."

"Thank you, Preston," I said. "It means a lot."

"I love dogs," he said, his voice brightening. "Besides, you saved my life and showed me your boobs. The least I can do is help your friend."

"I didn't do either of those things, but thank you. We'll set up a time for you and Shelby to meet him. I've got to get to work."

"Have a good one, and stay safe."

I thanked him, hung up, and petted Roy. He grinned at me. Preston would love Roy, and Roy would love Preston. They were a good match. Roy needed more than I could give him, and that was okay. He'd be happy with Preston. It'd be selfish to keep him. Still, I'd miss him.

I slipped off the edge of my sofa so I could sit beside the dog. Roy put his head in my lap and closed his eyes. Then he seemed to sigh contentedly, as if I had finally gotten the hint and given him what he most needed. I petted the hair on his neck.

"You're a good boy," I said. "You'll be happy with Preston."

As much as I wanted to sit there all day, I couldn't stay, so I brushed my teeth, put on deodorant, and filled the water bowl outside before putting him in the dog run for the day. Hopefully I'd be back before nightfall.

When I reached my station, my fellow officers were just beginning to congregate in the second-floor conference room for the morning briefing. Usually, that was a pretty sedate affair. Today, though, people smiled and spoke excitedly to one another. I pushed through the crowd in the conference room and met Trisha near the dispatcher's desk. She smiled at me.

"Morning," I said. "What's going on?"

She looked over the crowd and then back to me and smiled.

"Shane Fox became a hero last night," she said. "He pulled over a driver going south on I-55 on suspicion of drunk driving. The guy blew clean, but the car smelled like marijuana. Shane took the driver into custody and called for a search warrant for the car. He found an eighth of an ounce of weed in a Ziploc bag in the glove box and seventy kilograms of heroin and three million dollars cash in boxes in the trunk."

I opened my mouth.

"You're kidding."

"Nope," she said, shaking her head and smiling. "DEA agents are going to come by later to interrogate him, but they think he was going to Memphis from Chicago."

I laughed.

"Good for Shane," I said.

"And good for us," said Trisha. "The Feds will put the money in an asset forfeiture fund, but St. Augustine should be entitled to some of it. We might get some new cruisers out of this."

"Fat chance of that," I said. "Once the County Council learns we've got money coming our way, it'll disappear. You know how this place works."

"You're a cynic, Joe," she said.

"I'm a realist. Anyway, I've got work to do. If you run into Shane, congratulate him for me."

"Will do," said Trisha.

I left and walked to my office, where I read through the updates to my cases. Sheriff Delgado had, apparently, interviewed Detective Mickey Lyons—Tessa Armstrong's brother—while Bob Reitz and I were doing the next-of-kin notification in St. Louis. The boss should have called me to let me know what happened, but his interview notes were thorough, and it looked as if he had asked the right questions.

I called the phone number Delgado had written down, but it went to voicemail.

"Detective Lyons, this is Detective Mary Joe Court with the St. Augustine County Sheriff's Department. I'm investigating your sister's death, and I had hoped to ask you a few questions about her. Call me when you're available."

I hung up and waited for just a minute, but he didn't return my call. I had other things to do, so I grabbed my purse, signed out a marked cruiser, and drove to the grocery store Sheppard Altman had said he visited after leaving Tessa Armstrong in the Wayfair Motel. The manager let me review the store's surveillance footage from the night of Tessa's murder, and true to Mr. Altman's assertion, he was in the store from 9:43 to 10:10 p.m.

We didn't have a tight time of death, so it was possible Altman left Tessa in the motel, went grocery shopping to secure an alibi, and then returned to the hotel to murder his girlfriend, but I doubted he was our killer. As far as I could tell, he had no reason to want her dead. Mickey Lyons, Tessa's brother, had an even tighter alibi. He was working in Chicago when Tessa had died. Delgado had called and confirmed it.

As best I could tell, only one person stood to gain from Tessa's death: her husband. With her death, he didn't have to worry about a divorce settlement or her monthly allowance. He was also one of the few people I had spoken to so far with no alibi for the night of Tessa's death. He had a motive and the opportunity to kill her, which made him my only viable suspect so far.

Now I needed evidence, and I had a good idea of where to start.

18

Mickey sipped his coffee and watched the house. After talking to Sheriff Delgado, he had gone to the library to check out its collection of high school yearbooks. He had known Tessa was dating a teacher, but he hadn't known which one. He knew her, though. Tessa was straight, so he eliminated half the teachers at the school right away. She wouldn't have dated someone too much younger than her, either, so he eliminated two teachers who looked as if they were in their early twenties.

That left him with a couple dozen candidates. Carl Armstrong was almost thirty years older than Tessa. She had loved him at one time, but their marriage hadn't worked out. She wouldn't have dated someone that much older than her again, so he eliminated all the teachers who looked over forty.

That narrowed the field to just four men. One taught chemistry, one taught industrial arts, one taught finance and business, and one taught driver's education and coached football. Tessa wasn't into football or football players at all, so the driver's-education teacher was out of the running. The chemistry teacher was ugly. Tessa wasn't superficial, but it would have taken a lot of money for her to date someone that ugly. He was out. Both the industrial arts teacher and the business teacher were possibilities, but the industrial arts teacher had a wife and three kids. Mickey had followed him home after school.

That left the business teacher, Sheppard Altman. Half an hour ago, Mickey had parked half a block from the front door of his single-story brick home. It was the smallest home on the street, but it likely fit the needs of a single man very well.

At ten after eight, the garage door rolled up. That was Mickey's signal to move. He flashed the lights on his unmarked cruiser and floored the accelerator. His car vaulted forward. When he reached the driveway, he slammed on the brakes, leaving a skid mark on the asphalt. Altman stood beside a red Subaru station wagon in the garage. He held his hands in the air and opened his eyes wide with surprise.

Mickey killed his lights, opened his door, and held up his badge.

"Put your hands on the roof of your vehicle. I need to pat you down for weapons."

"I just talked to the police," said Altman. "Who are you?"

"Detective Lyons," said Mickey, nodding toward the red Subaru. "Put your hands on the roof of your car."

"You're Tessa's brother," said Altman. "She told me about you."

Mickey straightened and nodded.

"Yeah, I'm her brother. Funny. She didn't tell me about you at all."

"She thought you'd be upset that she was dating me without divorcing her husband."

Mickey shrugged.

"I wouldn't have cared about that. I just wanted her happy."

"She was happy," he said. "She was going to leave Carl for me."

"Sure she was," said Mickey, nodding toward the car once more and holding back his jacket to expose the firearm on his hip. "Put your hands on the car so I can pat you down. If you don't, I'll arrest you for interfering with my investigation."

Altman turned to face his vehicle and put his hands on top.

"Is this necessary?" he asked.

"I don't know the first thing about you except that you were supposedly dating my sister," said Mickey. He ran his hands across Altman's shoulders and arms, then down his torso. He had keys in his pocket but no weapons. "Lower your arms and turn around."

Altman did as he asked. Then he raised his eyebrows.

"Am I under arrest?"

"Not yet," said Mickey. "Let's talk about Tessa. If you killed her, I'll put you in a casket, cover you in dirt, and then drink a Mai Tai on top of your grave as you suffocate beneath me."

Altman leaned against his car and crossed his arms.

"And I thought Tessa was the charming one in the family."

Mickey didn't smile.

"Did you kill my sister?"

"No," he said. "I loved her. I planned to marry her."

Mickey looked from Altman's feet to his face, appraising him.

"You just found out she's dead. Why are you going to work?"

"We all grieve in different ways."

Mickey pulled his firearm from its holster and pressed it against Altman's forehead.

"If I pulled this trigger, who would grieve for you?"

Altman closed his eyes tight. His body trembled, and he looked like a breeze could have knocked him over at any moment, but he stayed on his feet.

"I'm a teacher. If I don't go to school, my kids fall behind. Please take the gun from my head. You're not stupid enough to shoot me with a firearm the police will trace back to you, anyway."

Mickey holstered his firearm.

"Where were you when Tessa died?"

"I already spoke to Detective Court," he said, turning and facing his car once more. He opened his door but didn't sit down. "If you want answers, talk to her."

"I'm talking to you. Answer me, or Sheriff Delgado will find out about your visits to Maddie Dawson. To refresh your memory, she's a nurse, and she sold you drugs she stole from her patients. She also recorded her conversations with you, so don't bother denying you had them. Now where were you when my sister was being murdered?"

He sighed and then raised his eyebrows.

"The grocery store. I met her at the hotel, we made love, and then I left. Since you know about Maddie

Dawson, you know what Tessa did for a living. She planned to get more pills the next day and then deliver them to her boss in Chicago."

Mickey narrowed his eyes at him.

"What do you know about her boss?"

Altman shook his head.

"Nothing."

Mickey didn't believe him, but that didn't matter. If Altman threatened their operation, he'd die.

"Why are you even involved in her business?"

"She needed help. A guy on her route pushed her against the wall and groped her in the break room of the hospice care center where he worked one day. Tessa thought he would have raped her if another nurse hadn't walked in. When I saw her that night, she was crying, and I held her until she stopped. Then I persuaded her to talk to me. Ever since then, I've gone with her when she buys from men. Did you even talk to your sister? Did you know how scared she was?"

Mickey furrowed his brow.

"If she was scared, why didn't she just quit?"

"Because the guy she worked for was a psycho. She thought he'd kill her. I know Tessa had problems with drugs in the past, but she didn't deserve this. We were saving up. I was going to sell my house, she was going to divorce her husband, and we were going to leave. We were going to get married. I told her I'd protect her. Do you know what it's like to love somebody and know she died because you couldn't keep her safe?"

Mickey stepped back and ran a hand across his chin. Altman's face and throat were red, and blood vessels striated the whites of his eyes. He looked close to tears.

"Her life wasn't that bad," said Mickey, his voice soft.

"How would you know?" asked Altman, stepping forward.

Mickey stepped back again, surprised.

"You know, for a schoolteacher, you've got some balls." Altman didn't reply, so Mickey continued. "You wanted to marry my sister, huh?"

"Yeah," he said. "I proposed two months ago. I gave her the ring and everything. She wasn't comfortable wearing it until Carl granted her a divorce, but she carried it with her everywhere she went."

Mickey tried to keep it from his face, but he didn't believe that one bit. Maybe Tessa had loved him, but she'd never leave Carl for him. Carl was a goldmine. Not only did he pay for her condo in St. Louis, he gave her an allowance and was almost always willing to give her a little extra if her funds ran low. She may have had to sleep with him, but he made the rewards worth the sacrifice. As heavily as he smoked, he didn't have much time left, anyway. When he died, she'd inherit part of his estate. At the low end, that'd be ten or fifteen million dollars.

Tessa had always been a romantic, but she hadn't been a moron. Mickey didn't know what to make of Sheppard Altman, but he didn't trust him.

"If you loved my sister, I'm sorry for your loss. Tessa was a special person. And keep this drug business to yourself. Maybe I couldn't protect her when she was alive, but I can do my job now. I'm a narcotics detective, and I'll be shutting her network down. Stay out of my way."

"Fine," said Altman. "I will."

Mickey held his gaze for another moment, getting a measure of the man, but he wasn't impressed by what he saw. As he walked to his cruiser, his gut grew tighter and tighter. Tessa might have dated Altman, but she'd never leave her husband for him. If she told him that, she must have been running some kind of play on him. Or maybe he was just lying. Either way, it didn't matter. Altman knew too much. As soon as Mickey's team arrived from Chicago, they'd get rid of him.

Unfortunately, that would leave the region in tatters. Over the past two years, Tessa had purchased almost two hundred thousand pills from twenty-four different nursing homes and hospice care centers in and around St. Augustine County. Those pills had netted Mickey's employers well over six million dollars in sales and kept countless bored housewives and young professionals high.

Mickey hated to lose that kind of production, but with Tessa dead, he needed to shut the whole area down. It was too risky. The nurses and doctors Tessa purchased from wouldn't know anything about the organization, so once he killed Sheppard Altman, no one connected to the drug trade would even know his name. He had his exit strategy.

Now he had to put his plans into motion.

19

I drove back to my station and went to my office, where I opened a web browser on my computer and navigated to the St. Louis County assessor's website. According to Carl Armstrong's last personal property tax declaration—a public record—he owned six cars. Two were inexpensive, ten-year-old sedans, so I figured he had bought those for his kids. He also owned a Bentley Continental, a Mercedes S-class, a Range Rover, and a Honda Accord.

I minimized the browser. Years ago, detectives in my station would create murder books when they picked up a homicide. Usually, they were thick three-ring binders with sleeves into which they could put their notes, photographs, and reports. For a big, complicated case, a detective could go through two or three binders and store hundreds of reports and thousands of photographs.

Now, we kept things digital. Each case we worked got a folder on our department's cloud server. That folder had subfolders in which we stored digital photographs, interview notes, reports, and an entry describing every piece of evidence we collected. Whenever I added a photo or report, the system time-stamped the entry and created a log so I could tell who looked at my work and what edits they had made. It was similar to the digital records systems hospitals maintained.

The system kept the case neat, but more than that, it protected us in court. When I became a cop, I'd had a naïve, romantic belief that detectives were modern-day knights on a quest for truth. That was part of the job, perhaps, but truth only got you so far. If a detective broke the rules, or if he didn't document his findings, the truth didn't matter. The bad guy would walk free.

By keeping such meticulous records, a complete stranger could re-create my entire investigation and understand why I had come to the conclusions I had come to. More than that, he'd know I followed the rules. Our departmental records protected me, my team, my department, and my investigation. My badge didn't make me a knight. It made me a pencil pusher who carried a gun, and that was just fine by me.

I dove into the case notes. Kevius Reed, our young forensic technician, had taken over a hundred pictures of Tessa Armstrong's room and the surrounding grounds. Each picture had a detailed description of where and when he had taken it, why he had taken it, and what camera he had used. They were good high-resolution pictures, the kind a prosecutor could use to illustrate his points in court.

Besides the pictures of the motel room, Kevius had taken about a dozen pictures of the parking lot, including several that contained a maroon Honda Accord registered to Carl Armstrong. That was Tessa Armstrong's car, which left him with the Bentley, Mercedes, and Range Rover.

After that, I searched the log for any entries by Kevin Owens, one of the first uniformed officers to make it to the crime scene. He had been told to go to Club Serenity and get any footage of the hotel shot by its surveillance cameras, but instead he had breakfast with the club's owner. I could have forgiven him for taking a break to eat, but, by the looks of things, he hadn't even logged the damn video.

I searched through our directory for his cell number and called. He answered on the second ring.

"Kevin," I said. "This is Joe Court. You took a call at the Wayfair Motel about a dead body. The victim's name was Tessa Armstrong."

He paused. "Yeah, I remember her. What's up?"

"Where's the surveillance video from Club Serenity?"

He grunted. "Didn't I upload that already?"

I didn't feel like smiling, but I forced myself to smile anyway, hoping it'd come through my voice and persuade him to talk to me.

"If you did, it's not in the correct case file."

"I'm working traffic now, but I'll search for it when I get back to the station. Don't get your panties in a bunch."

I almost told him off. Instead, I clenched my jaw and then drew in a deep breath.

"Don't worry about it. I'll find it."

I hung up before he could respond. Then I took two breaths, shook my head, and searched for any reports Kevin Owens had submitted in the past week. His paperwork was in good order, but it still took me almost fifteen minutes to find the correct video. For some reason, he had attached it to one of his traffic stops. I moved it to the correct case and then wrote a note explaining where it had come from and why we were interested in it. If we had to introduce the video into evidence in court, Owens would have to explain his mistake on the stand, but that'd be fine.

Once I had the video, I watched it at high speed. We didn't know when Tessa died, so I started the video at 9:00 p.m. and watched for about five minutes. According to the time stamp, a pizza delivery driver arrived at the motel at 9:13 p.m. and went to a room on the second floor. He left within three minutes. At 9:21 p.m. a couple crossed the road from the strip club. Almost certainly, she was a prostitute he had picked up in the club, but we wouldn't be able to prove that.

At 9:27 p.m. Tessa's door opened. The video had been shot from Club Serenity's parking lot across the street, so it was grainy. I slowed the playback. Two people emerged from the room. They embraced, and then one person—Sheppard Altman—walked to a red Subaru station wagon and drove off. Altman wasn't lying: Tessa had been alive when he left.

At 9:31 p.m., Altman's wagon left the parking lot in a direction that would have taken him back to town. At 9:36 p.m., a black Range Rover SUV pulled into the lot. My heart began thumping against my chest. I paused the video and flipped through my notes to confirm that the color and vehicle matched the one registered to Carl Armstrong. It did.

The Range Rover pulled to a stop in the fire lane outside Tessa's room. Unfortunately, it had parked with the driver's side door facing the room and the bulk of the vehicle facing me.

I slowed the video to half speed and held my breath. The dome light popped on at 9:37 p.m. as the driver opened his door. My fingers gripped my mouse. Within moments, the room's door opened. The SUV's driver walked inside and shut the door. The video was good quality, but I couldn't see the driver's face.

At 9:42 p.m. the door opened again. This time, the room light was off. The figure returned to the SUV and drove off.

I leaned back in my chair and blinked. Since we didn't have a picture of his license plate, Carl Armstrong's attorney would argue that the black Range Rover could have belonged to anyone. He'd say it was a coincidence that Carl owned one, too. No jury would believe him, though.

I watched the next thirteen hours of video at high speed and made notes every time a vehicle entered or left the parking lot. Nobody knocked on or opened Tessa's door again until the housekeeper let herself in the next morning. We had him. Carl Armstrong had killed his wife. We had it on film.

I rubbed my eyes and gave myself a moment to put this together. After Sheppard Altman left, Carl Armstrong pulled into the lot and parked in front of Tessa's room, knowing she'd be alone. He then entered the room.

It would have only taken moments to shoot her, so maybe they talked for a few minutes before the shooting.

Or maybe she was already in the shower when he arrived, and he had to psych himself up to kill her. Either way, he shot her while she was in the shower. We didn't need to know the details or precise order of things to know Carl pulled the trigger. This was planned and premeditated. He stalked his wife until she was alone and then shot her when she was most vulnerable. We'd send him to death row for this.

I watched the video again at full speed and came away even more convinced. My arms and legs felt light, my shoulders and back felt relaxed, and I breathed easily. I even smiled. We'd need solid forensic evidence to make it stick, but we had him.

"Good night and good luck, Mr. Armstrong," I said, pushing back from my desk. "You'll need it."

I let myself enjoy the moment before picking up the desk phone to call my boss. Before I could dial the sheriff's number, though, my cell rang. It was Anna Kelley, the mother of the young woman who'd died in her apartment a couple of days ago. I answered before it could ring a second time.

"Ms. Kelley," I said, forcing the smile from my face. "This is Detective Joe Court. How are you?"

"I'm fine," she said. "I just wanted to call and let you know that Emma Hannity is home right now with a couple of her friends. My daughter Erica was just visiting her. Emma was Jasmine's best friend."

I called up the case files on my computer and flipped through my notes to reorient myself to that investigation.

If anyone knew who sold Jasmine the drugs I found in her apartment, it'd be Emma. My investigation into Tessa could wait for a few hours, especially now that I had the video.

"Okay," I said. "Thanks for calling. I'll go to her house and talk to them."

Mrs. Kelley paused.

"Have you learned anything new about Jasmine's death?"

I shook my head.

"I'm still working the case. I can't give many details."

She paused.

"I guess I just don't understand what's going on. She wasn't hurt, was she?"

"We're still not sure what happened to her yet," I said. "She wasn't shot or stabbed or beaten, but it is still possible that someone intentionally killed her. If someone slipped a drug into her drink without her knowing, for instance, and that drug killed her, it's a murder. Until we learn how and why she died, we'll be investigating every aspect of this case we can."

"Who would do something like that?"

By the waver in her voice, she was close to tears.

"I don't know, but if someone hurt her, I will do everything in my power to find out. I promise you that."

"Thank you, Detective," she said. "I loved that girl. She was my baby."

Nothing I said would have helped, so I said nothing. A moment later, Anna wished me luck and hung up. My shoulders slumped, and a sense of heaviness began taking the place of the delighted feeling I had enjoyed after finding Carl Armstrong's SUV outside Tessa Armstrong's hotel room. I may have come close to closing Tessa's case, but I had hardly begun investigating Jasmine's death.

I had work ahead of me.

20

After talking to Anna Kelley, I emailed my boss to let him know about the video from Club Serenity and about Carl Armstrong's car collection. Sheriff Delgado had been a good detective when he was younger, so he could look up the case, interpret my notes, and come to a reasonable conclusion. We didn't have enough to pick Carl Armstrong up for murder yet, but we had ample probable cause to apply for a search warrant for his car and house. Delgado and I would talk about that later, though. For now, I needed to focus on Jasmine Kelley's death.

I searched the license bureau's database for Emma Hannity and found her address. She lived about a block from Jasmine's apartment. The drive didn't take long. Emma lived in a cute little bungalow with white clapboard siding, a red metal roof, and a big front porch overlooking a massive oak tree in the front lawn. Two cars had parked in the driveway, while a big Chevy pickup had parked with two wheels on the road and two wheels on the grass in front.

I parked behind the Chevy and walked toward the front door. The blinds were drawn, but someone had cracked open a window overlooking the front porch. Even outside, I could smell marijuana. That gave me leverage, but it also made it likely somebody would try to run out the back. I thought about calling for backup, but weed rarely made people violent. Instead, I walked back to the driveway and snapped pictures of the cars. If their owners were dumb enough to run, I'd track them down at their homes.

Then I knocked on the door.

"Sheriff's Department," I said. "I'm looking for Emma Hannity."

"Shit!"

It was a girl's voice. I sighed and waited.

"What do we do?"

This voice belonged to a guy. His voice was raspy, like he was trying to whisper. I wondered whether he remembered the window was open.

"Just eat it," said the girl's voice. "There's not much left."

I knocked again.

"I don't care about your weed," I said. "Possession is a low-level misdemeanor, and I don't want to fill out the paperwork. I'm here to talk about Jasmine Kelley. Open the door."

"What about mushrooms?"

It was a second girl's voice. I closed my eyes and shook my head before responding.

"I'll pretend you didn't ask me that," I said. "Don't eat them, though. You're no help to me if you're hallucinating. Just hide them or something."

"Give me a minute."

I rubbed my eyes and sighed again. About three minutes later, a young woman with blond hair opened the door. A wave of incense and air freshener wafted outside like a cloud.

"Can I help you, Officer?" she asked. Her pupils looked dilated. She held up a hand to shield herself from the sun.

"Emma Hannity?" I asked. She nodded, so I looked past her. A young man with black hair and a young woman with brunette hair sat on a sofa in the living room. Both were in their late teens to early twenties, and both looked as if they were ready to fall asleep. They must have had some good weed. "You guys hide your illegal drugs?"

The girl didn't react, but the boy nodded.

"Great," I said, looking to Emma again. "Can I come in?"

She nodded and stepped back.

"Other than those two, is anyone else in the house with you?" I asked.

"No," she said. "We're it."

"Good," I said. "Have a seat. I'm going to walk through the place. If I find anybody hiding, everybody's going to my station for a fun afternoon in the holding cells."

Emma sat on the loveseat kitty-corner to the sofa on which her friends sat. I walked through the house and checked the bedrooms, bathroom, and closets but didn't open any cabinets or move any furniture. Nobody popped out of anywhere or screamed. Afterwards, I took a chair from the dining area and placed it near the sofa.

"Okay, guys. I'm Detective Joe Court with the St. Augustine County Sheriff's Department. As you guys know by now, your friend Jasmine Kelley is dead. I'm trying to figure out why. Our coroner hasn't determined her manner of death yet, so we don't know whether someone murdered her, whether she overdosed, or whether she died of natural causes. Because of that, I'm looking into every aspect of her death that I can, including the ecstasy we found in her apartment. You guys can help us all out by telling me the truth."

They nodded, so I started the interview. The boy was named Bryan Golden, and the girl on the couch was Vicky Henderson. They, along with Emma, were two of Jasmine's best friends. They had gone to high school together and continued to hang out afterwards. Bryan worked in the stock room of the grocery store, while Vicky was a part-time college student at the University of Missouri in St. Louis and a full-time barista at a coffee shop off campus. Emma worked in a laundromat in St. Augustine.

"Great," I said, once we finished the introductions. "Emma, when did you see Jasmine last?"

She blinked and then looked down. "I don't know. I don't remember."

"Three or four days ago? A week?" I asked. She shrugged. "Maybe you can check your phone. Maybe you texted her before meeting her somewhere."

She didn't move.

"I don't know when I last saw her."

I gritted my teeth and smiled before looking to Bryan and Vicky.

"How about you two? Are your memories any better?"

Both of them shrugged and said nothing. I took a deep breath and held it for a moment.

"Look, guys, I'm not here to get you in trouble. I don't care if you guys smoked weed or drank or did whatever. I need you to talk to me, though. When we found her body, she smelled like alcohol, but she didn't have any dirty glasses lying around her apartment. Her makeup was done, her hair was done, and she had a cute dress on. She was going out. If she wasn't with you guys, who was she with? Does she have a boyfriend?"

Emma looked toward the kitchen. Vicky snaked her arm through the crook of Bryan's elbow and looked at the floor. He stared at his hands.

"I'm talking about your friend," I said. "Her family deserves to know what happened to her."

None of them moved. I had expected a little reluctance but not complete silence. I looked at Emma.

"Did you want her dead?"

She furrowed her brow and shook her head.

"No."

"Are you sure?" I asked. "You guys are stonewalling me as if you killed her. Did you murder her?"

"No," said Vicky. "We loved Jasmine."

I locked eyes with her.

"Is that right?"

She nodded. So did her boyfriend.

"If you cared about her, you'd talk to me. You won't

even admit when you last saw her," I said. "Is it about the drugs in her apartment? Because those shouldn't be your concern right now. This is a death investigation. Your behavior today makes me think there's way more going on here than I had thought. When did you last see her?"

No one answered. I stood and shook my head.

"Fine. I'll keep working the case. If I find out any of you were involved in her death, I'll send you to prison for the rest of your lives. Think about Anna Kelley, too. She deserves to know what happened to her daughter."

They kept their eyes on the ground as I walked out of the room. The muscles in my shoulders quivered, and my skin felt flushed. Most of the time when I raised my voice in an interrogation, I was acting. People responded to emotion. Sometimes it opened them up and made them speak; other times, it shut people down. Part of my job as a police officer was to read a situation well enough to understand how to act in order to get the response I wanted.

Here, I was pissed. I didn't know why Jasmine died—and maybe these guys didn't, either—but they knew something. I left the house, got in my car, and called Dr. Sheridan, our coroner.

"Doc, it's Joe Court," I said, once he answered. "I sent you a pair of bodies, and I was wondering how you were doing on them."

"Hey, Joe," he said. "I had planned to call you this afternoon when I made it back to my office. Sam and I have autopsied both Ms. Armstrong and Ms. Kelley. Tessa

Armstrong was straightforward. At the time of her death, she was a healthy, well-developed female. I've listed her official cause of death as catastrophic injuries to her heart and major blood vessels caused by the gunshot wounds to her torso.

"One gunshot passed through her. I don't know where the bullet is, but I sent the other four to your crime lab. They look like .22-caliber rounds, but Darlene McEvoy will have to confirm that. The damage to Ms. Armstrong's internal tissues was extensive. If it matters, she didn't suffer for long. Unfortunately, I still haven't been able to narrow down her time of death."

I nodded to myself. We had interviewed every guest staying at the motel the night Tessa had died, and none of them had heard gunshots. A .22-caliber pistol alone wouldn't have been that quiet, but a .22-caliber pistol with a suppressor explained a lot. Even if a guest or member of the staff walked by Tessa's room while the shooter was inside, he could have mistaken the gunshots for sound effects on a TV show or movie.

"I'm glad she didn't suffer long," I said. "And I've learned her time of death. I've got surveillance video from Club Serenity. She and her boyfriend came to her door at 9:30 p.m. She was alive when he left. About five minutes later, her husband came to the hotel and killed her. It's all on video."

"That's great," he said. He paused. "Well, actually, that's awful, but that's great for you."

"Yeah," I said, smiling a little. "What can you tell me

about Jasmine?"

He paused and then sighed.

"That's complicated," he said. "I'm at St. John's Hospital in St. Augustine picking up a body right now. Can you meet me here?"

I grimaced. "Can we talk on the phone?"

He made a noise in his throat. "It's complicated. It'll be easier to talk about in person."

"Okay," I said, sighing. "I'm on my way."

"Meet me in the cafeteria. I'll see you soon."

I grunted and thanked him before hanging up. After meeting Emma Hannity and her friends, I had realized Jasmine's death investigation would be complicated. It looked like Dr. Sheridan agreed with me. At least I was close to an arrest in Tessa Armstrong's case. I turned on my car and drove.

21

St. John's wasn't a major hospital, but their doctors and nurses had taken good care of me on the few occasions I had gone there. I parked in the lot out front and followed signs to the cafeteria. When I got there, I found Dr. Sheridan sitting alone at a table in the back corner. He had a sandwich, salad, and a cup of coffee on a tray in front of him. As he saw me walking toward the table, he put his drink down and gave me a tight smile.

"If you're hungry, get lunch. The food's all right as long as you stay away from the 'heart-healthy' items. Those are shit."

He made air quotes when he said *heart-healthy*. It was a little after noon. Most days, I had no idea how my schedule would progress, so I grabbed food whenever and wherever I could. Still, I hesitated before getting in line.

"You think we'll be here long enough to eat?"

He sighed and nodded. "Yeah. Sorry."

"I guess I'll eat hospital food, then."

He nodded and picked up his sandwich. I grabbed a grilled chicken sandwich, pretzels, an apple, and a bottle of water and joined Sheridan at the table. It was healthier than my usual fast-food lunch, so hopefully it wouldn't shock my body too much.

"Tell me what you've got," I said, sitting across from him. He nodded and pulled an iPad from a briefcase at his side.

"First, I've only got preliminary results on Ms. Kelley's tox screen. We'll get to those results in a minute. Second, though, I examined Ms. Kelley for injuries and for signs of habitual drug use. Her septum is intact, so she likely doesn't snort cocaine regularly; her fingers lack the callouses or bruises associated with someone who smokes meth or other substances from a glass pipe; and I found no needle injection marks anywhere on her body. That's the good news."

I nodded and started eating my sandwich.

"That is good," I said. "Go on."

Sheridan tapped a button on his iPad to wake it up.

"Among people Ms. Kelley's age, unintentional injuries—car accidents and drug overdoses, most notably —are the leading cause of death. That's followed by homicide and then suicide. I've autopsied Ms. Kelley. She died of a heart attack. I looked for ventricular defects but couldn't find any. Moreover, the muscle tissue of heart was healthy and of an appropriate thickness, none of the valves of her heart appeared abnormal, and I've not found any signs of electrical malfunction."

I ate my pretzels and nodded. "Why'd she have a heart attack, then?"

The doctor leaned forward.

"Let me ask you something," he said. "Did you find illegal drugs at the scene?"

I nodded. "Ecstasy."

"Did they have stars on them?"

I raised my eyebrows.

"Yeah. What do you know?"

"Ms. Kelley isn't the first teenage heart attack victim I've had this week. Until we get a final toxicology report on Ms. Kelley, I can't give you definitive answers. That said, I've conducted autopsies on four people this week who overdosed on pills very much like the ones you've described. You're familiar with ecstasy. The chemical name is methylenedioxymethamphetamine. MDMA. It's a psychoactive drug. It heightens your sensations, increases your energy, and gives you a euphoric feeling."

I smiled just a little.

"I'll take your word for how it makes you feel."

He nodded but kept a stern expression on his face.

"It's possible to have a lethal overdose of MDMA, but it's not common. The danger with MDMA is that it can raise your body temperature. In an enclosed environment with lots of people dancing in a small space, your temperature can spike to dangerous, even lethal, temperatures before you know what's going on."

"Jasmine died of a heart attack, though," I said, narrowing my eyes. "You said your other victims did, too. Could MDMA cause that?"

"Sure. It's rare, but it happens," said the doctor, shrugging. "But I don't think that's what happened to Jasmine. I haven't got the complete results of her tox screen back yet, but I have received the tox screens of three victims who took pills similar to the ones you described. Presumably they're the same ones she took."

"Your other victims have MDMA in their systems?"

He nodded. "Yes, but they had also taken N-Benzyl-4-methoxyaniline. It's a phenethylamine like MDMA and produces similar hallucinogenic effects, but it's toxic at lower levels. In the brain, it binds to serotonin receptors and alters the way they function. That can lead to psychosis-induced injuries, but NBOMe does its real damage to the cardiovascular system, where it constricts the blood vessels while simultaneously thickening the blood. The combination of the two puts a user's heart under a lot of stress and can lead to ventricular fibrillation, which can lead to a heart attack or stroke.

"If a user knows his pills have NBOMe and MDMA, he'll take a smaller dose, get high, and have a good time. If a user doesn't know what he's taking, though, he could kill himself easily. It's nasty stuff, and I'm willing to bet it killed Ms. Kelley—just as it killed my other overdose victims."

I gave myself a moment to process what he had just told me. Then I nodded.

"Could the drug maker have included NBOMe by accident?"

Sheridan shook his head.

"The drugs are synthesized differently. More than likely, the maker included it to dilute the amount of MDMA in each pill while maintaining the potency. It's a cost-saving measure, but if you include too much NBOMe, you'll kill your customers instead of getting them high. Just as with everything, different people have different tolerances. A pill that could kill Jasmine Kelley might just make a larger person sick. That's why we're not having more deaths than we are. These pills are killing those with low tolerances while making people with higher tolerances high.

"For now, these deaths are a local phenomenon. After my third overdose victim, I called coroners in St. Louis, Chicago, Memphis, Kansas City, Little Rock, Indianapolis, and Louisville, but they're not seeing the same deaths we are. Someone is selling tainted drugs to college kids in east-central Missouri."

I thought of Emma Hannity, Vicky Henderson, and Bryan Golden. They were Jasmine Kelley's friends. All three of them had been high during our interview. They took drugs. I wondered whether they sold drugs, too. It would explain why they had been so evasive.

"I don't know a lot about the manufacture of illegal drugs," I said, leaning forward, "so bear with me if I sound naïve. If we've got bad drugs here, though, we've probably got them all over the place. The labs that make these drugs ship everywhere, don't they? We've only found deaths in central Missouri so far, but maybe I should call the DEA."

Sheridan picked up his coffee and sipped before wiping his hands on a napkin.

"It's possible we're looking at the start of a major epidemic, but the lack of similar cases outside our region makes me think we've got a lab somewhere around here, and that lab made a bad batch."

I almost asked whether he was joking, but then I

thought of Reid Chemical, which was once one of St. Augustine County's largest employers. The company manufactured private-label pharmaceuticals, but it had plans to develop its own drugs and chemical compounds. Then, we learned that its CEO, along with some of his more senior chemical engineers, had been manufacturing fentanyl and selling it to a gang in Chicago.

I grabbed a pen and notepad from my purse.

"What would this lab look like?"

"Similar to a meth lab," he said. "And this is a good area for it because of our abundance of sassafras trees."

I narrowed my eyes and shook my head. "Why do sassafras trees help?"

"Because they produce safrole, a chemical precursor of MDMA."

I shook my head again.

"I've got a degree in biology, but it's been a long time since I took organic chem."

He leaned forward.

"Most makers of MDMA aren't professional chemists. They're people looking to make money. The easiest way to make that money is to do everything yourself, and it starts with the sassafras tree. A cooker will find a sassafras tree and start digging at the base to get to the roots.

"Once they have a piece of sassafras root, they'll use a potato peeler to strip off the bark. They'll wash the bark to get rid of the dirt and then let it dry. It'll take a week or two. They can then boil that dried bark in a pot. That'll pull the sassafras oil out of the bark and into the water. Because of the relative density of the oil, it'll float to the top of the pot and congeal. A cooker will then take that congealed oil, warm it up again, and filter it to remove impurities. At that point, it's sassafras oil."

I wanted him to hurry, but I didn't want to interrupt and miss something, so I nodded.

"I'm with you so far."

"Good," he said. "Now, sassafras oil contains about 80 percent safrole. In fact, the government regulates sassafras oil for just that reason. To extract that safrole from the oil, our cooker would vacuum distill it. Once you've got purified safrole, it's easy to synthesize MDMA.

"The sassafras tree is the key, though. If a cooker's trees die, he'll have to either find another source of safrole —which isn't easy—or he'll need to look at other drugs with readily available ingredients to synthesize."

"Like NBOMe," I said. The doctor nodded.

"Yep," he said. "Our drug maker isn't trying to hurt people. He's just trying to make up for a lack of his regular ingredients."

"His intent doesn't make his victims any less dead," I said.

"It sure doesn't," said the doctor.

I picked up my chicken sandwich and ate a few bites. Then I put it down.

"My victim had a full bag of pills on her," I said. "That's a lot of potential dead people."

"Not everyone who took one would have died, but if she had sold all of them, we'd have more bodies," said Dr.

Sheridan, nodding.

"We've got to find her supplier," I said.

"That's a lot easier said than done," said Sheridan, picking at his salad and eating a tomato.

Unfortunately, he was right.

22

Neither the doctor nor I had much left to say about the case, so we finished lunch in relative silence. I didn't eat with other people often, so a quiet lunch with a colleague was nice, even if it was in a hospital. When I got back to the station, I nodded hello at the construction workers cutting tile in the parking lot as I passed and then walked inside. My office was quiet and comfortable, the perfect place to sit in a chair and lean back to think. Jasmine Kelley lived in a two-bedroom apartment. She may have had sassafras trees nearby—I hadn't known to pay attention when I was first called out —but we hadn't found laboratory equipment anywhere near her place. She got her drugs from somewhere, though.

I spun around in my chair and stood up to pace my office. Jasmine's friends didn't want to talk to me, and nothing I could do would change their minds. I had Jasmine's phone, so I had a window into her life, but her text messages were words without context. Jasmine and I had spoken, but I didn't know her or how she thought. That needed to change.

I opened a browser on my computer and navigated to YouTube. Jasmine kept a nice video camera in her spare bedroom to film makeup tutorials. I didn't spend a lot of time on YouTube on a regular day, but I had learned a lot about how to renovate my house by watching videos posted by professional contractors. Most of the channels kept their content professional, but everybody let personal details slip through occasionally. Jasmine wouldn't mention a side hustle as a drug dealer, but anything that helped me understand her better would help at this point.

I searched until I found her channel, and then I started watching. The first couple of videos I watched held little of interest for me. Jasmine was exuberant and charming, but I didn't care to learn new ways to maximize my sex appeal through eye shadow. After about three videos, I turned the speed up and watched them at double the usual pace. That made things go quicker, but I still learned little.

Then I noticed something. Some of her videos had hundreds of thousands of views, while others only had a couple hundred. For someone with a popular channel, that struck me as being a little strange. I clicked on one with few views and found a video that she had filmed outside and in which she wore little makeup.

"Hey, YouTubers," she said, holding her camera a few feet from her face and smiling. "It's Jasmine, and I'm filming from the grounds of a college near my house."

She panned the camera—probably her cell phone— around to show young people walking to class. Most people wore shorts and short-sleeved shirts, but a few wore pajamas. It was a bright, clear day. Day lilies bloomed in a flower bed beside the red brick base of the nearest building. It was Waterford College. She turned the camera toward herself again.

"This isn't a makeup video. I just wanted to talk. Once the campus police find me, I'm sure they'll make me leave. I'm not from here, and they know it. These kids don't know how good they've got it. They go to class every morning, and they party all night. Some of them have jobs on campus, but they don't really work. They're making money so they can buy beer."

She panned the camera again, and this time, I saw the back of one of the campus's side entrances.

"I work two blocks that way at a diner," she said, turning the camera toward herself again. "On a good day, I make ten dollars an hour. And I earn that money, too. Every dirty old man within twenty miles has patted me on the ass at least once. Even if I worked ten hours a day, every day, without a break, I couldn't afford this school's tuition. They don't have a clue what I'd give to live in their world."

Somebody—a boy—walked up to her. They spoke for a moment, but I couldn't understand what they said. When the boy left, she looked at the camera again.

"I can pretend to be one of them, but I don't fit in here. Even that guy who walked up. He didn't want me. He wanted something from me. That's all I am. I'm the girl you get things from, the one who makes you feel good. I'm not real to them."

It was a vague statement. She might have meant drugs, but she could have been talking about sex or something else. Either way, I paused the video and grabbed a cup of stale coffee from the break room. When

I returned, I played the video again at normal speed.

"I'm tired of my life," she said, staring right into the camera. "Everybody wants something from me, but nobody wants me. I come here between shifts at the diner because it's pretty and quiet, but I feel like shit every time I leave. It's like I can watch my dreams coming true for other people, but I can't ever join in. Some days, I just want to get in my car and drive and never look back, but I can't because I can't even afford a tank of gas. I'm trapped, and I'm tired. Don't tell me it'll get better because it won't. That's not my lot in life.

"If you're one of these people, if you get whatever you want, just be happy. Be grateful. And be kind to the people who serve you coffee. You never know whose dream you're living."

The video ended. I closed the browser before another could start.

"That was depressing," said a voice from behind me. I turned and saw Darlene McEvoy near the door. "Someone you know?"

"Young woman who died of an overdose. I'm working the case," I said. I forced myself to smile. "What's up?"

"I've been processing the fingerprint evidence from the Tessa Armstrong crime scene. The condom wrappers held her fingerprints and the latent fingerprints of an unknown subject."

"Probably Sheppard Altman," I said. "He admitted being in the room with her and having sex with her. I've also got him on video leaving the motel. Tessa hugged and kissed him, so she was still alive."

"That's one mystery solved," she said, nodding. "Someone crushed the soda can in the trash, but I found a palm print, three partials, and one very clear thumbprint on it. The prints match the exclusionary prints Carl Armstrong gave us."

I sat straighter and almost held my breath.

"How good is the match?"

"Very," she said, a tight smile forming on her lips. "Nineteen points of comparison on the thumbprint. The partials and palm have fewer points of comparison, but the thumb alone is definitive. Carl Armstrong crushed that can and threw it away."

I brought a hand to my face. The surveillance video from Club Serenity gave us enough to secure a search warrant, but with this we could charge him with murder.

"Did it have anyone else's fingerprints on it?"

She shook her head.

"Just his."

I nodded and reached for my phone. Sheriff Delgado answered before his phone finished ringing once.

"Boss, this is Joe Court. You in your office?"

"For the next few minutes, yeah."

"Good," I said. "Darlene McEvoy and I are on our way over. We need to talk to you and the prosecutor. We've got enough to arrest Carl Armstrong for killing his wife."

The sheriff paused.

"We haven't even searched his house yet. You sure an arrest is wise at this point?"

"Yeah," I said. "I'll brief you."

I hung up before the boss could say anything else. Then I looked to Darlene.

"Come on," I said. "The boss needs to see us."

Sheriff Delgado's office was just down the hall. The room was cavernous and had a conference table, a separate seating area with two couches and a coffee table, and an area with a desk and chairs for smaller meetings. Big picture windows overlooked the town. One day, it'd be a gorgeous office fit for a king. Now, it had water stains near the ceiling, and those big picture windows whistled whenever the wind blew hard.

George was sitting behind his desk, but he stood when Darlene and I stepped inside.

"Come on in," he said, waving us toward his desk. Darlene and I sat on the chairs in front, while he sat behind. We filled him in on the investigation so far and the evidence we had collected. Afterwards, he nodded, picked up the phone, and dialed a number, without saying anything to us. "Shaun, it's George Delgado. I need you down in my office. Detective Court and Darlene McEvoy just brought me some evidence in a homicide investigation you need to see. We'll be making an arrest this afternoon."

Despite the evidence, my stomach quivered, and my left thumb picked at the nail of my index finger. We had Carl Armstrong's prints, and we had a video of him at the hotel, but something didn't sit right with me. The sheriff finished his call.

"Good work, you two. You did right by Ms. Armstrong. That's something to be proud of."

Darlene smiled, but I blinked and shook my head.

"But something's not right," I said. "Think about the video: Armstrong hides somewhere off camera in his SUV and waits for Sheppard Altman to leave. That makes sense. He doesn't want witnesses. After Altman leaves, Armstrong pulls into the Wayfair Motel's lot and parks in front of Tessa's room. It's not in a parking spot. It's right out in the open by her room. If he had parked in a parking spot like a normal person, no one would have even noticed it. Instead, he parked in the fire lane. Why?"

Delgado considered me and then crossed his arms.

"The fire lane put him close to the door. It let him get in and out quickly."

"But he didn't get in and out fast," I said. "We've got it on video. He stayed in the room for several minutes, long enough, apparently, to drink a soda. Why did he do that? And where'd he get the soda? Did he bring it with him? Did he find it in the room? I can't figure that out. If you plan to kill your wife, you go there, you shoot her, and you leave. You don't stay long enough to drink a soda. And even if you do, you don't leave that soda can with your prints on it in the trash."

Delgado considered and then reached to a coffee cup on his desk before nodding.

"Those are good points," he said, after taking a drink.

"If you had murdered somebody, Joe, you would have been a lot more careful, but you know how police officers and forensic technicians think. Armstrong's a civilian. He doesn't know what he's doing. He probably saw a scenario like this on *Law & Order* and thought he could pull it off. You're overthinking it. Trust me."

I sighed and shook my head. "I hope you're right."

"Don't forget that we'll search his house and car, too," said Darlene. "If he shot her, his car will still have gunshot residue, and his clothes will have blood spatter on them. We might even find the gun. We've got this guy. His wife was having an affair, so he killed her. I've worked half a dozen cases like this."

I shook my head.

"This wasn't about jealousy. If he killed her—and our evidence says he did—he did it for money. He paid for her car, and he gave her an allowance. We'll pull his finances. Maybe he's having money problems, and her death was his way of solving them."

Delgado nodded. "We'll get his bank records, then. It's a good idea. You feel better now?"

I nodded and rolled my shoulders to loosen them even as my gut tightened and a vague sense of unease hung in my thoughts.

"Yeah. Let's get this asshole."

23

It took a lot to get the great machinery of law enforcement moving, but once the process started, little could make it stop. Shaun Deveraux, our county prosecutor, arrived in Delgado's office about fifteen minutes after Darlene and I arrived. For ten minutes, we explained what we had found and how we had found it. Then, all of us sat behind Sheriff Delgado's monitor to watch the surveillance video. Afterwards, Deveraux blew out a slow breath.

"By itself, the video is damning, but with the fingerprints Ms. McEvoy found on the aluminum can, it gives us ample cause to arrest Mr. Armstrong. I'll get the paperwork started. By the time you get to St. Louis to pick him up, I should have signed arrest and search warrants in hand. I'll fax them to the county police in Clayton."

"Thank you," I said. I looked to the sheriff. "You want to go with me, boss?"

He shook his head. "I've got meetings this afternoon. Bob Reitz should be there, though. He worked the case and deserves to get some of the reward. And take two cars this time. I don't want him stuck in St. Louis."

I nodded. "We will."

The sheriff told me to drive safely, so I left the office and called Sergeant Reitz to let him know what was going on. He agreed to meet me at the St. Louis County police headquarters in Clayton. That left me with just the drive.

I signed out Old Brown, my decrepit cruiser, and headed north on the interstate. When I arrived, Bob was still half an hour away, and my search and arrest warrants were still waiting for a signature, so I took a walk. Officially, Clayton, Missouri, was a suburb of St. Louis, but it felt like a separate city in its own right. Many of the buildings were ten or fifteen stories tall, and cars packed the tree-lined streets. It had a lot of nice restaurants and bars, but I didn't think I could have lived there. It felt too stuffy. The residents wore suits to work, not uniforms. I wouldn't have fit in.

Eventually, Bob called to tell me he was in the area. I met him on the steps in front of the county police headquarters.

"Hey, Joe," he said. "I hear we got the guy."

"Close," I said, pulling out my phone to see whether I had missed a call or text. I hadn't. "Delgado's called the St. Louis County police liaison office, so the locals know we're in the area. They agreed to get a team together when we need it, but Deveraux's apparently still working on the warrants."

Bob nodded across the street toward a Starbucks.

"Coffee?"

"Sure," I said. "I think I've walked around enough."

Bob and I sat and talked about his kids and complained about the construction on our station. After that, we ran out of conversation topics, so we lapsed into silence. Thankfully, Deveraux eased the awkwardness by calling to let me know he had faxed the signed warrants to

St. Louis. They were ready to go as soon as we were.

Things moved quickly after that. Bob Reitz and two uniformed St. Louis officers went to Carl Armstrong's office to pick him up, while a team of officers, two forensic techs, and I went to Armstrong's palatial historic home in Ladue. Outside, big oak trees swayed in the breeze on his parklike front lawn. His house overlooked the pristine, rolling greens of a golf course. A foursome sat on a cart near the greens, watching us and drinking. Nobody looked like they were there to play golf.

I looked to my team. I didn't know them, but they knew what they were doing.

"Thanks for coming. I'm Detective Joe Court, and as you guys know, we're serving a search warrant on the home of Carl Armstrong. My partner is picking up Mr. Armstrong as we speak for murdering his wife with a .22-caliber pistol. It was likely suppressed. If you find a pistol or suppressor, bag and tag it. We're also here for blood evidence. That's clothes, shoes, socks, papers...if it's got blood on it, we want it. If you find illegal drugs or anything else legally questionable, we'll take them, too. Questions?"

No one responded, so I rang the doorbell. Within seconds, a man in a black suit opened the door and introduced himself as Joel Sanderson. He was Mr. Armstrong's estate manager, which, he informed me, meant he managed the property and rest of the household staff. He opened doors for us and introduced us to the rest of the staff. They had done nothing wrong, so we escorted two housekeepers and a groundskeeper to the front lawn. If we needed them, we'd question them later.

Sanderson, meanwhile, followed me around to supervise the search and ensure we didn't break anything. He would have annoyed me, but he had keys for every locked door, drawer, and cabinet in the building. It saved me from having to pick a lot of locks. About an hour after we started the search, Bob called to let me know he had Armstrong in the back of his squad car and was driving to St. Augustine. I told him to drive safely and that I'd be with him when I could. About twenty minutes after that, one of the forensic technicians called me into Mr. Armstrong's home office.

Sanderson followed me as I walked. The home office was just off the master bedroom and had probably been built as a nursery. It was light and cheery. Big windows crisscrossed with ironwork overlooked the golf course. The hardwood floor creaked beneath my feet. Sanderson stopped in the doorway and covered his mouth with surprise. The evidence tech had placed a pistol and suppressor on the desk. I took my phone from my purse and snapped pictures.

"Where'd you find it?" I asked the tech, a young woman with brunette hair. She wore jeans and a navy windbreaker with *POLICE* written across the back. A tie held her long hair from her face. She nodded toward the desk.

"I opened the center desk drawer and found two small magnets in the corner. When I tried to move them, I found resistance, which I thought was odd. I found the pistol under the drawer. It's a Ruger Mark IV. My dad lives in west Texas. He uses one to shoot rattlesnakes when he goes out walking."

The pistol was small and ugly.

"And the suppressor?" I asked.

"It was on the underside of the desk supported by a second magnet."

I nodded. "It's a good find. Mr. Armstrong and his lawyer are having a bad day."

"They sure are," she said, chuckling.

I stayed and helped her search the office for a few minutes, but she had things under control. Every sign pointed to this being the weapon that killed Tessa Armstrong, but I couldn't help but feel that we were missing something. Carl Armstrong lived in a multimillion-dollar home, he owned more luxury cars than the average professional baseball player, and he employed hundreds of people.

Gangbangers and other low-level thugs kept their firearms after committing crimes because they couldn't afford to replace them. Armstrong could buy a thousand pistols and still pay the mortgage without issue. If he knew enough to hide his pistol beneath his desk, he should have known enough to just get rid of it.

The St. Louis County team and I stayed in Armstrong's house until almost five in the afternoon, but aside from the gun, we found nothing of interest. After my search, I interviewed the housekeepers outside but let them go quickly. They knew nothing, and neither of them had been inside the home when Mr. Armstrong would have come home after killing his wife. Mr. Sanderson, likewise, knew nothing. He hadn't seen the firearm before, and he had been at home in Glendale with his wife and three kids when Mr. Armstrong would have come home.

At six, I thanked the St. Louis County team for their hard work and promised to put a good word in for them with their superiors. Then I drove to St. Augustine, checked the gun and suppressor into the evidence locker, and went to my office to fill out some paperwork. Bob Reitz came in at about 7:30.

"How'd it go?" he asked, leaning against my doorframe.

"Found a Ruger Mark IV and suppressor beneath his desk," I said. "There's a strong possibility that it's our murder weapon."

"Right on," he said, nodding and smiling. "Any bloody clothes?"

"Nah," I said, shaking my head. "He got rid of those. His car had trace amounts of GSR on the steering wheel and dash but no blood. Has he had dinner yet?"

Bob looked at his watch and nodded.

"By now, yeah. Why? You want to interrogate him?"

"Sure do," I said. "If you've got a minute, bring him up here. I'll call his lawyer. I've got his number somewhere."

"If you haven't had dinner yet, you can let him stew overnight," he said. "There's no hurry, is there? I can stay, but my daughter's got a volleyball game tonight. I'd like to go."

"Go to the game," I said, shaking my head and allowing a measure of softness into my voice. "And tell your daughter good luck. We'll worry about Armstrong tomorrow."

"Thanks, Joe," he said, nodding. "Have a good one."

I nodded and smiled at him as he walked out. Once I felt confident he couldn't hear me anymore, I sighed and picked up my phone. It was still early, so I called Preston Cain and asked whether he and his girlfriend were home. They were, but I wished they weren't.

I drove home. Roy was in the backyard where I had left him. When he saw me, he jumped and put his paws at the top of the dog run's gate. I petted his cheek, and he licked my hand.

"Hey, boy," I said. "I'm glad you're in a good mood. I have a friend I want you to meet."

He panted and stuck his tongue out. He looked content now, but in the long term, he'd be happier with Preston than with me. I let him out of the dog run, and the two of us went inside, where I fed him and microwaved a frozen rice bowl for dinner. We sat together for maybe ten or fifteen minutes before loading up in my Volvo and driving to Preston's house.

He had a nice place about five or six miles from my house. Like me, he lived in the country in an old house. There was a big pole barn out back and a fenced yard that kept the neighbor's cattle from traipsing through his garden. Roy could get under the fence, but he wouldn't go far. He was a homebody.

I looked over my shoulder at him. He panted at me from the hammock that covered my rear seat.

"How do you like it?"

He seemed to grin. That was a good sign. Preston and a woman a little younger than me stepped onto their home's front porch as I opened my door. I waved and then opened my Volvo's rear door. Roy jumped out and then nuzzled my hand before padding beside me toward them.

"Hey, guys," I said. Before he was shot, Preston had been the youngest sworn officer in our department, but he'd still had good instincts. To top it off, he was brave and sweet and had a good sense of humor. I smiled at them both.

"Hey, Joe," said Preston. "This is Shelby, my fiancé."

I walked to the steps and held out my hand. She shook it and smiled. It seemed genuine.

"I hear you flashed my fiancé after he was shot," she said, winking.

"I hear that, too," I said, looking to Preston. "Care to explain?"

He kept his expression neutral as he shook his head.

"What happens on the job stays on the job."

I nodded and looked to Shelby.

"After Preston was shot, I removed my shirt hoping I could stanch the blood. I was wearing a sports bra, so he didn't see anything."

She punched him on the shoulder and laughed. Then she looked at me and reached for my hand. I hadn't met her before, but she pulled me into a hug anyway and squeezed tight. I rarely liked it when people hugged me, but she seemed insistent, so I let her.

"You saved his life," she whispered. "Thank you."

"It's what friends do," I said.

She squeezed me once more before letting go and looking to Roy. He sat as she knelt in front of him.

"You're pretty, aren't you?" she asked, petting his cheek. He leaned into her hand. Preston knelt beside his girlfriend and petted Roy's shoulder before standing again and looking to me.

"Let me show you around," he said. "Roy'll like it here."

Preston and I took a walk around the yard and property, leaving Shelby and Roy to get acquainted. He owned about five acres, one acre of which was fenced. Roy would have plenty of space to walk around and enjoy himself. Already, he and Shelby were talking about having children, so Roy would even have kids to play with one day. Since Preston worked at home, Roy would never be alone. He'd have everything he could need.

As we reached the front yard again, Shelby was trying to throw him a ball. Roy watched her throw, and then tilted his head to the side and laid down once the ball stopped moving. She chuckled and walked to get it.

"He'll retrieve some, but he's lazy," I said. "If you want him to keep playing, give him a treat. He's more of a companion than a playmate. He loves walks in the woods, though."

"Is that right?" Shelby asked, her voice high as she petted his back. Roy thumped his tail against the ground. I smiled, but I felt acid in my throat, and my chest felt tight.

"Are you sure about this, Joe?" asked Preston, his voice barely above a whisper. "We'll give Roy the best home we can, but I feel like I'm kidnapping your friend."

I cleared my throat so my voice wouldn't crack.

"No, you're not kidnapping my friend. You're giving him a home I can't."

"He makes you happy, though, doesn't he?"

I forced myself to smile as I ignored his question.

"He's food motivated, so if he's upset, just give him something to eat. It doesn't matter what it is. He loves peanut butter and beef jerky. And don't leave a beer sitting around. He'll knock it off the table and lap it up."

Preston put his hands on his hips.

"Are you sure about this, Joe?"

"Yeah," I said. "I'll just head out now. It looks like Roy and Shelby are having a good time. And make sure he doesn't tire her out. She'll have to chase after that ball all night if she keeps throwing it."

"I'll take care of him," said Preston. "And when you want to see him, come around. You're always welcome."

"Thanks, Sasquatch," I said. "I'll see you around. Okay?"

He smiled. "Nobody calls me Sasquatch anymore. It's nice to hear it again."

"I'm glad," I said, heading toward my car. "I'll see you around."

He waved as I got in my Volvo. Roy and Shelby were walking around the front yard. When he heard my car start, Roy started trotting over, but Shelby grabbed his collar. Preston hurried over and knelt in front of the dog to hold him and keep him from running out. The first day would be rough, but he'd forget about me soon. Roy was kennel trained, and Preston already had a big kennel for him as well as toys, food, and a bed. The county had provided the equipment for him when he applied to be a canine officer. They had everything they needed.

As I drove home, I thought of Jasmine Kelley. On one of her videos, she said it was her lot in life to watch as others lived out their dreams. I knew how she felt. Life didn't work out for everybody. Some people just didn't catch lucky breaks. It was unfair, but that was life. The world didn't give a shit about anyone's happiness.

As I drove off, my chest felt heavy, and my throat felt tight. I didn't want Preston to see me cry, so I drove away quickly and pulled over on the side of the road about a mile away. I had just dropped him off, but already I missed my dog. He'd have a better life with Preston and Shelby than he would with me, so giving him up was the right thing to do.

Intellectually, I knew that, but I wished doing the right thing would, for once, also mean doing the thing that made me happy.

24

Mickey Lyons parked two streets south of Sheppard Altman's home. Outside the car, the neighborhood was quiet and still. It was two in the morning, and winter had begun replacing fall's soft embrace with a stranglehold that promised to choke the area until spring. The sky was clear, but the moon was a waning crescent that cast little light across the ground. A dog howled somewhere distant, but no answering barks greeted him from Altman's neighborhood. It was a good night for the work ahead of them.

In his pocket, Mickey had a list of six names in St. Augustine County. He didn't enjoy killing people, but the orders had come from on high after he gave his most recent report. Before she died, Tessa had performed admirably and procured millions of dollars' worth of opioids, but her death had left a void in the territory no one could fill. Her suppliers seemed loyal for the moment, but six months or a year down the road, that could change. It was a risk Mickey and his employers couldn't take.

Everyone on the list had to die, but the purge started at the top with Sheppard Altman. Even if Tessa had loved him, she never should have brought him into the fold. If she had a problem with a man on her route, she could have called Mickey. He would have straightened it out, and if he couldn't have straightened it out, he would have made the problem disappear. That was protocol.

Instead, Tessa had brought in her boyfriend. She was a decent judge of character, so Sheppard was likely a good man. That didn't mean he'd be a good partner, though. By bringing Altman into the business before Mickey and his superiors could vet him, Tessa had signed his death warrant. Neither Mickey nor the men in the car with him had a choice in that.

"How do we want to handle this?" asked Adrian.

"Quietly and with dignity," said Mickey. "He loved my sister, and she loved him. We'll strangle him and hang him. Even without a suicide note, no one will question his death after what he's been through. Then we search the place for drugs."

"And the other names?" asked Lukas.

Mickey sighed. "I don't know. Hitting six people in one night is a recipe for arrest. Even these hillbillies will see a pattern if we drop six bodies in one night. We'll do it slowly. Some can disappear, others can overdose. We'll figure it out in the coming weeks."

Lukas sighed and looked out the window. "The county's pretty, but I'm not looking for a long-term project."

"Too bad because that's what we've got," said Mickey. "Tonight, we'll go in the back door, but once we're in the house, we split up. According to tax records, the home has two bedrooms. Altman will be in one of them. If you see him, put a cord around his neck and choke him out before he wakes up. We'll string him up together. Once he's taken care of, we can search the house room by room for drugs. I doubt he's got any, but we're looking to remove any ties to us or our organization. Sound good?"

Both Lukas and Adrian nodded.

"Okay, then. Let's go," said Mickey, opening his door. He stepped out into the cold night. His navy, one-piece coveralls felt stiff, but they'd protect his clothes from blood spatter and prevent him from leaving any of his body hair or skin cells in Altman's home. They also helped him blend into the night. Lukas and Adrian wore identical clothing. If any of the neighbors looked out the window, they'd look suspicious, but the chances of that happening this late were low.

Mickey opened his trunk and handed each of his colleagues enough rope to wrap around Altman's neck. Once they finished the job, they'd burn their coveralls and any rope they didn't use and head back to their hotel for the night.

The three men snapped black nitrile gloves over their hands and left the car. Altman lived in an older, well-established neighborhood full of mature trees and lush, healthy lawns and gardens. Mickey and his team wove their way through trees and past play sets and swimming pools before reaching the edge of Altman's sloping yard. The ground felt spongy. Grass led to a small concrete patio.

Mickey knelt in the shadow cast by a fir tree and reached to the grass.

"Ground's wet," he said. "When we get inside, put on

your slip covers. This needs to look like a suicide. We can't leave footprints."

The two guys agreed, and they crossed the lawn at a run. Lukas had a knack for picking locks, so he knelt beside a pair of French doors that led into the kitchen while Adrian and Mickey stood beside him. The home's eaves cast long shadows on the patio, giving Mickey and his crew ample cover.

Within a minute, Lukas had the deadbolt unlocked. The door swung open. Mickey held his breath, waiting for the beep of an alarm or the squeal of a hinge. Only silence greeted him. He nodded to the two men beside him and pulled a pair of slip covers from his pockets and put them on his shoes before stepping inside.

Slate tile covered the floor of the eat-in kitchen. There was a carpeted living room with a vaulted ceiling and exposed beams to the right, while a large hallway led straight ahead to a dining room overlooking the front yard.

No dog or cat came running at them, but Mickey shot his eyes around the room anyway to see whether he could find a dog bowl or toys on the ground. He hadn't expected an animal—it would have barked at him through the windows when he accosted Altman in the driveway earlier—but he breathed a sigh of relief, anyway.

"Lukas, Adrian, you go right. I'll go left. The floor's slick, so tread lightly."

The two men glided across the ground. Lukas and Adrian went through the kitchen and then took a hallway to the right. Mickey followed but went left in the hallway. The slate flooring continued through the kitchen and to a laundry room before finally terminating at the closed door of what Mickey presumed was a bedroom. He paused and stretched the rope taut in his hands.

The trick with a job like this was to move quicker than his target could respond and overwhelm him before he could come to his senses. If Mickey could get the rope around Altman's neck before Altman started to fight back, the job was as good as done. Then, they could tie him to one of the exposed beams in the living room to make it look like a suicide. Mickey didn't like the cloak-and-dagger approach, but he was professional enough to understand what the circumstances demanded and adjust his plans. This would be just fine.

He opened the bedroom door. The room held a king-sized bed, a dresser, and a chest of drawers, but the bed's covers were drawn up to the headboard. No one slept inside.

Mickey's heart thumped against his breastbone as he hurried toward the two open doors on the far side of the room. One led to an ensuite bathroom, while a second led to a walk-in closet. No clothes hung inside. This was evidently just the guest bedroom. Adrian and Lukas had the target. He hurried outside, knowing his colleagues should have reached Altman by now. That he hadn't heard a scuffle meant they were doing their jobs.

The hallway outside the guest bedroom felt warm. The front windows lit up as a car drove past on the street.

As he crept toward the other side of the house, Mickey spotted something on the ground in the hallway near the kitchen. It was a figure in navy coveralls. Blood, like a black mirror in the faint light, pooled around the body.

Mickey inched forward, feeling his heart pound hard and his breath grow tight. As he got closer, Mickey recognized Adrian's face. He wasn't breathing, and he bled from a gaping, ugly wound on the right side of his neck. For a moment, he could only stare, but then he realized something. If Adrian was down in the hallway, Lukas was probably down, too. Mickey shot his eyes around the room.

His fingers trembled as he tried to formulate a plan. Even if he killed Altman without making a sound, they were in trouble. Adrian and Lukas were cops. Their fingerprints and DNA samples were on file with the Chicago police, the DEA, the Illinois State Police, and half a dozen other law enforcement agencies. Even the hillbillies in St. Augustine would ID Adrian and Lukas's bodies and trace them back to Mickey and the organization for which they worked.

Mickey needed a solution, and he needed it fast. This was a screw up, but it shouldn't have happened. A schoolteacher shouldn't have been able to take out two police officers in the dark like this. They had missed something.

Before Mickey could think through the situation, the floor creaked. A figure stepped out of the shadows at the end of the hall. He had something in his hand, but it wasn't a knife. It was much narrower, and it had a blocky handle. It looked like a flat head screwdriver.

"I already killed your friends," said Altman. "I'd run if I were you."

Mickey considered, but Altman was right. The rewards weren't worth the risk. Even if he killed Altman, he gained nothing. He couldn't make it look like a suicide, and he couldn't get rid of three bodies and however many gallons of blood they had spilled on the floor. This was about survival now.

Mickey dropped the rope and sprinted to the back door. Almost the moment his feet touched grass, the house's floodlights popped on. He ignored them and kept running until he reached his car.

It was over. Everything. Altman may not have seen Mickey's face, but he wasn't stupid. He knew who had broken into his house. The police would know soon, too.

Mickey dove into the driver's seat and jammed his keys into the ignition. His hands trembled with adrenaline, and he clenched his jaw tight. This motherfucker took out two guys in the dark with a screwdriver. He wasn't a schoolteacher. Mickey didn't know who Altman really was, but he knew that right away. He also knew it didn't matter. He had to get out of there.

The moment he pulled away from the curb, he flicked on his lights and accelerated hard. The road was empty, so he floored it and hit almost a hundred miles an hour. After a few minutes of white-knuckled driving with his breath held in his throat, he braked and then pulled onto a main road. There he slowed further, though his mind still raced.

It was over. Not just his business, but his life. Every single one of his employers wore a badge, and he had become a liability to them all now. With their resources, there'd be nowhere in the country he could hide. He couldn't hide in Canada, either, because his employers had too many contacts with Canadian law enforcement. Mexico might work for a while, but even there, he'd be vulnerable. He could probably disappear in eastern Europe, but it would take resources to get there, and everything he owned was in Chicago.

In one night, he had lost everything. Even his sister was gone.

"Goddammit."

He pounded the seat beside him as he swore. He never should have sent Tessa here. This whole fucking county was cursed.

25

I was dead asleep at 2:30 in the morning when my phone rang. At first, my mind tried to incorporate the ringtone into my dream, but by the fourth or fifth ring, even my subconscious couldn't ignore it. I opened my eyes and rolled toward my nightstand, half expecting to feel the bed shake as Roy jumped off. The dog wasn't there, though. I was alone. The room felt empty.

I let myself feel that emptiness a moment before grabbing the phone.

"Yeah?" I asked.

"Hey, Joe. Sorry for calling so late, but we've got bodies. George Delgado's already at the house, but he asked me to call you."

The voice belonged to Doug Patricia. I rubbed my eyes and sighed.

"Okay," I said. "I presume this is a homicide and not an accident."

"Yep. Homeowner caught three people breaking in. He killed one guy by stabbing him in the neck with a screwdriver, he stabbed the other guy in the gut, and he told the third guy to run. Homeowner thinks he's Batman or something."

"Jesus," I said, opening my eyes wide. I grabbed a notepad on my nightstand. "Where's the scene?"

I wrote down an address as he read it.

"And who's the homeowner?" I asked.

"Sheppard Altman."

I closed my eyes and nodded. That explained why Delgado needed me at the scene. He thought this was connected to Tessa Armstrong's death.

"Tell the boss I'm on my way."

Doug said he would and then hung up. I changed into jeans and a pale blue sweater and then grabbed a light jacket on my way out of the house. It had dropped fifteen or twenty degrees since I was last outside, so the night air was bracing. My breath came out in small puffs of frost. I pulled my jacket tight around me and hurried to my car.

At this time of night, the roads were empty, and I made good speed to Sheppard Altman's single-story home. Trees ringed his property, giving him privacy from the back and sides. Sheriff Delgado's SUV and three marked cruisers were parked on the street out front, while a van from the coroner's office was parked in the driveway. Officer Katie Martelle stood on the front lawn.

I parked near the boss's SUV and walked toward the home. Katie gave me a tight smile. At twenty-three, she was five years younger than me, but she could have passed for eighteen. She was intelligent, observant, and kind. I liked her, but I also worried for her. Police work was tough, especially for a young woman. A drunk college kid caught smoking marijuana outside his dorm might not dream of attacking a big officer like Marcus Washington, but a petite young woman like Katie made a different sort of target. She was learning the ropes, though. Only time would tell whether she stuck with the job, but she'd be an asset to our department if she did.

"Hey, Detective," she said, holding a clipboard for me to sign. I scanned the entries on the log sheet before signing. "The boss call you in?"

"He did," I said, nodding. "The homeowner was the boyfriend of a young woman murdered in the Wayfair Motel. I think he's afraid they're related."

She lowered the clipboard to her side and then looked to the home before focusing on me again.

"I haven't been inside, but Dr. Sheridan said it's an ugly case."

I nodded.

"Has anybody woken the neighbors yet?"

"Sheriff Delgado and Marcus Washington. Mr. Altman has a smart doorbell with a built-in camera, but the attackers came in through the rear. He thought a neighbor behind him might have a similar system, but he wasn't sure."

"Good. And where is Mr. Altman?"

She drew in a breath and narrowed her eyes as she thought.

"Shane drove him back to the station for a formal interview."

I looked around me. The front yard was empty, but an older couple stood on the front porch of the home across the street. The other neighbors had probably gone back to bed after Delgado and Marcus spoke to them. This late, we wouldn't get many gawkers. Katie would be fine outside by herself, so I walked through the open front door.

Altman's entryway had a slate tile floor that ran down hallways to the left and right. Straight ahead, there was a carpeted living room with a vaulted ceiling and exposed wooden beams. A body in navy coveralls lay in the hallway to the right. It was a good-sized man in his early to mid-thirties. The sun had baked his skin to a deep brown and left his lips chapped. He wore a diamond stud in his left ear but no other jewelry as far as I could tell.

Something had ripped his throat out. If I hadn't known a human being had killed him, I would have assumed it was an animal attack. Blood pooled on the ground in a thick, congealing puddle around him.

"Jesus," I whispered, taking a step back to consider the scene. Dr. Sheridan must have heard me because he stepped into the archway that separated the kitchen from the hallway. He couldn't reach me without stepping over the body, so he gestured to his right. I met him in the living room. When he saw me, he nodded but didn't smile.

"You caught this case, too?"

"I'm not the lead detective, but I'll be working it. I'm sure somebody's told you, but the homeowner is the boyfriend of Tessa Armstrong. What can you tell me about the body?"

He cocked his head to the side.

"It's ugly."

I looked to the body and nodded.

"I can see that."

"Best guess, based on what I'm seeing here, is that the deceased stood in the hall facing the back door. Mr.

Altman crept up behind him and stabbed him on the right side of the throat with a large screwdriver. The tip of the screwdriver plunged down and severed the deceased's external carotid artery. As best as I can tell, Mr. Altman then pushed the screwdriver forward, which caused further damage to the soft tissues of his neck. Once I perform a full autopsy, I'll be able to tell you more."

I nodded.

"Where's the second victim?"

"Paramedics took him to St. John's, but it wouldn't surprise me if they flew him to a hospital in St. Louis after stabilizing him. He had a deep penetrating injury to his left abdomen. To survive, he'll need surgery."

"And I'm guessing neither victim had any ID on him."

"Good guess," said Sheridan. "Both men wore coveralls, slip covers on their shoes, and nitrile gloves. They didn't have guns or knives, either. This guy had a rope in his pocket, but that was it. I guess they expected Mr. Altman to sleep through the robbery."

I covered my mouth and focused on the body in front of me, thinking. In the past year, I had worked thirty-nine home burglaries and arrested four people on burglary charges. Some bad guys planned their crimes before committing them, but I had never worked a burglary in which the suspects wore coveralls, gloves, and shoe covers.

I shook my head.

"This wasn't a robbery attempt," I said. "These guys

came to kill the homeowner."

Sheridan furrowed his brow. "Who would break into a house and try to murder somebody but not bring a gun?

"That's the million-dollar question," I said, my mind already jumping ahead. Carl Armstrong might want Sheppard Altman dead for sleeping with his wife, but Armstrong was in a holding cell. Tessa's brother, Detective Lyons, might have blamed Altman for his sister's death, but I'd need irrefutable evidence to charge a cop with murder. This would be a mess.

I thanked the coroner for his time and stepped out of the house. My boss was on the front lawn. Sheriff Delgado wore a blue polo shirt, a fleece jacket, and jeans. His badge hung on a lanyard around his neck. When he saw me, he stopped speaking to Officer Martelle and waved me over.

"Have you seen the body?" he asked.

I nodded. "Yeah. It was...something. Have you talked to Altman about it yet?"

Delgado shook his head.

"I tried to, but he asked for an attorney."

I crossed my arms.

"Odd move for a guy who defended himself against three men who broke into his house."

Delgado looked toward the home and then back to me. He narrowed his eyes and cocked his head to the side.

"What are you thinking?"

"I'm thinking home invaders don't enter a house through the back door while wearing gloves and coveralls.

The dead guy in there looks like he could be a member of our forensics team. This was a kill squad."

"Except that they didn't bring weapons," said Delgado.

"They brought a rope," I said.

Delgado considered me before nodding and looking toward the house.

"They should have brought a gun."

"In hindsight, I'm sure they'd agree if they were alive," I said. "I can stay and work this case with you, but I don't know how much I can help. You've got one guy dead while in commission of a felony. You've got a second guy in custody, and you've got a third guy on the loose. Charge your second guy with first-degree murder and give him a deal to turn on his still-living partner."

Delgado grunted and nodded. "Be nice to know who these assholes are and who they're working for."

"My guess is Carl Armstrong," I said. "We've got him dead to rights on Tessa's murder, so we know he's capable of killing someone. He's in a jail cell, but he wasn't yesterday morning. Altman slept with his wife and was trying to persuade Tessa to divorce him. That would have cost him a lot of money. It's a powerful motive however you look at it."

"That's possible," he said, glancing at me before staring at the house once more. "All right, Detective Court, you've talked your way off the case. Go home, get some sleep, and I'll see you tomorrow. Hopefully Mr. Armstrong will have a new cellmate by then."

"Good luck, boss," I said, nodding and walking toward my car.

As I drove back home, I wondered about Sheppard Altman. He took out two guys with a flat head screwdriver. These weren't garden-variety burglars, either. These guys were smart and experienced enough to wear clothing that limited their forensic footprint to almost nothing. That took skill few people possessed. It made me wonder whether we should look at him a little closer and see what skeletons he had hiding in his closet. He didn't kill Tessa, but his hands had blood on them—literally.

I'd worry about that later. It was a little after four in the morning when I made it home. The moment my head hit the pillow, I fell asleep, knowing I had done my job well that day. Because of the work my colleagues and I had done, Carl Armstrong would die in prison for murdering his wife in cold blood.

He deserved that and more.

26

I arrived at work the next morning at eight. Most of the contractors and their crews had been there since six, so the construction site was already in full swing. A semitrailer had parked out front, and teams of men were carrying steel I-beams inside through the front door and then down the stairs.

The builders had already done a lot of structural work in the basement to shore up the old limestone foundation, but they must have found additional problems if they needed more steel. As much as I loved this old building, I wondered whether they should have just torn it down and built it again. It probably would have saved the county money.

I entered through the small side door we used as a main entrance and took the stairs to the second floor. Delgado was in the conference room, going over his notes for the morning briefing, but when he saw me, he waved me toward him.

"There are two gentlemen from the US Attorney's Office in St. Louis driving to see you," he said. "They want to talk about Carl Armstrong. We also got a call this morning from an administrator at the Willow Bend Living Center. One of their nurses has gone missing. She's not answering her phone, and her house looks abandoned, but her car's still in her driveway. Since you closed the Armstrong case, you're on this one. See whether you can find her."

I nodded and thought for a moment.

"Did she have a boyfriend or girlfriend she might have gone away with?"

"We don't know."

I didn't know where this retirement home was, but I'd look it up.

"All right," I said. "I'll see what I can find. Once the lawyers get here, tell Trisha to make them comfortable and call me."

"Good luck, Detective," said Delgado, looking at his notes once more. I started to leave but then stopped.

"Hey, boss, that guy last night survive?"

Delgado nodded. "Barely, but yeah. Scott Hall's watching him at St. John's. As soon as the suspect is well enough, we'll charge him with felony murder, conspiracy to commit murder, breaking and entering, trespassing, and whatever else we can think of. He'll have a real bad day."

"Good," I said. "Hopefully he'll talk to us. If you need anything, you know how to reach me."

He nodded and looked toward the growing crowd of officers. Then he cleared his throat and looked at his watch.

"It's five after eight in the morning. Let's get this shindig started. Last night, we had fourteen calls, including a homicide at the home of Sheppard Altman..."

As Delgado recited the events of the previous night, I walked to the front desk, signed out a marked cruiser, and headed out. According to the GPS on my phone,

Willow Bend Living Center was halfway between the town of St. Augustine and Dyer, a farming community so small it didn't even have a post office. I had driven by the facility dozens of times and had never given it much thought. Now, I slowed and turned into a parking lot with spots for maybe fifty people. Willow Bend Living Center sat atop a rolling, grass-covered hill and overlooked a convenience store and derelict house. Nearby, an electrical substation hummed.

I hung my badge around my neck and walked toward the facility's front door. The interior felt warm and smelled like antiseptic. An elderly couple played cards in the front lobby. They smiled hello to me but didn't stop their game. The front desk was empty, so I waited a few minutes for a man in navy scrubs to come by. He wore latex gloves, and he pushed a big plastic cart full of laundry. He looked at my face, but then his eyes followed the lanyard around my neck to my badge. His eyebrows furrowed.

"Can I help you, Officer?"

"You in charge?"

He chuckled, shook his head, and reached for a walkie-talkie on his belt.

"I'm not even in charge of the laundry, ma'am," he said before holding his radio to his mouth. "Mr. Selznick, you're wanted at the front desk. There's a police officer here to see you."

The radio crackled, and a voice confirmed the message. I thanked him and then sat on a couch to wait.

The facility had wide hallways and small windows to the outside. Overhead fluorescent lamps provided most of the illumination, while colorful landscape paintings covered the walls. I wouldn't have bought any of the paintings in a gallery, but they brought a welcome splash of color to an otherwise beige world.

From the exterior, the building had looked like a dump on a lousy piece of property, but the interior was clean, and the two residents I had seen seemed content. Even the housekeeper I'd spoken to seemed glad to be there. That said a lot about this place. It was a home, and it didn't deserve my judgment.

Three or four minutes after the housekeeper placed the call, a man in gray slacks and a white polo shirt came down the hall.

"Detective?" he asked.

I nodded and shook his hand.

"Joe Court. You must be Mr. Selznick. I hear an employee of yours is missing."

He looked around and smiled at the two residents playing cards before taking a step toward me and lowering his voice.

"Yeah. Can we talk in my office?"

I nodded. "Lead the way."

He led me through the building toward its administrative center. Along the way, we passed an art and music room, a cafeteria, therapy rooms, and other rooms full of chairs and sofas for socialization. Most residents stayed in their private rooms, but a few people walked the halls. Mr. Selznick knew them all by name and wished them a good morning.

Mr. Selznick's office was clean and had big windows overlooking the hallway. There were motivational posters on the wall and photographs of his family on his desk and bookshelf. He had at least five kids, and he held his wife's hand whenever they stood close to one another in pictures. In one, she beamed at him and rested her head against his shoulder like a teenager in love. It was cute. I didn't know this guy, but I liked him.

I sat in front of his desk, and he sat in back.

"Okay, Mr. Selznick, my boss told me you're missing an employee. What's going on?"

"She's one of my nurses," he said. "Maddie Dawson."

He spelled the name for me, which I appreciated. After writing it down on a notepad, I glanced up at him.

"When did she go missing?"

"She missed her shift three days ago," he said. "I called her that day, but she didn't answer her phone. It was unlike her to miss work without first calling her supervisor, so I thought she might have had an emergency. One of her colleagues went by her house after work that day, but she wasn't home. When she didn't show up the next day, I called again, but she didn't answer. After the third day, I went by her house again, but she still wasn't home. Her car was in the driveway."

I raised an eyebrow.

"Was it in the driveway before?"

"I don't know," he said. "I didn't think to ask Tina."

I nodded and scribbled a few notes. "Did she have any family or a significant other I can talk to?"

"She lives alone. Her mom has passed, but her dad lives in Kansas City. They're estranged. Maddie can be a difficult person to be friends with, but she's a good nurse. She's worked here almost fifteen years. I'd hate for something to have happened to her."

I looked at my notepad before glancing at Mr. Selznick.

"How well did you know Ms. Dawson?"

He considered before answering.

"I hired her right after she finished nursing school, and she's worked here ever since."

I raised an eyebrow and tilted my head to the side.

"That's not what I mean," I said. "It's rare for a supervisor to call me and say his employees are missing. In most cases, missing persons are reported by family and friends. Employers just fire their missing employees and move on. They don't become concerned and involve themselves in their employees' lives. How would you characterize your relationship with her? Friendly? More than friendly?"

He straightened. "I'm married. Maddie is an employee."

"Okay," I said. "That's great. You're a good boss. Is there anything I should know about her?"

For a moment, he said nothing. Instead, he kept his eyes on his desk. I kept my mouth shut and let the silence draw him out.

"Maddie's been stealing drugs from patients."

I crossed my arms and leaned back.

"Okay," I said, raising my eyebrows in surprise. "How do you know?"

He glanced up at me. "I'm not positive, but I'm growing more confident by the day. When she went missing, I had to call in additional nurses to cover her patients, and since we've switched the nursing rotation up, several of Maddie's patients have told me they feel better than when she oversaw their care. If one patient had told me she felt better with a new nurse, I would have attributed it to the staffing change. Instead, I had almost a dozen patients tell me they feel better.

"I started interviewing the staff and the patients. Remember our patients are elderly, and most are in poor health. Some take dozens of pills a day. We have protocols in place to ensure that our staff give our patients their prescribed medicines in the correct dosage at the correct time. Maddie dispensed the cancer drugs and antibiotics, but I think she was stealing painkillers from her patients."

I sighed and made a note.

"Okay," I said. "How many pills could she steal like this?"

He tilted his head to the side. "It's difficult to say. We have thirty-four residents on prescription opioids. Each of those patients could receive between four and twelve pills a day, depending on their level of pain and the medicine their doctors have prescribed. If she stole half the prescription opioids she was supposed to dispense, it might be seventy to a hundred pills a day."

I thought about that. If she had stolen a couple of pills a day, I would have assumed she had taken them for her own consumption. If she stole seventy or more a day, she was selling them. It just so happened that I knew a woman who had been found dead with over a hundred prescription opioids and an envelope full of cash in her hotel room. It might have been a coincidence, but I took my phone from my purse and flipped through pictures until I found one of Tessa Armstrong.

"Have you seen this woman around?" I asked, turning my phone toward him. He concentrated and then nodded.

"Yeah. I don't know her name, but she was one of Maddie's friends. She picks Maddie up about once a week. Why? Do you think she hurt Maddie?"

I shook my head and put my phone away.

"She's dead," I said, standing. "I'll investigate Ms. Dawson to see what I can find out, and I'll also contact the Missouri Department of Health and Senior Services to discuss the drug situation. I appreciate your cooperation. My office will be in touch."

He nodded. "Thank you, Detective. We try our best here."

"I can tell," I said. "Good luck."

As I left the facility and walked to my car, I called my boss.

"George, it's Joe Court. I'm at the Willow Bend

Living Center, the retirement home that reported a missing nurse. We've got a problem."

27

I spent about ten minutes on the phone with Sheriff Delgado. He said he'd start an investigation into Willow Bend and its staff, while I continued looking for Maddie Dawson. That was easy enough. I started by looking her up on the license bureau's database and then by searching to see whether she had a criminal record. Beyond two speeding tickets, though, she was clean.

My next step was to call neighboring departments and make sure she wasn't sitting in a jail cell somewhere. On my third call, I got an odd response from a deputy with the Washington County Sheriff's Department.

"Your missing woman have curly blond hair?"

I had only seen the photo on her license, but I nodded.

"Yeah," I said. "She's thirty-six years old. According to her license, she's five-three and weighs a hundred twenty-five pounds. I've not seen her in person, so I'm just going on the information I have from the license bureau. She's missing. Why?"

The deputy paused. "It's possible we've got her in our morgue. Hiker found a body off the trail in Mark Twain State Park two days ago. No ID on her. She had a gunshot wound to her head, ligature marks on her wrists, and abrasions on her forearms, chest, chin, belly, and thighs. Our coroner thinks someone dragged her behind a car."

"Jeez," I said, my voice low.

"Yeah," said the deputy. "It was ugly. This lady got hurt before she died."

And that was a problem. Torture wasn't part of the average murderer's M.O. If this was Maddie Dawson, we had a bigger problem than I had expected.

"Is Trevor Sheridan your coroner?" I asked.

He paused. "He used to be, but now we contract that work out to a private doctor in Potosi. It saves the county money."

He gave me the doctor's name and number, and I promised to call her and set up a time when I could bring someone in to ID the body. The case was more complicated than I had expected, so I picked up my phone to call my boss and let him know I might have found our missing nurse. Before I could dial, my phone buzzed with an incoming call. I answered and put it to my ear.

"Trisha, I was just going to call Sheriff Delgado. I've got some news."

"That has to wait," she said. "I've got two lawyers from the US Attorney's Office in the conference room waiting for you."

"Did they say what they want?"

"Only to talk to you," she said. "You should get down here."

I sighed.

"Okay. Tell them I'm on my way. And tell George Delgado that I need to talk to him about Tessa Armstrong and Maddie Dawson. Dawson is the missing nurse from the nursing home. I think Ms. Dawson was selling Tessa Armstrong drugs, but I can't ask her because she might be in the morgue in Washington County. If she is, she was tortured before she died."

Trisha paused. "Okay. I'll talk to the sheriff and let him know what's going on. You drive here."

"Thanks, Trisha," I said.

I hung up and tossed my phone to the seat beside me. In the past few months, I had worked a few high-profile cases, most of which had ended up in federal court. Because of that, I knew a fair number of lawyers in the US Attorney's Office in St. Louis. They were professionals, and they didn't make house calls. If they needed to meet a local detective, they summoned that detective to their offices in St. Louis. I didn't know what it meant that they were driving down to see me, but it made me more than a little nervous.

The drive to my station took about twenty minutes. When I arrived, I found two men in Trisha's conference room. They turned to me and stood with their hands out to shake.

"Chris Sorenson," said one, a middle-aged attorney with brown hair and green eyes. His hands were soft, but his grip was strong. "You must be Detective Court. Officer Marshall said you were on your way in."

"Nice to meet you," I said, giving him a curt smile before turning to his partner.

"Jeff Wallace," he said, shaking my hand. Wallace had soft hands like Sorenson and an equally strong grip.

"How about we go to my office?" I suggested.

They agreed, so we walked to the storage room I had been using as a private office during the construction. I didn't have a lot of furniture, but I had a desk and chairs. The three of us sat down, and I leaned back.

"What can I do for the US Attorney's Office?"

Wallace leaned forward.

"I understand you have Carl Armstrong in a jail cell."

"We do," I said, nodding. "He murdered his wife. Because of the crime and his resources, the judge at his arraignment denied bail. Why is the US Attorney's Office interested?"

"Because he didn't kill Tessa Armstrong," said Sorenson.

I smiled and looked at my desk.

"We've got video that puts his car outside the victim's room at the time of her death, we've got a soda can with his prints on it from inside the room, and we found the murder weapon inside his home office."

"Do you have video of Mr. Armstrong killing his wife?" asked Sorenson.

"No," I said. "He killed her inside a hotel room while she was in the shower. Our video came from surveillance cameras on a strip club across the street from the hotel."

The two lawyers looked at one another. Then Wallace looked at me.

"How sure are you of your victim's time of death?"

"Positive," I said. "We've got video of her boyfriend leaving her room. She gave him a hug and a kiss, so we know she was alive. He then drove off, while she stayed behind. Mr. Armstrong's car arrived a few minutes later. He parked in the fire lane, went inside the room, and then drove off five minutes later. The next person to enter the room was the housekeeper almost twelve hours later. Armstrong was the only person who could have killed her."

Wallace cocked his head to the side.

"You have video of the car, but you don't have video of Mr. Armstrong specifically."

I hesitated. "Correct, but we have his prints inside the room, we've found GSR in his car, and he had the murder weapon, which also has his prints on it, hidden in his home office. Seems simple to me."

"It's not that simple," said Sorenson. "For the past six months, our office has been working with the NCAA to investigate financial impropriety and recruiting violations at major athletic departments at several universities in the Midwest. Mr. Armstrong is a major booster at his alma mater, so we were watching him.

"At the time of his wife's death, Mr. Armstrong was entertaining three potential football recruits in a suite at the Ritz-Carlton Hotel in Clayton, Missouri. We haven't talked to the football players involved for fear of tipping the university off to our investigation, but Mr. Armstrong brought six prostitutes with him. We've flipped all six. They are all willing to testify that Mr. Armstrong paid them a thousand dollars each for their services and that he stayed the entire night with them."

I sank into my chair.

"Shit," I said.

"This is a sensitive investigation," said Wallace. "College football is big business, and we need to keep a lid on this while we determine whether the university or anyone associated with the football program knew of Mr. Armstrong's efforts on their behalf. He might be a bad guy, but he didn't kill his wife. Sorry."

I scratched my head and looked down at my desk.

"How sure are you that he was in the hotel at the time his wife died?" I asked.

"Positive," said Wallace. "We've got surveillance video from the garage in which he parked. He and a young lady drove in his Bentley. She performed oral sex on him inside the garage, and then they entered the hotel. They didn't leave until the next morning. It's on film."

I grimaced and sighed.

"I'll take your word for that."

"Again, we're sorry," said Sorenson. "Normally we wouldn't involve ourselves in your investigation, but in this case, we decided that we had to step forward."

I swore again and then sighed and stood.

"Well, gentlemen, thank you for your time, and thank you for coming down here. I'll call the prosecutor and have the charges against Mr. Armstrong dropped."

Both lawyers nodded. Before leaving, they gave me their business cards and told me to call if I needed anything from them. I thanked them and escorted them out. As I walked back to my office, I passed the conference room in which Trisha was working. She jogged out to meet me.

"Hey," she said. "Did your meeting go okay?"

"Yeah, but we're back to the beginning on the Tessa Armstrong murder," I said. "Her husband didn't do it. He was in St. Louis with six prostitutes at the time of her death."

Trisha's mouth popped open. "What would an old man even do with six prostitutes?"

"I don't want to know," I said, shaking my head and sighing. "It's complicated, and they've asked me to keep it under wraps for now. Bottom line is that Carl didn't kill Tessa. And neither did her brother or her boyfriend. It's back to the drawing board."

"That sucks."

"Yeah," I said, sighing. "I'll call the boss and the prosecutor and tell them what's going on."

"Before you do, Dr. Sheridan is in the crime lab. He's dropping some things off for Darlene McEvoy, but he wanted to see you before he left. He said he's got the autopsy results from Jasmine Kelley."

With everything else going on, I hadn't thought about Jasmine, my overdose victim, for a little while. I nodded.

"Thanks. I'll head down there before I do anything else."

Trisha headed back into her office, and I took the stairs down to the basement. St. Augustine County had a small but modern forensics lab. I knocked on its metal door and stuck my head in to see Dr. Sheridan and

Darlene McEvoy smiling at something on his cell phone. They looked up at me, and Darlene waved me forward.

"It's my new granddaughter," said the doctor. "Six pounds, nine ounces."

Many women my age went gaga over kids, but I wasn't such a big fan. Maybe one day. Still, Dr. Sheridan's granddaughter was cute, and her mom looked happy to be holding her.

"Congratulations," I said, smiling at him. "I didn't know you even had kids."

"Two," he said. "Hazel is my first grandchild, though. My wife and I plan to see her in two weeks."

He put his phone away and told Darlene to call him if she needed anything. Then he and I stepped into the hallway outside the lab.

"I'm glad I got to talk to you," he said. "I heard from a doctor at St. John's that two young women were brought in last night complaining of chest pain after taking what they thought was ecstasy. Both survived, but it was touch and go. If they hadn't gone to the hospital, they'd be dead. Have you made any progress tracking down the source of Jasmine Kelley's drugs?"

A tight feeling began growing in my chest, and I closed my eyes.

"I'm working it," I said.

"I know you've got a lot on your plate, but this is important," said Sheridan. "Every day that passes means more kids could die. I know you don't have kids, but losing a kid is just about the worst thing that can happen to somebody. Believe me. I'm a dad. You can't just sit on this and hope the supply of tainted drugs runs out."

I gritted my teeth so I wouldn't snap at him.

"I know what's at stake. You don't need to remind me," I said, bringing a hand to my face to rub my eyes. The doctor took a step back and held up his hands as if he were warding off a blow.

"I'm not trying to tell you how to do your job," he said. "This is important. I'm just asking you to make this a priority. Can you do that?"

"This case is a priority," I said. "As is every case I work. Each moment I devote to this case is a moment I can't work another equally important case. No matter what I choose to do, somebody gets the shaft. You don't need to remind me of that. I think about it enough. If you want to complain, talk to my boss. Tell him to hire more help."

"I might do that," he said, straightening.

"He's upstairs. Go for it."

Sheridan drew in a breath and then walked away. Once he left, I leaned against the cool concrete wall and allowed it to sap some of the heat from my skin. With Tessa's case reopened, Maddie Dawson tortured to death, and Jasmine Kelley's drugs still unaccounted for, I had more work in front of me than I could keep straight. I needed to focus and think.

Tessa, Maddie, and Jasmine would all be as dead today as they would be tomorrow. Jasmine's drug supplier could kill a lot of kids still. Dr. Sheridan was right: That case needed my attention. Too many lives depended on it. I straightened and started walking toward my car. Jasmine's friends hadn't been willing to talk to me before, but that wouldn't fly anymore. I didn't have time to play nice.

28

Emma Hannity, Jasmine Kelley's best friend, worked at the Wash Basin in St. Augustine. It was a clean, modern coin-operated laundromat and dry cleaner with free Wi-Fi and big tables on which you could fold sheets. About four times a year, I went there to wash the comforters and blankets that didn't fit in my washing machine at home. Nobody enjoyed doing laundry, but the Wash Basin was as pleasant as a laundromat could be.

As I drove, I found my mind drifting back to Tessa Armstrong. Her case made little sense, and that was pissing me off. I called Dr. Sheridan again. He answered after about four rings.

"Hey, doc," I said. "It's Joe Court. Sorry I snapped at you. You were right. Jasmine Kelley's drugs need to be my first priority. I'm driving to visit her friends now and see what they can tell me."

"Thank you," he said. "And I'm sorry I didn't try to understand your position better. Your job's hard. I get that."

"Good. Thanks," I said. "While I'm driving, I wanted to talk to you about Tessa Armstrong. She's the young woman who died of gunshot wounds at the Wayfair Motel."

"I remember her," he said. "I thought you closed her case."

I grunted. "I had. Now I've reopened it. It's

complicated, so don't ask. At the time of her death, Tessa had over a hundred pills in her purse. When you autopsied her, did you find evidence of habitual opioid abuse?"

He paused, but then he clicked his tongue.

"Judging by the state of her liver, she drank too much, but her kidneys were too healthy for someone addicted to opioids. Sorry."

So the drugs we found in her purse weren't for her personal consumption; she planned to sell them. Or maybe she was just a mule. Or maybe she was something else entirely. The case was frustrating. Until an hour ago, I thought I had her murder solved. Now, I didn't know shit. This was a mess.

"Thanks, doc," I said. "That's all I needed."

He wished me luck and hung up. I tossed my phone to the passenger seat and tried to think things through, but I couldn't come to any conclusions.

About ten minutes after I left my station, I pulled into the parking lot of the Wash Basin. The building had a brick facade that someone had painted dark gray. Big windows allowed in copious amounts of light and let me see the interior. Emma Hannity sat behind the front desk to the right of the door, reading a magazine. I walked inside and stopped in front of her. She looked up and lowered her magazine.

"Hey," she said, her voice low. The color drained from her face. "Do you need quarters?"

"I'm not here to do laundry, which I suspect you know," I said. "Jasmine Kelley, your best friend, died of a drug overdose after taking tainted ecstasy. She's not the only person who's died, either. We've got cases all over the area. You need to talk to me before more people die. Where'd Jasmine get her drugs?"

She looked down to the counter and started to shake her head.

"I don't know—"

"Bullshit," I said, interrupting her. Two women folding laundry at a table near the rear of the shop looked at us. "At the time of her death, Jasmine's makeup was done, her hair was done, and she was dressed to party. Are you telling me she planned to go out by herself?"

Emma kept her eyes on the counter.

"I don't know."

"Oh, really?" I asked, crossing my arms. "The coroner found alcohol in her stomach and in her bloodstream, but we didn't find any booze in her apartment except an unopened bottle of wine. Somebody cleaned up, which means somebody was with her at the time of her death. Instead of calling the police or driving her to the hospital when their friend overdosed, they left Jasmine to die on her sofa."

Emma's face grew red, and she brought a hand to her mouth. Her shoulders trembled as she stifled her sobs. I leaned forward.

"I don't care what you did in that apartment," I said. "If you left your best friend to die on the couch, that's for you to deal with. I'm interested in preventing anyone else from dying. Where did Jasmine get her drugs?"

She tilted her head and opened her mouth to say something, but no words came from her lips. A middle-aged woman in a blue apron came from an office behind Emma. The newcomer looked at me.

"Everything okay, Emma?" she asked. Emma wiped tears from her eyes.

"Yes, Mrs. Roberts," she said. Her voice sounded strained, but it was stronger than it had been a moment earlier. "I'm talking to a customer."

Mrs. Roberts paused.

"Okay," she said. "I'll be in the back if you need me."

Emma nodded but said nothing as her boss returned to her office. I kept my eyes on the young woman.

"Where'd she get the drugs, Emma?"

Emma drew in a breath. "Her boyfriend. Blake Meeks. He goes to Waterford. He's a college student. She got her drugs from him. He sells to a lot of college students."

"Thank you," I said, straightening. "I'll be in touch."

She stayed at the counter with her eyes downcast as I left the store and walked to my car. My face felt hot, my chest felt tight, and my fingernails bit into the palms of my hands. Jasmine didn't have to die. None of these kids did.

When I got to my car, I called the Office of Public Safety at Waterford College to let them know I suspected one of their students was dealing tainted ecstasy and that I planned to search his dorm room as soon as I could secure a warrant. They agreed to pick the kid up and make sure he couldn't remove anything until I arrived.

Then, I drove to the prosecutor's office. Shaun Deveraux, the county prosecutor, wasn't available, but a paralegal and I put together a search warrant affidavit. Then I walked it over to the judge on duty and got a signature. Within an hour of leaving the laundromat, I stood beside Rusty Peterson, Waterford College's director of Public Safety, in the middle of Blake Meeks's dorm room. There were two desks built into the eastern wall and a big window overlooking a parking lot to the north. He had bunk beds, although Meeks was the room's only occupant.

"Mr. Meeks is in my office," said Rusty. "We've suspected we had someone dealing ecstasy on campus, but we thought it was a kid in a fraternity."

I nodded and then tilted my head to the side.

"Could still be," I said. "You've got a lot of students with disposable income. They could keep two or three dealers in business."

"Isn't that the truth?" grumbled Rusty as he reached into his pockets for a pair of nitrile gloves. "Let's get this search going."

I agreed, so we got started. We stayed in the room for about half an hour. I found a bottle of vodka in a suitcase beneath the bed, but underage consumption didn't concern me. Rusty, though, found a Ziploc bag of pills in an old tennis shoe beneath the window. He put it on the desk for me to see.

The pills were multicolored, but they didn't match the

ones I found in Jasmine's room. Her pills had stars on them, and they came in vibrant, psychedelic colors. Meeks's pills were square, and they had diamonds, hearts, spades, and clubs stamped into them as if they were playing cards. The colors were closer to pastels. Maybe they were just different batches from the same maker.

"They almost look like candy," said Rusty, reaching into his pocket for a small vial. "You mind documenting this?"

I took pictures with my cell phone as he put a pill on the desk and squeezed a drop of chemical reagent onto it. The liquid turned black, and Rusty sighed.

"Presumptive tests are positive for MDMA," he said. "Looks like Mr. Meeks is in some trouble."

"More than he could know," I said, taking out my phone to call Trisha and request backup. She sent a pair of uniformed officers my way to pick up Meeks and the drugs. She also told me the Washington County sheriff and two of his deputies were on their way to search Maddie Dawson's home.

I stayed at the college another half hour to finish the search. We found almost two thousand dollars cash in his sock drawer and a quarter ounce of weed in the center drawer of his desk, but we didn't find more ecstasy. Still, we had enough to charge him with trafficking. Once I interviewed him, we might up that to include multiple counts of manslaughter.

That was for another day, though. I had other cases to work. I thanked Rusty for his help and promised to keep him updated about anything we found before jogging back to my car.

Maddie Dawson lived in a single-story brick house on a country road outside the town of St. Augustine. Three marked cruisers from the Washington County Sheriff's Department had parked in the driveway. I parked out front and hung my badge from a lanyard around my neck. The moment I opened my door, a uniformed deputy walked toward me. She was in her early fifties, and she had brown hair pulled back from her face.

She looked at my badge and then to my face and held out her hand.

"Sheriff Mae Lepley," she said, shaking my hand. "You must be Detective Court."

"Just Joe," I said, nodding and giving her a quick smile. "You find anything interesting inside?"

She nodded and led me to a cruiser in the driveway. A uniformed deputy stood beside the trunk. On it, they had arrayed two bags of white pills and a stack of hundred-dollar bills.

"We were hoping to find a murder scene," she said. "There wasn't a lot of blood on the ground near where we found the victim, so our coroner thinks somebody dumped Maddie in our neck of the woods and killed her elsewhere. We haven't found any signs of a death scene here, though, either. Our search did, however, turn up twenty-four thousand dollars cash beneath a mattress in a guest bedroom and a bag of pills inside a toilet tank. Our lab will test the pills to see what they are, but they've got

'OC' stamped on one side and '40' on the other. They look like forty-milligram doses of OxyContin."

I whistled and nodded.

"You know how many pills there are?"

"We haven't counted them yet, but a few hundred at least," said the sheriff. She paused. "So what's your interest in our victim?"

I glanced from the drugs to the sheriff.

"I picked up a murder a couple of days ago. My victim was named Tessa Armstrong, and she had an envelope full of cash and a bag of pills in her purse. According to Maddie's boss, she and Tessa knew each other. I suspect Tessa bought pills from Maddie regularly."

The sheriff nodded. "You have any idea who killed your vic?"

"Nope," I said, shaking my head.

The sheriff looked toward Maddie's house and crossed her arms.

"At least it looks like we're all on the same page."

"Yeah," I said. "If you need anything, call my office. We'll send somebody out as quickly as we can. I've got a teacher to interview."

"For this case?" she asked, raising her eyebrows.

"Maybe, sort of…I don't know," I said, sighing. "I've got bodies and drugs galore this week, and nothing makes sense."

She gave me a sympathetic look and nodded.

"Good luck, Detective."

Unfortunately, I'd need a lot more than luck to close

a case. I thanked her anyway and got in my car. It was time to hear what Sheppard Altman had to say about his girlfriend and the company she kept.

29

On a normal workday, Sheppard Altman would have been standing in front of a classroom full of kids at one in the afternoon. After killing an intruder with a screwdriver and seriously injuring a second, he was home.

I parked in front of his home. Less than twelve hours ago, this had been a major crime scene, but now, it looked like the average suburban home. Two white paneled vans had parked in front. They were from a commercial cleaning company from St. Louis that specialized in biohazard removal and trauma remediation. The company wasn't cheap, but from all I had seen, it did good work. I even kept its business cards on hand in case I assisted a family with a sudden, traumatic death. If a loved one committed suicide, the last thing a family needed to worry about was the cleanup.

Altman must have seen me because he walked outside and came toward my cruiser as I opened my door.

"Afternoon, Detective," he said. "I thought you'd be here last night."

"I came by, but someone had already taken you to our station. Did Sheriff Delgado treat you well?"

Altman crossed his arms.

"He was fine. What can I do for you?"

A breeze blew down the street, sending a chill down my back despite my jacket.

"Can we talk inside?"

He blinked.

"No. You won't be staying long. We're good out here."

I closed my cruiser's door and leaned against the vehicle to speak over its roof. Our conversations hadn't been pleasant before, but his tone here was edging on hostile already. That didn't bode well for the questions I needed to ask.

"You may have heard that we made an arrest in Tessa Armstrong's murder."

He nodded.

"Yeah, Carl killed her. Somebody said you had it on video."

"Video can be deceiving. Multiple witnesses and surveillance footage put Mr. Armstrong in St. Louis at the Ritz-Carlton Hotel at the time of his spouse's death. He didn't do it."

Altman considered me and then brought a hand to his chest.

"You think I did it? I loved Tessa."

"I'm not saying that," I said, cocking my head to the side. "But you've held back on me long enough. Who came to hurt you last night?"

Altman lowered his chin and put his hands on his hips.

"Are you seriously asking me that?" he asked. "Three people came into my house while I was sleeping. I'm the victim here."

"Do you know Maddie Dawson?"

He answered immediately and shook his head.

"No."

"She was a nurse at the Willow Bend Living Center. She's dead, too."

"I'm sorry to hear that," he said, tilting his head to the side.

"She stole opioids from the residents. According to Ms. Dawson's boss, Tessa paid her regular visits. To refresh your memory, we found pills and two thousand dollars cash in Tessa's purse at the time of her death. That's a lot of money and drugs."

He looked down.

"I can't help you."

"Why would Tessa have those pills?"

He sighed and shook his head before locking his eyes on mine.

"I don't know. She's had problems with alcohol in the past. Maybe she started popping pills, too."

I shook my head.

"Nope. She had some damage to her liver, but her kidneys were healthy. If she was a chronic opioid user, her kidneys would have shown damage. Try again."

He put up his hands. "I don't know what you want me to say. She had drugs. I don't know why."

"How well did you know Tessa?"

"I loved Tessa. I'm not interested in hearing you try to tear her down."

Going at him straight ahead was only making him shut down. I needed to try a new tactic, so I nodded and softened my voice.

"I know you cared for her, and I am sorry for your loss. She seemed like a remarkable young woman. I'm just trying to get to the truth, though. Sometimes I have to do and say offensive things to gauge an interview subject's reaction."

He grunted.

"Is that what you're doing?"

I smiled at him.

"How are you doing after last night?"

"What do you mean?"

"You killed a guy with a screwdriver," I said, tilting my head to the side. "If you'd like, I've got the name of a good therapist who specializes in counseling trauma victims."

"I'm fine," he said. "Now if you'll excuse me, I've got stuff to do."

"Sure," I said. "And you've got my number if you change your mind about anything you've told us."

He nodded and walked back into the house. A dull ache began forming at the back of my head, and my jaw ached from clenching it to keep from snapping at him. It was more than mere annoyance. Altman was elbow deep in this mess, just like Tessa. I got back in my car and slammed my door shut before driving to my station. I needed to find out who this guy was.

When I reached my building, I hurried through the hallways so nobody could stop me and dump more work on me before I reached my office. I started by searching the FBI's National Crime Information Center's databases for any entries involving Sheppard Altman. That took about ten minutes, and it came up empty.

Then I looked him up on the Missouri license bureau's database to double-check his address and the spelling of his name. Mr. Altman had first applied for a Missouri driver's license four years ago, which meant he must have moved in from out of state. That also meant we didn't have a list of his previous addresses. We did, however, have his Social Security number. Tessa Armstrong's husband gave her more than enough money to live on. She had no good reason to sell drugs. Maybe Altman did.

I ran a credit check on him. Altman had two credit cards, neither of which had a balance, and a thirty-year fixed mortgage on which he owed a little over a hundred and fifty thousand dollars. He had never missed a payment on either his mortgage or credit cards, and he had a credit score in the eight-hundred range. He may not have had a lot of money to spare, but he wasn't in debt. A lot of teachers probably had a similar report.

Few male teachers, though, had likely changed their names midcareer. Until five years ago, Sheppard Altman was named Sheppard Zimmerman.

I leaned back in my chair. It was a hassle to change a name. Women did it when they got married or divorced, but I didn't see men do it as often, and when they did, it was usually to conceal an embarrassing name. Altman was hiding something.

I opened up the NCIC database portal, but this time I looked up Sheppard Zimmerman, and this time, I got results. Mr. Zimmerman had spent two years in the Dixon Correctional Center in Dixon, Illinois, for laundering money. My case had just become a lot more interesting.

I minimized the database, opened a web browser, and googled his name. Before his arrest, Mr. Zimmerman had a high profile in Chicago. When he was twenty-four, *Chicago Magazine* named him one of the city's most eligible singles. According to the magazine's write-up, Zimmerman liked women and enjoyed gardening and playing on a beach volleyball team. His job as an investment banker kept him busy, but he was always open to having a good time. His perfect date involved a walk along the lakefront and a fabulous dinner. The article probably got him laid a few times, but evidently it didn't change his long-term relationship status.

The other articles I found were less flattering. In 2012, special agents from the FBI, the Treasury Department, the IRS, and the SEC arrested him—along with almost a dozen other men and women from the bank at which he worked—on money-laundering and tax-evasion charges. It was a big scandal that ensnared a lot of wealthy, powerful people. Where many of Zimmerman's colleagues ended up with serious prison time, though, he pleaded guilty to money laundering in exchange for turning on his clients and partners. He spent a few years in federal prison and then disappeared.

From the start, I had assumed this case was about

Tessa. She was the first victim, she had drugs and cash in her purse, and her husband had the motive and means to kill her. Maybe I was wrong, though. Maybe this was all about Altman.

Altman may have been an investment banker, but he hadn't worked for choirboys. He had probably had some legitimate clients who wanted to avoid paying taxes, but he'd likely had some drug traffickers and gangsters mixed in the bunch. If they found out where he lived now, I could see them ordering a hit on him and his loved ones. Maybe Tessa just got in the way.

But if that were the case, why would they frame Carl Armstrong? If they planned to frame somebody, why wouldn't they frame Altman? Not only would they hurt him by killing a loved one, they'd send him to prison. I'd be hard pressed to think of a better way to kick a guy in the nuts, and it would have been easier to do than framing Armstrong.

Nothing about this case made sense. Tessa was dead. Maddie Dawson was dead. An unidentified man from Sheppard Altman's home was dead. A second unidentified man from Sheppard Altman's home was in the hospital. None of them were innocent, but they didn't deserve to die. I didn't know who killed them or why. Hell, I didn't even know if they were killed by the same person or group.

The more I learned about this case and the people involved, the less I knew. Considering everything they were willing to do, that was a scary thought. So far, they had only killed co-conspirators, but I doubted it'd be long before an innocent person got caught in the crosshairs. I needed to close this now.

30

I called my boss to see whether I could get an update on his investigation into the events at Sheppard Altman's house, but he didn't answer his phone, and he wasn't in the office. That was okay, though. I had plenty to do.

I walked into the conference room. Our dispatcher had four phone lines, two computers, and three different monitors on her desk. It was a tough job. She had to keep calm even during stressful situations. With just a few clicks, she could look up the owner of a vehicle, trace a phone call, or route every officer in the county to any point on the map. It took a lot of specialized training, but Trisha—and our other staff members—did it well.

Until construction began, our dispatcher had sat behind a permanent, comfortable desk in the first-floor lobby. Panels in her desk and under the floor had hidden the wires required for her system, and she had enjoyed a comfortable perch from which she could work. Now, we had wires dangling from the ceiling and duct-taped to the floor, and every monitor and computer rested on card tables. It made her job harder, but I hadn't heard Trisha complain yet. She was a pro, and I liked working with her. I enjoyed being her friend even more.

She smiled when she saw me.

"Hey, Joe," she said. "I hear you've been busy today."

"Yeah," I said. "Did Rusty Peterson from Waterford bring in a young man yet?"

She nodded. "Yep. Marcus processed him and put him in a holding cell. The pills you found in his dorm are in the evidence vault. The kid was cursing up a storm when Director Peterson brought him in. If you're curious, he plans to sue me, Rusty, you, Sheriff Delgado, the judge who signed the warrant to search his dorm, the prosecutor who helped you fill out the affidavit, and everybody else who works in our building. Then he'll sue the County Council, the board of directors at Waterford College, and the resident advisor who lives in his dorm."

I nodded. "The RA, too, huh? That seems a little excessive."

"Well, you know," she said, tilting her head to the side and shrugging, "if someone's wronged you grievously, you've got to go nuclear. Otherwise people just don't learn."

"That's a fair point," I said, nodding. "If you don't mind, call down and have somebody bring Mr. Meeks to my office. I need to interview him."

"You want him if he's still screaming?"

My lip curled into a frown at the thought of sitting with an entitled, screaming asshole, but I nodded anyway.

"Yeah. His drugs might have killed a bunch of people. If he screams at me, it'll make ruining his day that much more satisfying."

She smiled and nodded before reaching to a walkie-talkie on her desk. I left her there and walked down to the evidence vault in the basement. Our evidence technician was a man named Mark Bozwell. He was old and cantankerous, but I'd heard he worked cheap, so he had that going for him. Our evidence room looked almost like an underground warehouse. Deep metal shelving units holding white file boxes ran from the front of the room to the back like aisles in a grocery store. A welded metal cage separated the front public space from the shelving units.

Bozwell sat at a desk and typed on his computer. When he looked up and saw me, I felt his eyes travel down my torso. Bozwell was gross, but at least the boss kept him in the basement.

"Afternoon, Detective," he said, leaning back but staying seated. "What can I do for you?"

"Rusty Peterson, the director of Public Safety at Waterford College, brought in a young man this afternoon. He also brought in some pills we suspect contain MDMA. I'm going to interview the arrestee, and I'd like the bag as a prop."

Bozwell seemed to consider for a moment. Mostly, I think he enjoyed looking at my chest. I crossed my arms, and he lumbered to his feet.

"Your drugs are in the vault. Give me a minute."

I nodded, and he unlocked the wire gate and held it for me.

"You want to come back with me?"

"Nope," I said. "Take your time."

He grunted and disappeared into the stacks. I shivered just a little. We kept most pieces of evidence for ten or fifteen years—however long the statute of limitations was on the crime being investigated—but we never destroyed evidence collected from a murder. Our oldest case was from 1904. A local man got into a fight with his wife while drinking, and he beat her to death with a hammer. We still had the victim's clothes, the bottle her husband had been drinking from, and the hammer he used to crush her skull.

Intellectually, I knew those shelves held inanimate objects that couldn't hurt anyone again, but I couldn't help but feel their former owners. The evidence room was a graveyard for the possessions of the damned. I hated going down there.

Bozwell came back a few minutes later carrying a clear plastic evidence bag. I signed out the drugs and told him I'd bring them back as soon as I finished my interrogation. He nodded and pretended to return to work, but I was sure he watched me leave. The guy was a lecherous sleaze, but he hadn't ever said anything inappropriate to me. If he had, I could have filed a complaint. Until he retired, I'd just have to endure his stares and sidelong glances. Men had stared at me most of my life, so at least I had practice.

When I got to my office, I found Officer DeAndre Simpson standing beside my desk. A young man with buzzed blond hair and diamond stud earrings in both ears slouched in a chair in front. He wore a red hoodie sweatshirt with Waterford College's logo on front. When he saw me, he rolled his eyes. Shackles bound his hands and feet together.

"You the cop who broke into my room?" he asked.

I smiled to DeAndre.

"Thanks for bringing him up," I said. "I think I've got him from here."

DeAndre looked to the kid. "You going to behave?"

"I'm not the who's going around stealing other people's shit," he said. "This bitch broke into my room."

DeAndre looked to me and raised his eyebrows as if to ask my opinion.

"I think I can handle him," I said, glancing to Meeks. "If you call me a bitch again, I'll end this interview, send you back to your cell, and charge you with five counts of murder."

He rolled his eyes again and shook his head.

"Sounds like something you'd do."

DeAndre smiled and chuckled.

"Good luck, Joe. If you need me, just shout. I'll be around."

I thanked him and sat down behind my desk. For a moment, I said nothing. Then I pulled out my cell phone, opened an app to record our conversation, and leaned forward.

"Okay, Mr. Meeks," I said, putting my phone on the desktop between us. "I'm Detective Joe Court. As you've been informed, you've been placed under arrest for possession of a controlled substance. Just to be fair, we will add additional charges as time goes on. You're facing some serious felonies.

"You have the right to remain silent. You don't have to talk to me if you don't want to. If you talk to me, though, I can use whatever you tell me against you in court or in another investigation. You have the right to an attorney, and you can call him or her whenever we speak. If you can't afford an attorney, the court can provide a public defender free of charge. Do you understand your rights as I've explained them?"

As he leaned forward, his shackles jangled.

"I can afford an attorney."

"I know," I said. "Do you understand your rights, and do you still want to speak to me?"

"I understand my rights," he said. "And I did nothing wrong. Your search was illegal. Even if you found something in my room, it's the fruit of the poisonous tree. You can't introduce it in court."

He smirked and leaned back. Evidently, the kid had read a little about the law. That didn't make him a lawyer, but it sure gave him some confidence. Contrary to what he thought, my search would hold up just fine. My interrogation was about trying to figure out what other crimes he had committed.

"We'll leave that to the lawyers," I said. "In the meantime, I'd like to talk. Before we start, are you hungry or thirsty?"

"I'm fine," he said.

"If you get thirsty, tell me," I said. I slid the plastic evidence bag across the desk toward him. "We found these pills in your room. Can you tell me what they are?"

"No," he said. "They're not mine."

"Okay," I said. "Why were they in your room?"

He shrugged.

"Somebody must have put them there."

"Sure," I said, nodding. "We also found some marijuana in your desk and almost two thousand dollars cash in your sock drawer."

He shrugged.

"Possession of weed's a misdemeanor. I'll pay my fine and leave. And last I heard, it's not a crime to have money."

"You're right," I said. "It's not a crime to have money. It is a crime to possess MDMA, though."

He closed his eyes.

"What's MDMA?"

"Methylenedioxymethamphetamine. Ecstasy. This bag weighs ninety-five grams. Mere possession of ninety-five grams of MDMA is a class-B felony. If I can find a single person to whom you've sold a pill, we'll charge you with trafficking in the first degree. That's a class-A felony. It's ten years in prison at a minimum, but it goes all the way to life without parole."

He looked down, his shoulders slumping.

"Your search was illegal," he said, his voice much softer than it had been earlier.

"I had a signed search warrant," I said. "But even if I didn't have a signed warrant, the director of Public Safety at your college accompanied me. Director Peterson may search your dorm with cause for violations of your school's honor code. He doesn't need a warrant. He just needs reasonable suspicion that you've violated the agreement you signed when you enrolled at Waterford."

Meeks said nothing, so I softened my voice.

"Kid, you're in serious trouble. If you want to see the sun rise again outside prison walls, talk to me."

He blinked a few times and then tried to lift his hands to his face, but the shackles wouldn't let him. His throat bounced as he swallowed. I let the importance of what I said sink in.

"What do you want?"

"In the past couple of weeks, we've had multiple young people die of overdoses after taking what they thought was MDMA. Instead, they took NBOMe. We're testing the drugs we found in your room now, and if they match the drugs taken by our overdose victims, I will charge you with involuntary manslaughter. That's on top of the drug charges. You will be in prison until the day you die. You will never finish college, get married, have children, or have a career. They will wheel you out of your prison cell in a casket and bury you in a pauper's grave on the grounds of the Potosi Correctional Center."

At first, he didn't react. But then his shoulders began trembling and his torso began heaving.

"That's one option," I said. "Your second option is to talk to me. If you cooperate, I'll tell the prosecutor and the judge assigned to your case. We might drop some charges. You could have a real life. Maybe you could even finish college. What do you want to do? Answer my questions, or be a hardass and spend your life in prison with the other hardasses?"

I gave him about a minute before repeating the question. Finally, he took some deep breaths and nodded.

"What do you want to know?"

"Where do you get your drugs?" I asked.

He drew in a slow breath. "A guy in China. I spent a semester in Beijing. I met him there."

If these pills came from a major lab, we had a bigger problem than I thought. We'd have victims elsewhere. I'd worry about that later, though.

"Who do you sell to?"

He shrugged. "Just people around school. Frat guys and sorority girls."

"Did you sell to Jasmine Kelley?"

He shrugged, so I repeated the question.

"I don't know anybody named Jasmine Kelley."

"You sure about that?" I asked. "She worked at Able's Diner. She was pretty. I hear she's your girlfriend."

He glanced up and shook his head.

"My girlfriend goes to Mizzou. Her name is Carrie. You can call her."

Meeks had no reason to lie to me now. Something wasn't right here. I grabbed the pills.

"Stand up," I said. "I'll take you back to your cell."

"I thought you were going to make me a deal," he said. "You said I could go."

I shook my head. "No, I didn't say that. I said I'd tell the prosecutor you cooperated, which I'll do. Any deals will be between you, your attorney, and Shaun Deveraux. Mr. Deveraux will have more questions, but I'm sure you'll be able to work something out. This is a first-time offense, and you're cooperating. Mr. Deveraux won't jam you up as long as you keep cooperating. Clear?"

He hesitated but then nodded. I led him through the building and down to the holding cells. There, Officer DeAndre Simpson removed his restraints and returned him to a cell. I hurried to our evidence room. Bozwell was deep in the stacks, but he came when I called. I handed over the drugs, and he signed the chain-of-custody form.

"Before you go back, I need the evidence box containing stuff we took from Jasmine Kelley's apartment."

"It'll be a minute," he said, nodding toward his desk. "Have a seat."

I thanked him and sat down as he carried the drugs back to the vault. Two minutes later, he came back carrying a white cardboard box. I opened it on Bozwell's desk, and he returned to doing whatever he had been doing before I got into the room.

We hadn't taken a lot from Jasmine's apartment, but we had collected her phone. I pulled it out and opened the plastic evidence bag. If Jasmine had an actual boyfriend, we should have proof.

I held the power button. Once the phone booted up, I looked through her text message. She talked to Emma Hannity half a dozen times a day or more, but those messages hadn't been helpful. Now, I focused on those conversations with people I didn't recognize. While browsing messages from someone named Austin, I found dozens of nude selfies—of both him and her—and a lot of dirty talk. They didn't talk about drugs, but they sure enjoyed talking about sex.

Just to settle my curiosity, I kept browsing the phone to see whether I could find calls to or from Blake Meeks, but his phone number never showed up. I powered the phone down and returned it to the box. Emma Hannity had lied to me: Blake Meeks wasn't Jasmine's boyfriend. They didn't even know each other. Lying to me during a murder investigation was a terrible idea—especially when lives were on the line.

"Mark, you still back there?" I called.

Bozwell emerged from the stacks a moment later.

"You done?"

"Yeah," I said, nodding and putting the top back on the evidence box. "Thank you."

"You get what you needed?"

"Nope, but I got leverage over somebody who can help me, and that's almost as good."

He nodded and started carrying the box back to its spot behind the wire cage. I took out my phone and walked to the stairs. Once I had a stable signal—cell phones rarely worked well in my building's basement—I called Emma's number. After five rings, it went to voicemail.

"Hi, Emma, this is Joe Court. I picked up Blake Meeks. Call me back within the next half hour or I'll start proceedings to have you arrested for interfering with a police investigation."

I hung up and walked to my office, expecting a call back at any moment. None came, so I started filling out a report detailing what I had just done and why. After half an hour, I looked at my phone, but no one had called. Emma wanted to do this the hard way. That was fine by me.

31

It was getting late in the afternoon, but I hurried through an affidavit for Emma's arrest and got that to a circuit court judge just before he went home. Once I had a signed arrest warrant, Jason Zuckerburg, our night-shift dispatcher, contacted every officer on duty and told them to be on the lookout for Emma Hannity. Since she wasn't a violent felon, she wouldn't be a high priority, but if someone saw her, they'd pick her up.

After that, I went by my boss's office, but he was still out, and he still hadn't returned my phone calls. I'd just work around him. As I walked to my car, my stomach rumbled. It had been a while since I had eaten, so I grabbed a sandwich from the deli at the grocery store and wolfed that down before driving to St. John's Hospital.

Being a rural county an hour from St. Louis, we were lucky to have a hospital at all, let alone one as decent as St. John's. If I need an organ transplant or other major surgery, I'd go to Barnes-Jewish Hospital in St. Louis, but for just about anything else, St. John's had me covered.

I parked in the main lot and walked to the front desk. The receptionist smiled hello to me and asked whether I needed anything. I unhooked my badge from my belt.

"Late last night, paramedics brought in a John Doe who had been stabbed with a screwdriver. An officer is watching his room. You know where it is?"

She nodded and typed on her computer while I

hooked my badge back to my belt.

"Room 414. Take the elevator to the fourth floor. The patient is in the room at the end of the hall."

I thanked her and stepped away from the desk. The fourth floor was quieter than the lobby. Light gray carpet covered the floor. The walls were forest green. A nurse smiled as he pushed an empty wheelchair past me. I followed signs to the fourth-floor lobby, where I found Officer Dave Skelton in civilian clothes. He was reading something on an iPad, but he put it down when he saw me.

"Are you my relief?" he asked, standing and looking at his watch. "I thought I was on duty until midnight."

"You probably are," I said. "I'm here because I can't get in touch with George, and I need information about this case."

"The sheriff's been a busy man today. We've got two detectives from the Chicago Police Department's Bureau of Internal Affairs in town. He's been showing them the sights."

I cocked my head to the side, almost afraid to ask the obvious question.

"And why did the Chicago PD send down two IA detectives?"

"Because the man who died at Sheppard Altman's home last night was Detective Adrian Valentino. He was part of the vice squad on the south side of town. The guy I'm babysitting is Detective Lukas Wagner. He worked burglary on the north end of Chicago."

My shoulders slumped, and I let gravity pull me down into a nearby chair. Skelton sat beside me.

"Terrific," I said, leaning forward to rest my elbows on my knees. "That's just what I needed: dirty cops from out of town."

Skelton nodded but said nothing. I swore under my breath and then sighed.

"Has this guy said anything yet?"

Skelton shook his head. "Nope. The sheriff came by earlier with the IA detectives, but he wasn't awake yet. I haven't been by the room for a while, but the scuttlebutt among the nursing staff is that they doped him up pretty well after his surgery. He's asleep."

I pushed myself to my feet. Even if I couldn't talk to our perp, the trip hadn't been a complete waste because I had learned something.

"I'll check him out. If I don't see you again today, have a nice night."

"You, too, Joe," he said, picking up his tablet again.

The hospital had long, straight corridors. They had put Lukas in an isolated room at the end of the hall. The doctors must have thought he was in stable condition, despite his injuries, because they hadn't put him in the intensive-care unit. His room was small, but it had big windows and a private bathroom. Light gray carpet covered the floors. The walls were white. The curtains were drawn, and none of the lights were on, so I flipped one of six switches beside the door. A lamp popped on beside the bed, illuminating the once-dark room.

"Fuck," I said, rushing forward. Detective Lukas Wagner lay on a standard hospital bed. A blanket covered his legs and chest. A pillow covered his face. I pulled the pillow off and checked his neck for a pulse. His skin felt cool to the touch, and he wasn't breathing. His heart felt still.

"I need some help in here now!" I shouted. Within moments, a nurse scrambled into the room. She saw Wagner's pale face and pushed past me to check his pulse. When she found none, she slammed her fist onto an alarm button beside the bed and pulled out her phone.

"Code blue in room 414."

Within seconds, a voice came over the hospital's public address system and requested that the hospital's critical response team come to room 414. I stepped into the hallway just as a pair of nurses and a doctor ran toward me. Skelton followed a few steps behind.

"What's going on?"

I swore loudly enough to draw attention even from people in the waiting room. I didn't care.

"They got to him. Somebody smothered him with a pillow."

Skelton narrowed his eyes and shook his head.

"Nobody's been in there but the medical staff. I even chased the chaplain away."

"Somebody got past you," I said. I paused and blinked. Another doctor came running toward us and into the room.

"I'm sorry," said Skelton. "I didn't see anything."

"He died in our custody. It's a little late for sorry," I said. I swore again and started running toward the elevator. Skelton started to follow me, but I turned and shook my head. "No. You stay here. I'll call the sheriff and let him know what's going on. He'll have questions, and you need to be here to answer them."

Skelton nodded and stopped moving. As I walked, I pulled out my phone. This time, Sheriff Delgado answered my call.

"Hey, Joe," he said. "I got your call this morning, but I've been busy. Listen, though, we've identified both attackers last night and—"

"They're both Chicago cops," I said, hitting the elevator's down button. "I know. I'm at St. John's. Get over here. Lukas Wagner's dead. I walked into his room and found a pillow over his face. He's doped up, so he didn't do it himself. It looks like someone smothered him."

Delgado paused.

"We've got an officer watching the room, though."

The elevator popped open, and I stepped on.

"Yeah. And he says he didn't let anybody in but medical professionals," I said. "I'll check out the surveillance cameras."

"Tell Skelton to stay where he is," said Delgado. "I'm on my way."

"He's on the fourth floor. I'll keep you updated."

The sheriff hung up, and I slipped my phone into my purse. The elevator stopped twice on the way to the lobby.

I tried to keep my anger and frustration from showing on my face, but I wasn't successful, and my fellow riders gave me a wide berth until we reached the lobby. Then, I strode out and hurried toward the receptionist's desk. She smiled at me again.

"Can I help you, ma'am?"

Again, I pulled my badge from my belt.

"You've got surveillance cameras. Where can I view the footage?"

She hesitated and sat straighter.

"You'd have to talk to my boss about that," she said, tilting her head to the side.

"Then get her," I said. "Someone murdered a patient on the fourth floor."

She furrowed her brow and looked at me as if I were crazy. Then she opened her mouth. Before she could speak, I leaned forward.

"Pick up the goddamn phone and dial," I said.

She grabbed the phone and hit buttons.

"Jamie, there's a detective from the St. Augustine County Sheriff's Department at the front desk. She needs to see you. And bring Seth from the security office."

They spoke for a minute. Then the receptionist hung up.

"My boss will be here soon. You can have a seat if you'd like."

"Thank you," I said, trying to force the hard edge out of my voice. By the pained look the receptionist gave me, I didn't succeed at all. Within three minutes, a woman in a pantsuit and a man in black jeans and a black shirt came bounding out of a nearby stairwell. The receptionist directed them toward me. I stood.

"Detective?" asked the woman. I nodded. "I'm Jamie Ferguson. I'm the deputy director of administration here. With me is Seth Kirby from our security office. Can we step into my office and speak in private?"

"No," I said. "My boss is on the way. You can talk to him to your heart's content. There's a patient on your fourth floor named Lukas Wagner. Paramedics brought him in last."

She nodded. "I've heard."

"He's dead," I said. "I walked into his room a few minutes ago and found a pillow over his face. He wasn't breathing, and he had no pulse. You've got doctors working on him now, but his skin was cold. He's not coming back."

She drew in a slow breath. "Okay. What do you need from us?"

I looked to Seth. "You have any security cameras on the fourth floor?"

He nodded. "Over the elevators and stairwells."

"Any of them point toward room 414?"

He thought for a moment. "If we don't have one pointed at the room, we'll have cameras pointed near it."

"Show me," I said. Seth looked to his boss. She nodded and then looked to me.

"Your boss is on the way?" she asked.

"Sheriff George Delgado," I said, nodding. "He'll be

here any moment."

"Then I'll wait here for him."

I nodded and let Seth lead me toward the elevator. He used a key to access a panel inaccessible to the public and then hit a button to take us to a subbasement. The elevator door opened a few moments later in a long hallway with concrete walls painted lime green and a bare concrete floor. It was cool and quiet. It reminded me of the morgue.

"This way, Detective," he said. I followed him to the first door. A sign outside declared it off limits to anyone but authorized personnel. Inside sat a young woman with brunette hair. Like Seth, she wore a black polo shirt and black pants. She turned when we entered.

"Hey, Seth. Something's happening on the fourth floor," she said. Then she looked at me and smiled. "Hi."

"Hi," I said, focusing on the two massive computer monitors in front of her. "A man was murdered up there. I went up there a few minutes ago, but I need to see the person who entered room 414 prior to me."

She narrowed her eyes and then looked to Seth.

"Is this authorized?"

Before Seth could say anything, I lifted my sweater to show her the badge at my hip.

"Yeah. I'm authorized."

She clicked a few times and then enlarged a live video feed of the fourth floor. It looked as if the camera was hanging in the middle of the hallway two doors down from Lukas Wagner's room.

"Rewind it," I said. The video technician complied and rotated a knob backwards to reverse the footage. The hospital had a modern surveillance system, so the video was clear. I watched until I saw myself on the screen. "Okay. Stop. That's me. Rewind slowly until we see the next person in."

"Okay," she said, nodding again. This time, when the technician rotated the knob that controlled the video speed, she didn't turn it much. The video showed me walking backwards from the room to the waiting room and then off camera. Nothing happened for about thirty seconds. Then a figure emerged from Wagner's room. I couldn't see his face, but the figure's shoulder size and gait made me think it was a man.

"Track him," I said. "I need to see his face."

The tech hit a few buttons until she had video from a dozen different cameras on the screen at once. The stairwells didn't have cameras, so we paid attention to the other floors. After about thirty seconds, I found him on two separate video feeds from cameras in the lobby. Unfortunately, both caught him in profile again. He walked through the front door and to the stairwell.

As he walked through the front door, though, he glanced up.

"Pause it," I said. The video technician clicked something, and the feed stopped. "Do you have cameras over your main entrance?"

She nodded and clicked a few things until a single video feed remained on the screen. Staring back at me on the screen was Detective Mickey Lyons, Tessa Armstrong's older brother. He wore blue scrubs that made him look like the hospital staff. That was why Skelton hadn't stopped him. The image was clear enough that I could see the spot on his chin he had missed while shaving that morning. Lukas and Adrian, apparently, weren't the only dirty Chicago cops in St. Augustine.

"Print this screen out," I said. "Give a copy to everyone on your security staff."

"Do you know who he is?" asked Seth.

I nodded. "Yeah. He's a murderer. Do what I asked. I've got shit to do."

32

I met Sheriff Delgado and two detectives from Chicago in the hospital's lobby about ten minutes after I viewed the video. Word of what had happened must have been spreading amongst the hospital's visitors and patients because the lobby was filling up with concerned families with questions.

According to Jamie Ferguson, the administrator I had met earlier, the hospital had ninety-three admitted patients at the moment. We couldn't just shut the place down to work our case, and we couldn't keep the families of those ninety-three people from coming inside. We were playing damage control at the moment, but it was a losing effort. Already, the families of the sick and infirm had begun asking to have their relatives moved to hospitals in St. Louis or elsewhere. Jamie Ferguson was trying her best to placate people, but it wasn't going over well.

"Hey, boss," I said, stepping toward the sheriff and lowering my voice while nodding hello to the two detectives from Chicago with him. "You need to calm the crowd down, or we'll have a riot."

He looked around. There were thirty or so people in the lobby, but already I could see cars circling the parking lot outside. Patients must have been calling their friends and families with news. Delgado nodded and walked to Jamie. They whispered together for a moment, and then Delgado stepped onto a short coffee table to give him some height.

"Okay, everybody, listen up," he said. "I'm Sheriff George Delgado with the St. Augustine County Sheriff's Department. As many of you have heard, a patient died in suspicious circumstances on the fourth floor. This is a sensitive, active investigation, so I can't give many details."

The small crowd around him groaned. A few started asking questions, but Delgado cut them off.

"I've got almost a dozen officers on the way. In addition, St. John's is calling in its entire security staff. We'll have multiple officers on each floor, but I want to stress that this was an isolated incident. We have identified a suspect via the hospital's security system. He has fled the building. Your loved ones are safe. If you have further questions, please direct them to Ms. Ferguson or an appropriate hospital representative. Thank you."

Several people shouted questions at him, but then they turned their focus to Jamie Ferguson and Seth Kirby, the hospital's security officer. Delgado walked to me.

"Tell me I didn't just lie to the crowd and that you've identified a suspect already."

"I have," I said, nodding and looking to the IA detectives from Chicago as I pulled a folded printout from my pocket. The security office's printer wasn't great, but it worked. "This is Mickey Lyons. He's a narcotics detective with the Chicago Police Department. He's also Tessa Armstrong's older brother."

Delgado crossed his arms and looked to the two Chicago officers.

"Okay, gentlemen," he said. "I'm tired of playing footsie. It's time you either put out or get out. We have three of your detectives in my county behaving badly. Talk to me."

The officer on the left, a big man in his mid-forties, spoke first.

"For the past six months, we've been investigating a small contingent of officers who have ties to the narcotics trade in Chicago. We believe Detectives Mickey Lyons, Lukas Wagner, and Adrian Valentino ran different territories for the syndicate. They also acted as enforcers for the organization."

I waited for them to continue, but they didn't seem to have anything else to say.

"Care to elaborate?" I asked. "We've got a lot of dead people. Now isn't the time to play coy."

"This is an active investigation," said the second detective, a slight, bald man in his early to mid-fifties. "We don't know how deep this runs."

Delgado shifted his weight to the balls of his feet and tightened his arms across his chest. His expression turned a little dark.

"So, you refuse to cooperate," he said.

"We can't cooperate," said the younger of the two detectives. "We have twelve thousand sworn officers in our department. That's more people than live in your entire county. We've got to do what's right by our department, and at the moment, that means we have to keep operational details quiet until we learn who's involved in a criminal network. Clearly, Detective Lyons was working out of your area. It's possible members of your department are corrupt, too. Until we learn who's on whose side, we have to be careful about what information we share. I'm sure you can understand."

I started to snap at them, but Sheriff Delgado spoke before I could get a word out.

"Sure," he said, nodding. "You can go back to Chicago now. We'll handle our end of the case. If we need your help, I'll call your liaison officer."

"I don't think you understand what's going on, Sheriff," said the older officer. "This is a major narcotics ring. These are dangerous people."

"I've got a good idea of how dangerous they are," said Delgado. "If you don't want to share the information you have, you're useless to me and my department. I can't kick you out of St. Augustine County, but I can kick you out of my crime scene. Now get out, or Detective Court and I will escort you out in handcuffs."

"You're making a mistake," said the older officer. "We came here to help."

"No, you didn't," I said. "You came here to gather information. And that's fine. You've already gotten what you came for, though, so get out."

The younger detective threw up his hands before turning to go. The older detective followed a few steps behind him. As they walked to an unmarked cruiser in the parking lot, Delgado turned to me.

"Good work identifying Mickey Lyons. We'll put out

an APB on him. In the meantime, try to track down where he's been for the past few days. I'll supervise here."

"We need to consider what happened here," I said. "Why would Lyons kill this guy? He's not an idiot. If you look at the surveillance footage, you can see he's not wearing gloves, he's not disguised his appearance, and he's not trying to hide. He had to know the hospital would have surveillance cameras, and yet he didn't seem to care."

Delgado considered that and then nodded.

"I agree, but what does that get us?" he asked.

"A very dangerous man," I said. "He didn't even try to cover his tracks."

Again, Delgado considered but then nodded.

"We'll tell our teams to be ready for him."

"They won't find him," I said, shaking my head. "He came into this hospital knowing it was a one-way trip. If I had to guess, he's already on a plane out of the country, and if he isn't, he's hiding out and waiting for his opportunity to escape."

Delgado tilted his head to the side.

"What are you proposing we do, then?"

I sighed. "I don't know. They may have beaten us on this one."

Delgado straightened. "Maybe you're right. Maybe you're wrong. It doesn't matter. We've got a job to do, so do it. Find him."

He was right, so I nodded and wished him luck before leaving and walking to my car. St. Augustine County had a booming tourist trade. Our Spring Fair alone drew in tens of thousands of people, all of whom needed places to stay. We had intimate, upscale bed and breakfasts on every other street in town, and we had campgrounds and RV parks in the countryside. As diverse as those places were, they had at least one thing in common: They all kept records of the men and women who stayed in their establishments. If you wanted to stay anonymous, there was only one place in town to put your stuff.

I got in my car and drove toward the interstate. It was a busy night at Club Serenity and the truck stop next door, but the parking lot outside the Wayfair Motel was mostly empty. It'd fill up later when the dancers at the strip club finished their shifts and started their second jobs as prostitutes. I parked outside the motel's office and hung my badge around my neck before going in.

The lobby was small but clean. It had a seating area and a television that hung from a bracket on the wall. A clerk sat behind a pass-through window on the western wall. The clerk lifted a remote and muted the news as I walked in. He was in his early twenties, and he had pale skin and red hair. He must have been a recent hire because he smiled at me. Very few of Vic Conroy's employees had smiles for anyone in law enforcement.

"Can I help you, Officer?"

"I hope so," I said, reaching into my purse for my phone. I flipped through my pictures until I found one of Mickey Lyons. Then I turned my phone so he could see. "You recognize this guy?"

He studied my picture for a moment and then nodded.

"Yeah. We don't have a lot of guests this time of year, but that's Mr. Lyons. He came here after his sister died in one of our rooms. The boss comped him. It was the least we could do after everything that happened."

I leaned forward.

"Have you seen him recently?"

"Not since yesterday," he said, turning toward his computer. He clicked the mouse a few times and then looked to me. "He checked out this morning at 10:34. I didn't come on duty until 3:00 this afternoon."

"Has anyone cleaned his room yet?"

"Of course," he said, nodding. "Whenever a guest checks out, we scrub the room pretty well."

My shoulders slumped, and I sighed.

"And I bet he didn't leave anything, did he?"

He turned to the computer, clicked the mouse a few times, and then shook his head before looking at me.

"No. He left the room in good condition and didn't leave anything behind. You seem disappointed."

"It's not your fault," I said, looking at my phone. I flipped through pictures until I found one of Lukas Wagner, the man who had just died in the hospital. "How about this guy? Is he familiar?"

The clerk looked at the picture and then nodded.

"Yeah. He and Mr. Valentino have a room together," he said. He paused. "Why do you have a picture of him asleep in a hospital bed?"

"He's not asleep. He's dead," I said, slipping my phone into my purse. "Mr. Valentino is dead, too. Did they check out, yet?"

The clerk opened his eyes wide but said nothing. I repeated my question.

"No," he said. "They haven't checked out."

"Great. Take me to their room."

He hesitated and stood straight.

"I feel like I should call my boss."

"He'll tell you the same thing I'm about to," I said. "Dead men have no privacy rights. I want in their room. If you don't let me in, I'll pick the lock and go in on my own. Then I'll arrest you for hindering prosecution. You don't want that."

I let him think it through before pulling up my sweater and pushing my jacket back to expose the firearm on my hip.

"I've got cuffs in my car," I said. "Am I going to need them?"

He shook his head and then held up his hands.

"I'll get you the room key."

"Great," I said. "Thank you."

I stepped away from the desk and took out my cell phone. Jason Zuckerburg at my station answered before his phone finished ringing once.

"Hey. It's Joe Court," I said. "Lukas Wagner and Adrian Valentino were staying at the Wayfair Motel. Send me a search team. Whoever's available."

Jason paused. I heard keys on his keyboard click as he

typed.

"Okay," he said a moment later. "I'm routing officers to you right now. You need anybody else?"

"If I do, I'll call you."

"Good luck, Detective," said Jason.

"Thanks," I said. I looked at the clerk. "Let's move. I've got a suspect fleeing now, and there might be evidence of his location in that room. We don't have time to waste."

33

Adrian and Lukas had a second-floor room with two queen-sized beds. Both beds had mussed covers, and the room smelled like sweaty gym socks. There was a duffel bag on the round table beside the door and a hard-case suitcase on the dresser beside the TV. Despite the smell, no dirty gym socks or other clothes littered the floor.

I knew who had stayed in this room, so I didn't care about fingerprints or trace evidence. I was here for information that would lead me to Mickey Lyons, and my eyes zeroed in on four cell phones on the nightstand between the two beds. One looked like an iPhone, while a second looked like a new model from LG. The third and fourth, though, were slimmer and smaller. One had a red case, but the other was black. They looked cheap. Burners. They'd come in handy.

Both the iPhone and the modern LG phone required a thumbprint or security passcode before I could access anything, but the two burner phones had no such security. I started by looking through their call histories. From what I could see, one of the burner phones made its first call a week ago, while the second made its first call three days ago. I wrote down the four phone numbers the two phones had called before focusing on their text messages.

Nobody used names in the text messages, but the context of the messages let me put some names to my phone numbers anyway. The red phone belonged to

Adrian Valentino, while the black one belonged to Lukas Wagner. A third phone—another burner, assuredly—belonged to Mickey Lyons. He had likely thrown it out by now, but I'd see whether we could trace it anyway. A fourth phone belonged to somebody else, and everybody deferred to him. I didn't know who it was, but considering the three known suspects were Chicago police officers, I suspected their boss was a Chicago cop, too.

The group had encoded their messages, but it didn't take long to figure the system out. Mickey Lyons employed his sister as a "courier." She collected "products" from a group of facilities in Jefferson, St. Augustine, St. Francois, Perry, and Bollinger counties and delivered them once a week to her brother in Chicago. It was a valuable territory for the organization.

When Tessa stopped responding to messages, Mickey Lyons came to St. Augustine to look for her. He found out she was dead after arriving. Then, he started visiting the nursing homes she bought pills from to see whether he could salvage the territory and bring in someone new to manage it. Most of his visits went pretty well. The nurses and administrators he spoke to refused to divulge any information about their illicit drug sales.

Then he came to Maddie Dawson at Willow Bend Living Center. He showed Ms. Dawson his badge and introduced himself as a narcotics detective from Chicago. Not only did she offer to turn on Tessa and her organization, she said she had recorded their transactions. Mickey then dragged her behind a car—which his partners found hilarious—until she admitted that Tessa had a local boyfriend involved in the drug trade. Mickey then killed Maddie and dumped her body in Washington County.

After killing Maddie, Mickey met Altman to assess what risk he posed to their operation. That meeting went badly, and Mickey recommended they kill him. Mickey's boss took it a step further and ordered him to kill everyone involved, starting with Altman. Mickey's boss even sent help—Adrian Valentino and Lukas Wagner.

The plan was for Adrian Valentino, Lukas Wagner, and Mickey Lyons to enter Sheppard Altman's home, kill him, and then make it look like Altman had committed suicide. Apparently, Sheppard Altman was a little more than they could handle. After Valentino died and Wagner was stabbed, Mickey went silent. Undoubtedly, he was still getting orders, but he was getting them on another phone.

I put the phones down and scribbled a few notes. We'd dump the phones' contents and print everything out at our station, but for the moment, I needed to get my thoughts in order.

The text messages explained the murder of Maddie Dawson and the attack on Sheppard Altman, but they didn't tell me a thing about Tessa Armstrong's murder. On the text messages, Mickey Lyons seemed to waffle between blaming Sheppard Altman and Carl Armstrong. My investigation, though, told me neither had killed her.

Tessa's murderer—whoever he was—had access to Carl Armstrong's home and cars, which limited my suspect pool. Motive, though, was harder to figure. Tessa might have pissed somebody off, but then again, her killer might not have even known her. It was possible her murderer went after her as an indirect route to take out her husband.

Despite everything I had found, I didn't know a damn thing about that case. Maybe even worse than that, I couldn't justify taking the time to figure it out. Mickey Lyons and Sheppard Altman were still out there. Altman had already killed Adrian Valentino, so he was clearly dangerous if backed into a corner. Lyons, though, was a stone-cold killer. Until we found him, nobody connected to this case was safe.

I slipped my notepad back in my purse and checked out the duffel bag by the front door. It held clothes and some toiletries but nothing interesting. As I searched the hard-case suitcase by the television, somebody knocked on the door. It was Kevius Reed, our young forensic technician.

"Hey, Detective," he said. He paused. "I don't mean to criticize, but shouldn't you be wearing gloves?"

I glanced at him and stepped away from the suitcase.

"Probably, but I don't care about fingerprints or trace evidence. We know who stayed here, and they're both dead. We also know who killed them. Finish searching this bag. If you find car keys, a car rental agreement, a cell phone, anything you think would help, shout. I'm going to the parking lot to make some calls."

He nodded and snapped on some gloves from the kit

he carried with him. I left the room and called Jason Zuckerburg.

"Jason, it's Joe Court," I said. "I need a pair of officers to swing by Sheppard Altman's home and pick him up on suspicion of drug-trafficking charges. He's not safe, and I'm sure he knows it. If he's not at his house, contact the Highway Patrol. We need him brought in before he kills somebody or gets killed."

Zuckerburg typed.

"I'm sending a pair of officers out."

I hesitated.

"Tell them to be careful. Altman's already killed one cop and sent another to the hospital. If he resists arrest, be ready to put him down."

Zuckerburg grunted and typed again.

"To be on the safe side, I'll send four guys instead of two."

"Good idea," I said. "Thanks, Jason."

He wished me luck and then hung up. I called Sheriff Delgado next to fill him in on the cell phones and text messages and to tell him I had sent officers to pick Altman up. Delgado sighed.

"All right," he said. "Good work. We're stretched thin, so I'll bring in the day shift. Surveillance cameras at the hospital showed Mickey Lyons getting into and driving off in a red pickup. He's probably dumped it by now, but we're looking for it. We're also watching the roads in and out of St. Augustine. It's a big county, but he can't have gone too far. We'll find him."

I nodded even though I didn't share in his confidence.

"That's good," I said. "Once I have someone here to supervise the search of Valentino and Wagner's motel room, I'll head out. Someone ordered Mickey Lyons to kill everybody his sister bought drugs from in St. Augustine County. Sheppard Altman was at the top, but it was a long list. I'll check the other names out and make sure they're alive. If they are, I'll bring them in. Once everybody's in custody, we'll figure out what to charge people with."

Delgado paused and then exhaled.

"I don't want you doing this alone," he said. "Lee Fernandez is at home. Call him and tell him we need him to do some field work."

Lee was a sworn officer, but he acted mostly in a community relations role. He gave presentations at schools and organized neighborhood watch associations. He was a good cop, though, and I liked working with him.

"Will do. Thanks, boss."

I hung up and called Lee. He told me he'd be meet me as soon as he could. Typically, we would have taken nine separate teams and arrested each person on our list simultaneously. That way, nobody could have warned anybody else that we were moving against the drug-trafficking ring. With Lukas Wagner's death at the hospital and Adrian Valentino's death at Sheppard Altman's home, though, we didn't have the manpower for that. What's more, we didn't need it. The men and women we planned to arrest were nurses and nursing home administrators who got into something over their heads. They weren't hardened criminals. Most of them would turn state's evidence and plead out to minor crimes. They'd lose their nursing licenses and spend some time in prison, but their lives weren't over.

For the next several hours, Lee and I drove clear across St. Augustine County and made nine arrests. Even though we came to their houses in the middle of the night, most of the men and women we picked up understood why we were there before we even opened our mouths. Two of them even had bags packed.

We worked through the night and arrested our last nurse at about six in the morning. Afterwards, I drove home. I was so exhausted I didn't even bother taking off my jacket before I fell into bed. The moment I closed my eyes, I was dreaming.

I slept until about eleven, but then my cell phone rang. At first, I incorporated the noise into my dream, but eventually the ringing broke through, and my eyes fluttered open. My body felt stiff, and my mouth felt as if I had stuffed it full of cotton balls. I almost felt hung over, but I had had nothing to drink in several days. I needed another four or five hours of sleep, but the world had never stopped for me before, and I doubted it'd be willing to stop now.

I rolled over and grabbed the phone from my end table. The caller ID was blocked. Odd.

"Yeah?" I asked, rubbing sleep out of my eyes. "It's Joe Court."

"Hey, Joe, it's Bryan Costa. You got a moment?"

I closed my eyes and considered telling him no, but I knew the FBI agent wouldn't have called me without a very good reason.

"I had a late night, so I'm just waking up. What do you need?"

"Sorry to drag you out of bed, but I wouldn't be calling except for something urgent," he said. "Did you like Terre Haute on your last visit?"

"It was fine."

"That's a better assessment than most give it," he said. "We need you back. How soon can you get here?"

34

I shouldn't have laughed at him, but my body didn't give my brain a chance to object.

"You okay, Detective?" asked Costa.

The smile left my lips as I shook my head.

"I'm working multiple homicides, I've got nine drug-trafficking nurses in my holding cells, I've got two dead Chicago detectives in my morgue, and a major manhunt throughout the state. No, I'm not okay, and no, I can't make it to Terre Haute. I'm up to my eyeballs in shit, and somebody keeps throwing more at me. What do you need? If I can help you quickly, I will. If it's not quick, you're on your own."

He paused.

"If you need the Bureau's assistance with your manhunt, let me know. I've always got your back."

I smiled genuinely and nodded.

"I know," I said. "What have you got?"

"Well, first, we've been working the Jane Doe we dug up in Oaktown, Indiana. She was somewhere between fourteen and nineteen years old at the time of her death, and there are signs of significant early childhood abuse. Several of her ribs had been broken and healed, and she had healed spiral fractures on both of her forearms. Whoever our victim is, someone abused her as a child, but we think she escaped that abuse in her teenage years."

I blinked and focused on a spot on my ceiling where

the paint was a slightly different color than the surrounding area. It kept me from thinking about what had happened to that kid.

"What's Brunelle say about her?"

"He's not interested in talking," said Costa. "Philippa Cornwell and I are at the prison right now. Brunelle's in an interrogation room, but he's already said he won't talk to us unless you're here, too."

It felt as if a weight had begun pressing me into my bed. Brunelle had possibly killed a lot of people. Even as I lay in bed, there were families out there, wondering whether they'd ever see their daughters again. I wasn't so naïve that I believed we could provide those families closure or make them feel better about their loved one's deaths, but we could get them some certainty. We owed them that, at least.

It would take me three and a half hours to drive to Terre Haute and another three and a half to drive home. If I spent two hours in the prison, I could be back home by eight or nine. On a normal day, I would have done that. With Sheppard Altman and Mickey Lyons still out there, though, I couldn't spare the time.

"I'm busy for the foreseeable future," I said. "I'll talk to him on the phone. Put me on speaker."

Costa paused and clicked his tongue.

"Let me talk to Philippa first and see what she thinks about that idea."

"Fine," I said, swinging my legs off my bed. "Call me back."

He said he would, so I hung up and stood. The house felt cold, so I grabbed a thin robe from my bathroom before carrying my phone to the kitchen. As I made coffee, my phone rang again. I set it on the counter and put it on speaker.

"That you, Costa?"

"Yeah," he said. "Agent Philippa Cornwell and I are sitting in a room with Peter Brunelle. We're alone, but we're recording the conversation."

"Hey, Mr. Brunelle," I said, leaning toward my phone. "This is Detective Joe Court. We met earlier."

"I know. I haven't stopped thinking about you, Joe," said Brunelle. "And how are you doing, sweetheart?"

"Busy," I said. "Otherwise I'd be there to see you. Last time we spoke, you mentioned a young woman you buried in Oaktown. We found her."

"Did you?" asked Brunelle, his voice bright. "How'd she look?"

"Dead," said Costa. "But she was right where you said she'd be. We haven't been able to identify her. Do you know her name? Her family deserves to know what happened."

"Ooohhhh," said Brunelle, drawing the syllable out. "Her family didn't give two shits about her. Don't you worry about notifying them. They wouldn't care if they still were alive."

"You think they're dead?" I asked.

Brunelle made a low growling noise in his throat as he thought.

"There's a good chance," he said, a moment later. "They were heroin addicts, so they burn out early. I didn't kill them, if that's what you're thinking. I don't do men."

The information would help Costa identify our victim, so I nodded and kept my voice light.

"How'd you find her?" I asked.

"She found me," he said.

I forced myself to smile and hoped he could hear it in my voice.

"What's her name? It'd help us out a lot."

"I wish you were here, Joe," he said.

I poured myself a cup of coffee and carried the mug and my phone to the table. My hot drink took the edge out of my voice.

"Look, I don't mean to be impatient, but this conversation is pointless if you're not willing to cooperate," I said. "We want to ID the girl from Oaktown and any other women you might have killed. I'm sure Agents Costa and Cornwell can improve your situation in Terre Haute. If you want a soda or pizza, I'm sure they can give it to you. If you cooperate enough, they might even get you a better cell or have you transferred to a prison of your choice. So, what do you want?"

He paused.

"I'm glad you asked that question, Detective. I haven't gotten laid in a long time, but I've got a fan club. If you've not heard about them, I'm sure Agent Cornwell can fill you in. Some of my fans would love to spend some time alone with me, and I would love to spend some time alone with them. You give me two hours of privacy, a big bed, and a couple of my fans, and I'll tell you whatever you want to know."

Agent Cornwell scoffed before I could even open my mouth to say anything.

"Not going to happen, Brunelle," she said. "The last time you were alone with a woman, you murdered her."

"Any wiggle room with that?" he asked. "You could tie me up."

"No. Now stop asking," said Cornwell.

"All right," said Brunelle. "If I can't touch a woman, I'd like to see one, at least. Guys in general population can at least get dirty magazines. I can't even get that. Agent Costa's phone can show pictures. How about you send me a naked selfie, Joe? I won't show it to anybody."

"No," I said. "If you have a reasonable request, we can think about it. I don't have time to waste with you, so I'm going to hang up now."

"Don't hang up, Joe," said Brunelle. "I'll give you a freebie. Another body."

I sipped my coffee.

"Okay. I'm listening."

"I made it easy last time," said Brunelle. "This one will take some work, but it'll be worth it."

"Where is she?" asked Philippa.

"This one's special. It's buried in the woods between a trail and a silver maple that fell in a windstorm. The property slopes down to a creek in the north. When it rains, water runs down the trail like it's a river, and in the spring, the mosquitos buzz around you as thick as a fog. They'll cover your skin like a blanket if you're not wearing bug spray. It's a real pretty area."

"I'm sure it is pretty," I said. "It could be anywhere, though."

"That's the idea, honey," he said, chuckling. "Show me your tits next time I see you, and I'll give you the address."

"Not going to happen," said Costa. He bobbled his phone, and then I heard his breath as he knocked on the door for the guards to let us out. "I took you off speaker. Sorry about that. I had hoped he'd talk to us."

"It was worth a shot," I said. "My schedule should clear up in a week or two if you still need me."

Costa paused and then whispered something I couldn't hear.

"Agent Cornwell and I are leery of giving in to any of his demands until we can identify the victim we already have. We don't even know that he killed the girl from Oaktown. For all we know, he could be feeding us rumors from the prison yard."

It was an understandable position. Nobody wanted to waste time chasing rumors—even if those rumors panned out occasionally.

"Okay," I said. "You've got my number if you need me."

"I do," said Costa. "Good luck with your homicides, Joe."

I thanked him and hung up. Then I drank a few more

sips of coffee and sat in my empty, lonely kitchen. There were still two dog bowls beside my back door. Roy was in a better home, but I missed him already. I didn't have time to think about him, though. I had shit to do and murderers to catch.

35

I showered, put on a fresh set of clothes, and grabbed a cup of coffee in a to-go mug before heading out. On a normal day, we had half a dozen marked cruisers in the parking lot, just waiting for an officer in need to sign them out for the day. As I walked toward the side door that had become our temporary entrance, though, I found none.

Carpenters, tile installers, and insulation contractors buzzed around the first-floor construction zone, but I didn't run into a single colleague on the second floor until I reached the conference room, where Trisha sat behind her desk. She gave me a tight smile.

"Hey, Joe," she said. "I hear you had a late night. We have, what, ten guests in the holding cells because of you?"

"Nine," I said, nodding. "It was a long day. Lee Hernandez helped, too."

"And he had the good sense to stay home and sleep," she said, winking. "Since you're here, though, George will put you to work."

I nodded and sipped my coffee.

"Anything interesting happen this morning while I was asleep?"

"We found the truck Mickey Lyons drove from the hospital," she said, nodding. "He ditched it near Ross Kelly Farms and stole a Pontiac Grand Am from the parking lot outside the plant. We haven't found the car yet, but we're looking."

Ross Kelly Farms was a poultry processing plant in a remote part of the county. The staff raised a couple hundred thousand organic, free-range chickens a year, butchered them in the plant, and then sold the carcasses to restaurants and high-end grocery stores throughout the Midwest. I didn't hear about the company often, mostly because Ross Kelly's corporate security team kept the largely immigrant workforce in check themselves.

"Is the boss around?"

"He's in his office, but he's asleep and told me he'd like to stay that way for a few hours," she said. "Wake him up at your peril."

"How long has he been out?"

She looked at her computer screen and wrinkled her nose.

"A little over two hours."

I would have been pissed if someone roused me after a two-hour nap, but I wasn't the boss, and we had work to do.

"Thanks, Trisha," I said. "I would let him sleep, but I've got an idea to find Mickey Lyons, and we need to move on it now."

She tilted her head to the side. "For your sake, I hope it works."

"Me, too," I said. I left her there and walked down the hall to the boss's office. He had shut his door, so I knocked hard and waited outside.

"Sheriff Delgado, it's Joe Court."

I heard a groan before the sheriff answered.

"Give me a minute, Joe."

"I'll be right back, boss," I said. He may have grunted, but I couldn't hear well through the door. I hurried back to Trisha's conference room and poured two cups of coffee from the massive drip coffee maker that used to be in our first-floor break room. By the time I came back to Sheriff Delgado's office, his door was open, and he sat behind his desk. His uniform was open at the collar, and his black and gray hair stuck up in the back. I put a cup of coffee in front of him, and he nodded his thanks and sipped.

"You make it home last night?" he asked.

"Yeah, but I didn't get much sleep. Bryan Costa called me about Peter Brunelle this morning. Brunelle's the serial murderer I met in Terre Haute."

The boss nodded, grunted, and sipped his coffee.

"Something happen?"

"Last time we were there, Brunelle gave us the previously unknown location of one of his victims. Agent Costa hoped he'd identify her, but he refused unless I sent him a naked selfie."

Delgado nodded.

"Federal inmates have the worst manners," he said.

"It's a little like high school," I said. "But when I told him I wasn't interested in talking to him further, he gave us the location of another victim."

He nodded and then leaned back.

"I appreciate that you've got commitments outside

this department, but I need you here."

I straightened. "I know, and that's what I told them. I'm here because I have an idea about how we can get Mickey Lyons."

Delgado nodded. "I'm listening."

"He thinks we're idiots," I said. "In those text messages he sent to his partners, he calls us inbred, he calls us rednecks, and he calls us morons. He thinks we're amateurs doing a professional's work."

Delgado picked up his coffee and nodded.

"He's an asshole. What does that get us?"

"I think we can use it. He thinks he's so much smarter than us that he can get away with anything. It's why he didn't disguise himself at the hospital."

"What are you proposing?"

I hesitated because I knew the boss wouldn't like this. Then I cleared my throat.

"I was thinking about giving him a target," I said. "Think about the situation he's in. We know he killed Lukas Wagner at the hospital, and we've got cell phone messages from his burner phone in which he talks about torturing and killing Maddie Dawson. What's more, he should know what we know. He knows he's got to get out of the country."

"Okay," said Delgado, nodding. "I'm with you so far."

"If we give him the chance to make a major score before he flees, I bet he'll take it, especially if he thinks it'll be easy."

Delgado narrowed his eyes at first, but then his

expression went dour.

"And I bet you've got just the bait in mind," he said.

I nodded.

"Yeah, and I'm pretty sure you're thinking the same thing I am. We've got seventy kilograms of heroin and over three million dollars cash in our vault right now from Shane Fox's traffic stop. Let's let the public know. It's a lot of money and drugs, and it's a great story about a young officer who did his job well. We'll get some good reporting out of it. Before the story goes live, we'll tell the DEA to pick up the money and drugs. They'll put the money into an asset forfeiture fund and the drugs in their vault. When Mickey Lyons shows up to steal the money, it'll be long gone."

"That's assuming he shows up," said Delgado. "He may not."

"Even if he doesn't, we've lost nothing and gotten some good publicity."

Delgado seemed to consider. Then he narrowed his eyes.

"How would you go about robbing a police station?"

"I don't know, but I don't need to know," I said. "He'll come up with a plan he thinks will work. We'll put surveillance cameras in the evidence room, and we'll install a panic button for Mark Bozwell. The moment Lyons shows up, we'll take him into custody."

"Mark will have to agree," he said. "I won't endanger him without his permission."

"If Mark isn't up for it, I'll sit in the evidence room

Chris Culver

myself."

Delgado drummed his fingers on his desk and then nodded.

"Okay," he said. "For the record, I don't think Lyons will bite, but there's no harm in putting out a story."

"Thank you," I said, turning toward the door. I stopped before leaving. "I haven't even checked my email this morning, so I'm going to go to my office. If you need me, I'll be there."

He nodded, sipped his coffee, and turned his attention toward his computer. I walked to my office and sat down. After making nine arrests last night, I had a lot of paperwork to fill out and reports to read. Thankfully, Lee Hernandez, my partner last night, had already gotten a jump start on things with his own reports. Since I was the primary detective on those cases, I signed off on them and started filling out the seemingly endless stream of forms that accompanied any arrest.

About twenty minutes after I sat down, my phone rang. I answered without looking at the screen.

"Detective Joe Court," I said. "What can I do for you?"

"Detective, I'm glad I caught you."

It was Dr. Sheridan. I hadn't expected to hear from him, so I took my hands off the keyboard and sat straighter.

"Hey, Doc," I said. "Everything okay?"

"No," he said after a pause. "I know you're busy, but a friend called me last night to say a young woman in

Jefferson County nearly died after taking an ecstasy tablet that had been stamped with a star. Young lady had a heart attack. Some of her cardiac tissue is likely permanently damaged."

I grimaced.

"My investigation has come to a dead end. I arrested an ecstasy dealer at Waterford College in St. Augustine, but I'm not sure he's the right guy."

"Were his drugs stamped with a star?"

I shook my head. "No. They looked like playing cards."

"He's not the dealer we're looking for. Every tainted ecstasy tablet I've found was stamped with a star. We need to find the source."

My muscles ached from a lack of sleep, and I knew I'd start dreaming the moment I laid down and closed my eyes, but I nodded anyway.

"I'll see what I can do."

"Thank you," said Sheridan. "I've autopsied enough teenagers to last a lifetime."

I said I'd do my best and then thanked him for his call. After hanging up, I ran a hand through my hair and drank the rest of my coffee. This would be a long day.

36

Before doing anything else, I opened my investigative file into Jasmine Kelley's death and browsed for a few minutes to reorient myself to her case. Then I called Jasmine's best friend, Emma Hannity. Her phone rang about half a dozen times before it went to voicemail. She hadn't returned my previous voicemail, so I didn't expect her to return this one, either. It didn't matter, though.

"Emma, this is Detective Joe Court. Since you didn't return my last call, I assume you didn't get it. I know you lied to me about Blake Meeks. He wasn't Jasmine's boyfriend. I arrested him for possession of a schedule I substance, but he didn't sell to Jasmine. He didn't even know her. Worse than that, I've got another overdose to contend with. I don't know what's going on, but every officer in St. Augustine County is on the lookout for you. Please turn yourself in before someone else you love dies or before you get hurt."

I hung up and focused on Jasmine's file again. To my surprise, my phone rang within seconds. I furrowed my brow and answered.

"Emma?"

"Did he die?" she asked, her voice quivering and small.

"Who?"

"The guy who just overdosed."

I shook my head. "It's a young woman, and she's still

alive. She had a heart attack, and it's left her with permanent damage to her heart. She took the same drugs that killed Jasmine. You know anything about them?"

Emma said nothing, so I sighed.

"All right. If that's how you want to play this, that's how we'll play this. Keep pretending you don't know what's going on, and I'll keep investigating. I've got at least half a dozen bodies on the ground, so, when I find the person who sold these drugs, it'll be goodbye and goodnight. I'm going to be honest with you. I think you know far more than you're letting on. If I can connect these drugs to you, I promise that you will die alone in prison. Is that what you want?"

"No," she said.

"Where did Jasmine get the pills?"

I waited almost a minute for her to speak. When she did, her voice was so soft I had to turn up the volume on my phone.

"Me," she said. I couldn't see her, but I could hear the tears in her voice. "I gave them to her."

I blinked and clenched my jaw.

"Why?"

"Because I thought they were safe," she said. "It's just X, right? Everybody takes it. I thought it would loosen her up. I didn't know it'd hurt her."

"Where'd you get them?"

This time, she didn't hesitate.

"I made them. I got the equipment from a chemistry supply house online and learned how to make them by reading stuff on the internet. You can learn anything on Reddit."

I took my phone from my ear and started an app to record the conversation.

"Just to let you know, I'm recording this conversation," I said. "We'll fill in some blanks later, but did you get the ingredients on the internet, too?"

"Yeah," she said. "On the dark web. A guy offered to sell me the stuff, and I paid him in Bitcoin. Everything was anonymous, so I don't even know his name."

It made some sense. The government regulated sassafras oil, but a resourceful person could buy just about anything on the black market. Still, something nagged at me.

"What'd the pills look like?"

"They were small and round," she said. "I put stars on mine. That's my brand."

She was right, so I nodded.

"Tell me about the drugs themselves. You learned how to synthesize them on the internet?"

"Yeah," she said. "I don't know the chemistry, but I can follow directions."

"Did anything change in your pills recently?" I asked. "Why are your customers dying now?"

She hesitated.

"I don't know. Sometimes I just get in the groove and make stuff."

I blinked, and a tingling spread from my chest to my shoulders. She was saying all the right things, but I couldn't force myself to believe it. She may have dealt on the side to make ends meet, but manufacturing pharmaceutical-grade ecstasy was a different job entirely. It took knowledge, equipment, time, and a secure location to do it. I doubted she had any of that.

"To clarify, you're telling me you produced the drugs that killed Jasmine Kelley, your best friend."

She paused. Her voice nearly broke.

"Yeah. I'm sorry."

"Me, too," I said. "Where are you?"

"Walmart. I'm in the bathroom. I got your voicemail and ducked in here."

"Okay, then. I'll send some uniformed officers to pick you up. Please stay put, and please surrender to them. If you fight them or try to run, you'll get hurt. There's no need for that. When you get to the station, we'll get you a lawyer. There might be ways out of this mess."

"My best friend is dead because of me," she said. "I don't deserve a way out."

I softened my voice.

"Just go with the officers."

She said she would, so I hung up and called my station. Trisha routed four officers to the store. I didn't think Emma had committed the crime she'd just confessed to, but I didn't want this turning into a manhunt.

While my colleagues picked Emma up, I called the prosecutor's office. Shaun Deveraux agreed that we had probable cause for an arrest and for a search of Emma's house, so I started putting together an affidavit. About ten minutes into that, Trisha called to let me know we had Emma Hannity in custody. She had given herself up without a fight. At least that had gone well. I thanked her and focused on my computer again.

Once I had my search warrant affidavit filled out, I brought it to the courthouse for a judge to sign. An hour after Emma confessed to manufacturing MDMA, I started searching her house. She had three S.A.T. study manuals on her dining room table and little notecards strewn about the home. I picked one from the refrigerator.

"Have you studied today?"

Alisa Maycock, one of the two uniformed officers I had brought with me for the search, stuck her head out of the bathroom with her brow furrowed.

"You say something, Joe?"

I showed her the notecard.

"I was reading aloud. Emma left herself notes throughout the house."

Alisa nodded.

"She's got one on the bathroom mirror, too. It says 'Mizzou Class of 2020. You can do it.'"

The home was warm, but I still felt cold. I sighed and rubbed at my neck.

"Have you found any laboratory equipment or anything that looks like a meth lab?"

Alisa shook her head.

"I found a bong in the bedroom," she said. "It's got

some weed in it, but I haven't found meth or anything like that."

I brought my hand to my face and turned around the kitchen while shaking my head. Emma had mixing bowls, measuring cups and spoons, and even a scale that weighed to the gram. She could use those things to manufacture drugs, but her scale had a dusting of powdered sugar on it, and there were Ziploc bags full of cookies in her freezer. Everything in that kitchen had a purpose, and it wasn't to make drugs.

"The young woman who lives here confessed to manufacturing ecstasy," I said. "I don't believe her, but have you found anything to corroborate that? Even a chemistry textbook would be telling."

"She's got books, but they're all fantasy and romance novels," said Alisa. "If she's making drugs, she's not making them here."

I balled my hands into fists and clenched my jaw before speaking.

"She's not making drugs. She's making cupcakes and studying to go to college."

Neither Alisa nor I said anything for a moment. Officer Gary Faulk must have heard us because he came out of the bedroom.

"She had a small bag of weed in her closet," he said. "Otherwise her bedroom and closet were clean."

I drew in a slow breath and nodded.

"Okay. Finish the search and lock up when you leave. I need to think about this."

Alisa wished me luck, so I left the house and walked to my cruiser. I hadn't spent a lot of time with Emma Hannity, and I had barely known Jasmine, but I felt like I knew them both after watching so many of Jasmine's videos on YouTube.

These two young women may not have had perfect lives, but they had plans for the future. Jasmine had her makeup tutorials and a budding video content business online. Emma dreamed of going to college, but even more than dreaming, she was planning. People with big dreams, people like Jasmine and Emma, didn't manufacture drugs in their living rooms.

I opened my purse and found the notepad on which I had jotted down notes while watching Jasmine's YouTube videos. Jasmine rarely mentioned her sister Erica, but when she did, she rarely had nice things to say. One quote in particular, though, stuck out to me enough that I had written it down.

I'd do anything for my mom, and my mom would do anything for my sister even though my sister has never done anything right in her life. I guess that means I'd do anything for my sister, too.

On a hunch, I used my cruiser's laptop to search for Erica Kelley on the NCIC database. She had a sealed juvenile record and eight arrests since turning eighteen. I didn't care about the misdemeanors, but three years ago, she was arrested for possession of a controlled substance while visiting the River City Casino in St. Louis. It was a class-D felony, so she'd either had a lot of weed or a small amount of heroin, cocaine, or something similar. From there, she graduated to felony assault with a motor vehicle. She was lucky she hadn't killed anybody or her brief stint in jail would have been ten to twenty years in prison.

I leaned back and crossed my arms as I thought things through. This wasn't right. Emma Hannity wasn't making drugs. She was covering for somebody, and I had a feeling I knew who.

I put my car in gear and headed toward the Kelley house on the edge of town. As I drove, the surrounding woods became thicker and thicker. On my earlier trip, I had paid little attention to the vegetation alongside the road, but now I couldn't help but notice dead sassafras trees alongside the road amongst the healthy maple, pin oak, and black walnut trees.

I pulled onto the shoulder of the road about a mile from Anna Kelley's house. The woods around me were thick and lush, but a pair of sassafras trees alongside the edge of the road had brown, dead leaves. Where the ground near the neighboring trees held thick grasses and invasive honeysuckle, the ground near the sassafras trees was broken. Someone had dug there recently.

I popped my trunk and grabbed the folding camping shovel Sheriff Delgado had ordered us to carry after our cruisers started getting stuck in snow last winter. I carried it to the base of the nearest sassafras tree and dug until I exposed the tree's thick roots. As I suspected, someone had cut big chunks away all around the trunk.

I moved to the next sassafras tree and dug there, too.

The ground was loose from previous excavations, and, unsurprisingly, someone had cut the roots on that tree, too. About twenty feet away, I found a third sassafras tree. This one had fared a little better. Someone had dug at its base and cut away some roots, but the illicit gardener hadn't been as aggressive. The tree survived, but I doubted it would make it through the winter.

A surprising number of drugs came from plants. Heroin came from the opium poppy, and cocaine came from the coca leaf. Ecstasy came from safrole, one of the primary components of sassafras oil.

Emma Hannity didn't manufacture ecstasy. Someone at the Kelley homestead did, though. And she got greedy. She killed her trees and had to look for something else, some other chemical that could get her clients high but that didn't require safrole. She settled on NBOMe, a synthetic chemical many, many times more toxic than the drug it was replacing.

Emma wouldn't lie to protect just anyone, but she might lie to protect a loved one. Though they weren't related by blood, Jasmine had called Emma a sister. She said she and Emma had grown up together and that they loved each other. But Emma had grown up with Erica Kelley, too. If Emma and Jasmine were sisters, so were Emma and Erica.

I thought of my sister, Audrey. I loved her with everything I had and would do anything for her. Emma, apparently, was like me. She'd take a fall to protect her sister. Maybe that was noble; maybe, given circumstances I didn't understand, it was even the right thing to do. Still, it wouldn't fly on my watch.

People had died because of Erica Kelley's drugs. She didn't get a pass. Some debts had to be paid by the person who made them, and I intended to make sure Erica paid hers.

37

I put my car in gear and drove to the Kelleys' house. The windows were dark, no car sat in the driveway, and no one answered my knock on the front door. To make sure they were really out, I walked to the backyard.

At the very rear of their yard, the Kelley family had a big shed. Its dark brown paint almost made it blend into the woods. A padlock secured its door, which was unusual for a home that far out in the country in St. Augustine. I grabbed a flashlight from my cruiser and shined it through the window, revealing an interior packed with shelves and old garden tools. Dust seemed to cover everything except one shelf near the western wall. On that shelf, I found big cauldrons, the kind a restaurant might use to make chicken stock for the week. I also saw glassware, tubing, and a turkey fryer. It looked like the kind of stuff a meth cooker might have.

Or, in this case, it belonged to a home-trained chemist who made MDMA in her backyard.

Realistically, I had tools that could break the padlock, but that wouldn't have been legal. It could wait until I had a warrant. I had the evidence I needed to pick up both Erica and Anna Kelley on manufacturing charges.

I walked back to my cruiser and called Trisha to update her on the situation. We had two officers within five minutes of my location if I ran into trouble, but I didn't think the Kelleys would put up too much of a fight if I asked them to come in and talk to me about Emma Hannity. Once they were safely in our station, then I'd spring an arrest on them. It'd be easy.

So, I sat and waited in my cruiser. The way the trees rhythmically swayed in a light late fall breeze made my eyes grow heavy. I would have drifted into a light sleep if my phone hadn't started ringing about twenty minutes after I sat down. It was Preston Cain. I rubbed my eyes and answered.

"Hey, Sasquatch," I said. "What's going on?"

"You busy?" he asked.

"I'm camping out in front of a drug manufacturer's house in the county while I wait for the homeowners to show up. Why?"

Preston paused.

"It's Roy."

I sat straighter.

"Yeah? What's wrong?"

"He's run away. One minute, he was sitting on the porch while I was in my shop working, and the next minute, he was gone. I've been all over the property calling for him, but he's not here."

My heart started thudding.

"Don't panic," I said. "Call the Humane Society and let them know in case anybody brings him in. He's chipped, so a vet or animal shelter will be able to identify him. There's a St. Augustine County lost pet group on Facebook, too. People post pictures there all the time. Oh, and call Trisha. We're busy today, but let her know. We've got officers all over the place today. Maybe somebody will see him."

"I'm sorry, Joe," he said. "I know what that dog means to you. I didn't think he'd run."

Part of me wanted to snap at him and tell him he should have been watching him, but it wasn't Preston's fault. Roy was a dog, and dogs weren't known for their judgment. He was probably chasing an animal in the woods. I swallowed hard and forced my voice to sound chipper.

"It's fine. He's probably just making friends in the neighborhood."

"Yeah, probably," said Preston, his voice low. "I'm going to get in my truck and start driving around. I'll see whether I can find him. Shelby's already on her bike looking for him."

I blinked a few times and nodded.

"Keep me updated. If he's not back by the time I arrest my drug makers, I'll help you look for him."

"I'm so sorry, Joe," he said. "You trusted me with your dog, and I let you down."

"Don't worry about me. Roy is your dog. I'll help you find him as soon as I can."

Preston wished me luck with my arrest, and I hung up. For a few moments, I just stayed in the car, waiting, my muscles tense. That didn't help anything, so I shook out my forearms and rolled my shoulders as well as I could while still sitting. Roy was going to be just fine. He wasn't a puppy, and he wore a collar with his information.

He had probably just smelled a neighbor making food and wandered over, hoping he could get a treat.

As much as I told myself that, and as much sense as it made, I couldn't make myself believe it. I got out of my car and started pacing the driveway. Then I started walking up and down the road, counting the sassafras trees. In an approximately two-mile stretch, they had thirty-four trees, twelve of which were dead and all of which had loose soil at the base. Sassafras trees didn't typically grow in the middle of a forest, but they thrived in open fields and along the roadside. I had the feeling that if I kept walking, I'd find dozens more trees from which the Kelleys had harvested.

After walking for almost half an hour, I returned to the house. I had only worked for about four or five hours that day, but the Kelleys were still gone, and already shadows were growing long on the ground as the sun began to sink on the horizon. I yawned and sat on my front seat and waited another half hour for Anna or Erica to come home from work. Neither did, though, so I called my station. Mark Zuckerburg answered after two rings.

"Hey, Joe," he said. "Anything happening at the Kelley household?"

"Just sitting and waiting," I said. "Trisha briefed you, I take it?"

"Yep," he said. "Preston called, too. I'm sorry about your dog."

I sat straighter and drew in a hurried breath.

"What have you heard?"

"Just that he's missing," he said. "I sent his picture out to everybody on patrol."

I tried not to let him hear it, but I breathed easier and let myself sink into my seat.

"Thanks," I said. "Listen, though, I'm exhausted. I had a late night. Do we have an officer who can babysit the house for a few hours? I need to sleep."

He typed for a few minutes and grunted and typed some more before drawing in a breath.

"Okay," he said. "I've got Carrie Bowen en route. She's about fifteen minutes away. Can you wait that long?"

"That's just fine," I said. "Thanks, Jason."

I settled back into my seat, but I couldn't keep my feet from bouncing on the old cruiser's floorboards. Muscles all over my body felt twitchy and agitated, and my gut felt both empty and uncomfortably full at the same time. After a few minutes, I got out of my car and started pacing again. That calmed me some and let me focus on something other than my own growing sense of unease.

Carrie arrived in a black SUV with patrol lights hidden in the grille about ten minutes after my call. When she saw me, she unrolled her window.

"Hey, Joe," she said. "I'm your relief."

I looked at the car.

"Riding in style tonight, huh?" I asked, forcing my voice to sound bright.

"Yeah," she said. "Sheriff Delgado usually reserves this beast for himself, but we're still all-hands-on-deck at work. Our marked vehicles are all out on patrol."

I looked to the cruiser I had signed out earlier that day.

"I should get Old Brown back to the station, then," I said.

"Please don't. I'm in love with Sheriff Delgado's car, and if you drop off Old Brown, I'm going to have to drive it all night once I get back. This SUV has everything. The heater works, the radio works, and it's even got power windows."

I smiled.

"All good things must come to an end."

"The front seat can give the driver a massage, Joe. I can't even get my husband to give me a massage, and I sleep with him. Please don't take that from me."

I smiled.

"I'll tell you what," I said. "I'll drop off Old Brown, but I'll tell Jason it has a flat tire. That way, you can keep Sheriff Delgado's car for the rest of the night."

She patted the steering wheel and then winked.

"Thanks, Joe. You're the best."

I wished her luck, drove to my station to drop off my cruiser, and picked up my Volvo. The evening was growing dark, which worried me. Roy had the bright yellow eyes of a Chesapeake Bay retriever but dark brown fur. Drivers would have a hard time spotting him if he ran into the road. I hated this. I felt sick. Every muscle in my body felt tight and twitchy, and my stomach contorted itself into knots.

I drove to Preston's house and got out of the car and yelled for Roy until my voice gave out. Then I got back in my car and drove for about an hour, hoping I'd catch a glimpse of him somewhere. At about seven, my phone rang.

"Hey, Joe," said Preston. "I've been out looking for Roy, but I can't find him. I'm calling it for the night. I bet somebody found him and took him in."

I nodded even if I couldn't force myself to believe that.

"I bet you're right," I said. "He'll probably turn up tomorrow."

"Yeah," said Preston. He paused. "I'm sorry."

"It's not your fault. He'll show up. Everything's fine," I said. "I'm going to go home, too. I need to get some sleep."

He promised to start searching again the next morning, which I appreciated. I thanked him and wished him luck before hanging up. Then I pulled onto the side of the road and drummed my fingers on my steering wheel. I hadn't eaten much all day, but I wasn't hungry. Even if my stomach told me it was fine, I needed food, though, so I drove by a Chinese place and ordered enough so that I'd have leftovers for a night or two.

Then I drove home and pulled into my driveway. As my headlights panned across my front yard and reflected on a pair of yellow eyes, I felt myself sink into my seat. I could have cried, but instead, I parked and swung my legs out of the car. Roy lumbered to his feet, jumped off the porch, and jogged toward me with his tongue sticking out of his mouth. I knelt in front of him, and he licked my face.

"You asshole," I said, petting his cheek and practically hugging him. He sat down and panted. "You could have gotten hurt. Don't do that again."

Roy didn't respond, but I stood and pulled out my cell phone to call Preston. He answered on the first ring.

"Hey," I said. "It's Joe. I just got home and found Roy on my porch. It's a little late tonight, but I'll bring him by tomorrow."

"I'm glad you found him," said Preston. He sighed. "You don't need to bring him back tomorrow. Roy's a great dog, but he chose his home. If you bring him back here, he'll just run away again. Next time, he might not make it to your house safely."

I shouldn't have felt relieved, but my shoulders loosened, and my chest felt lighter. Then I looked at Roy, and a pit grew in my stomach again. I swallowed hard.

"Can we give it one more shot?" I asked. "If you give him time, he'll feel at home. Maybe you'll just have to keep him on a leash for a while."

Preston hesitated before responding.

"Shelby and I can do that," he said, his voice soft, "but why? Do you really want to get rid of him?"

"Of course I don't," I said. "I love Roy. He's my friend, but your farm is so much better for him than my house. He'll forget me eventually. If you give him a chance, you'll love him, and he'll love you. He's worth fighting for."

"Then why aren't you fighting for him?"

I closed my eyes and shook my head.

"What I want doesn't matter," I said, reaching down to pet the dog. "This is about Roy. If you don't want him, I'll find somebody who does."

"He's already got a home," said Preston. "And what you want does matter. At work, you were always the first one to help other people, but you never let anybody help you. I used to think you just wanted to show everybody up, but now I see that wasn't the case at all."

"Dude, you don't see anything," I said, shaking my head.

"I think I do," he said. "Roy makes you happy, doesn't he?"

"Of course he does. He's my dog."

"That's why you're pushing him away," said Preston. "You don't think you deserve to be happy."

"That is such bullshit I don't even know where to start criticizing it," I said.

"If you say so, I believe you," he said. "And I'll tell you what: I'll swing by and pick up Roy tonight. I've got a lot of free time. I'll find a good home for him."

"No," I said, my voice sharp. Roy startled and peered up at me. I cleared my throat and softened my voice. "I mean, he's content where he is. We'll set up a time later."

"Okay," said Preston. "You're a friend. More than anything, I want you happy."

I looked down.

"Thanks, Sasquatch. I am happy."

"I hope so," said Preston.

He thanked me for my call and hung up. I sat with

Roy long enough for even him to get tired of sitting. Then I went back to my car for the dinner I'd forgotten in there. As Roy and I walked in, my house finally felt like home again. I ate dinner and then sat on the couch in the living room to watch TV before bed. Roy ambled over, climbed onto the couch beside me, and put his head on my lap. I petted his ear as he fell asleep, and I thought about what Preston had said.

When I lived with Erin, my biological mother, I was too young to think about happiness. Then, when Erin overdosed and lost me, I moved into the foster care system. Some of my homes there were comfortable and safe, but I had never stayed in one place long enough to drop my guard. Then, as I got older and some of my foster fathers started viewing me as a young woman instead of a little girl, I had to keep on my guard for creeps. But even staying on guard all the time wasn't always enough.

All my life, I had focused so single-mindedly on survival that it didn't occur to me to even think about being happy. My biological mother was a danger to everyone around her, me most of all. Some of my foster parents were okay people, but one drugged and raped me. My adoptive parents were wonderful. I had been happy living with them, I think. That may have been the last time, though. Maybe Preston was right. Maybe it was time I let myself be happy again.

I hesitated and then searched through the directory on my phone until I found the number of a friend of mine. He was a detective in southern St. Louis County, and we talked at least once a week. Ian, my little brother, thought Mathias was my boyfriend, but he wasn't. He was just a good friend. Sometimes, when we talked, Mathias and I complained about work, but usually we just chatted. Once, we talked about sandwiches for almost two hours. It was the most absurd conversation I had ever had, and yet, it had made my entire week.

I dialed his number and waited for him to answer.

"Hey, Joe," he said, his voice bright. "I'm glad you called. It's been a while since we talked."

"Six days," I said, nodding. I sighed as my heart started pounding. "Look, I'm not good at this, so I'm just going to come out and say it. I like talking to you, and I like spending time with you. When you call, I smile for hours afterwards like I'm an idiot, and I'd like to do that more."

He paused. "Okay. I can call more often. That's no problem."

"That's not what I'm getting at," I said. I looked down at my fingers. They were trembling, so I balled them into fists and then sucked in a deep breath. "Would you like to go out with me sometime? Like on a date."

Again, Mathias paused. Warmth spread all over me, and my heart thudded in my chest so hard I could almost see my shirt moving. I wondered whether that was what a heart attack felt like.

"You can say no, if you want. I mean, that's fine. I'd probably say no, too," I said. I paused. "I'm sorry I asked.

Forget it. I'll talk to you later."

I pulled the phone from my ear to hang up, but Mathias called out before I could.

"Wait. Don't hang up," he said. I put the phone back to my ear. "I like you, too, and I'd love to go out with you. I asked you before, and you turned me down."

"I wasn't ready," I said, "but I was always interested."

"All right, then," he said, his voice bright. "We'll go out. Let me plan something. We'll do something special."

We agreed to set up a time and date later. I would have kept him on the line and talked to him for a while, but I was so tired, I could barely keep my eyes open. After I hung up, I practically sank into the couch. Throughout the entire conversation, my heart had thudded, my fingers had trembled, and skin all over my body had tingled. I couldn't remember being that nervous or excited in years.

It felt good.

I ran a hand across Roy's back, and he sighed and opened his eyes to look at me.

"Hey, dude," I said. "I think I'm going to like being happy."

38

After my call with Mathias, I had hoped to catch up on lost sleep, but life had other plans for me. At a little after eight, my phone rang. Roy jumped a little but stayed on the couch as I went to the kitchen. The call was from the dispatcher's desk at my station, so I answered immediately.

"Hey, it's Joe."

"Joe, it's Jason Zuckerburg. Carrie Bowen just brought in Anna and Erica Kelley. They seemed pretty upset. Carrie's got them in an interview room if you want to talk to them."

"Watch them, but don't let them leave."

"Will do," he said. "See you soon."

I thanked him for the call, hung up, and petted the dog.

"Dude, I've got to go out. Do you want to be inside or out?"

He lifted his head and then stepped off the couch. I grabbed my purse and led him to the kitchen where I let him outside. While I ran some water over my dinner plate and turned out the lights, Roy bounded off to use the restroom. It was a little cool out, so once he finished, I called him back and let him inside. Once his winter coat grew in, I'd let him stay outside in the doghouse if he wanted, but for now, he'd be okay inside by himself. I didn't plan to stay out very long, anyway.

I drove to my station, parked in the lot by the side

door, and walked to the conference room that held our dispatcher's station. Zuckerburg was routing a pair of patrol officers to a home in the county for a domestic disturbance, but he nodded hello to me as soon as I walked in. When he finished speaking to our officers, he looked up at me.

"Carrie's got them in interview room 2. They should be ready to go for you."

"Thanks, Jason," I said. "I'm crossing my fingers that this won't take too long."

"Well, good luck," he said. "And, hey, when you get the chance, check out KSTL's website. They sent a news crew to cover Shane Fox's traffic stop."

"Any visitors yet?"

"The DOJ sent an armored car to pick up the money and drugs. It should be in St. Louis by now."

If Mickey Lyons showed up—and I still thought he would—he'd have a bad day. I hoped I'd be there to see it.

"Thanks for the update," I said.

Zuckerburg nodded and turned his attention to his equipment as the phone rang. I left as Zuckerburg asked the person on the other end to stay calm and repeat what she had just tried to tell him. The hallway was quiet, and the lights were low. Once the construction crews finished working, we'd have comfortable, modern interview rooms with surveillance systems hidden in the walls and ceilings and big windows overlooking the town. Until then, we had cramped, windowless storage rooms into which we had stuffed tables and chairs.

I stopped by my office and printed out a few documents and pictures before walking to interview room 2. Erica and Anna Kelley and Carrie Bowen sat around a small conference table. Erica and Anna had bottles of water and bags of peanuts in front of them. Carrie was sitting across from them and looking at her phone, but she stood when she saw me.

"Evening, Detective," she said, nodding to me and then to Erica and Anna. "You guys have everything you need?"

The two Kelley women nodded, so Carrie looked to me.

"I guess I'm back on patrol."

"Enjoy the massage chair," I said, winking.

"Oh, I will," she said, nodding and smiling.

She left, so I sat down and put my folder on the table.

"You have news about my daughter's death?" asked Anna.

"I do," I said, nodding. "I've arrested Emma Hannity for manslaughter. She's sitting in a holding cell right now."

"Emma would never hurt Jasmine," said Erica. "They were best friends."

"As close as sisters, I hear," I said. Erica nodded.

"We all were," said Erica.

"Emma didn't mean to hurt her," I said, tilting my head to the side. "How familiar are you guys with MDMA? It's a recreational drug often used in clubs and music festivals. It gives users a euphoric high. Most people take it in pill form. The street name is ecstasy."

Anna's face paled. Erica nodded.

"We've heard of it," she said. She paused. "Why do you ask?"

"Jasmine died after taking what she thought was ecstasy. Her pill, though, was tainted by another drug called NBOMe."

Anna covered her mouth.

"And that killed her?"

"Yeah. It thickened her blood and narrowed her blood vessels. Her heart had to work overtime just to keep her blood flowing. It's like trying to suck mud through a straw. Eventually, it became too much. Her heart couldn't take it anymore and quit. MDMA wouldn't do that, but NBOMe does. What makes this especially bad is that Jasmine's isn't the only death we've had lately. A lot of families in the area have had to bury their kids lately."

"What does all this mean?" asked Anna. "For Emma, I mean. What will happen to her?"

I sighed and opened my eyes wide.

"I'm not sure, to be honest. My initial thought is to charge her with multiple counts of manslaughter and with drug trafficking, but with so many people dead, the prosecutor will probably make an example out of her. He'll charge her with multiple counts of murder. It'd be a tough case to make, but he's a good lawyer. No matter what happens, she'll be in prison the rest of her life. She might even hit death row."

I was laying it on pretty thick, but it seemed to get their attention.

"There are several things I can't quite figure out, though," I said. "You guys were the closest thing she had to a family, so maybe you can help. Neither Emma nor Jasmine had criminal records, which is strange if Emma's a drug dealer. Both young women were also doing things with their lives. Emma was studying to go to college, and Jasmine had a growing business online. Her videos were popular. Some had half a million views. Why would these two manufacture illegal drugs?"

Anna cried. Erica looked down at her hands.

"Maybe it wasn't them," she said. "Maybe it was someone else."

I looked at her. "Please don't tell me about Blake Meeks. I've heard his name too often lately."

Erica shook her head and then opened her mouth to say something. No words came out.

"Let's focus on Emma," I said. "She's a nice young woman. She loves you two like family."

Erica squeezed her eyes tight as tears fell down her cheeks. Anna closed her eyes. Her lips moved. I suspected she was praying.

"She'll die in prison, surrounded by strangers," I said. "That sucks."

Erica kept crying, and Anna kept praying. I needed to keep going. One of them would break soon enough.

"What's interesting is that Emma told me she made the drugs herself after learning how on the internet. When I searched her house, though, I couldn't find any equipment. I almost get the feeling she's covering up for someone she loves."

Again, Erica opened her mouth as if she wanted to say something, but her mother cut her off before she could.

"It was me," said Anna. "I did it. If you need to arrest somebody, arrest me."

"Emma's already confessed," I said, my voice calm and even. "Why should I believe you over her?"

Anna leaned forward.

"Did Emma ever tell you about her daddy?"

I hadn't expected her to ask that, so my back straightened as I shook my head.

"No. Why?"

"Because he killed her mom," said Anna. "He used her as a punching bag until she couldn't take it anymore. She killed herself. Emma was ten, and her daddy moved in on her after. I saw it happening, but I did nothing until Emma came to my house with bruises all over her arms one day. She said she fell down the stairs, but I could see her daddy's handprints on her. I sent her out to play with Jasmine and Erica, and I went to her house with a shotgun. I aimed that gun right at her daddy, and I told him if he ever touched that girl again, I'd blow a hole clean through his chest."

"You protected her," I said.

"I gave a beautiful, kind, and sweet little girl the home she deserved," said Anna. "You'd better believe I protected her. She's mine."

"Are you protecting Emma now by confessing to

something she did?"

"She's trying to protect me, Detective," said Anna.

"What are you doing, Mom?" asked Erica, sitting straighter.

"Hush," said Anna, looking to her daughter and then to me. "My grandson—Erica's baby—has cystic fibrosis. We've got insurance, but do you know how expensive care is for a baby with cystic fibrosis?"

I shook my head. "No."

"More than we could pay," said Anna. "Joseph, Erica's fiancé, came to me with an idea."

"Leave Joey out of this, Mom," said Erica. "Please."

"I can't, and you know I can't," said Anna. "Joseph teaches high school chemistry. He just finished college. He's a good boy."

I looked at Erica. "Is he the father of your child?"

She said nothing, but her mother nodded.

"He is," she said. "Joseph and I have talked about this. He thought he knew how we could make some money."

"And what did he suggest?" I asked.

"Drugs. Ecstasy. It's basic organic chemistry. He said it'd be easy to make since we had sassafras trees all over our property. Our neighbors did, too. Nobody cared if I dug up the roots for sassafras tea. Instead of making tea, though, he extracted the oil from the bark and used that to make the drugs. It worked pretty well until our trees started dying."

"I've been to your house," I said, nodding. "I noticed

some dead trees."

"We tried to buy safrole, but we got ripped off," said Anna. "Then Joseph suggested we try a different chemical. It was harder to synthesize, but the chemicals were easier to get. Nobody was supposed to get hurt."

"People died, though," I said.

"Not just people," said Anna, blinking as tears ran down her cheeks. "My baby died. Jasmine. I never meant for that to happen."

"And we're back to my earlier question: Why should I believe you instead of Emma?"

"Because Emma didn't have any drugs," said Anna. "You searched her house. I know that girl, and I know she didn't have drugs."

"You're right," I said. "Do you have them?"

Anna nodded and reached into her purse for her car keys.

"In my trunk. Peel up the carpet. There's a spot where you're supposed to put the spare tire. That's where you'll find them."

She slid her car keys across the table toward me. I grabbed them and considered for a moment before standing.

"You two stay here," I said. "There'll be an officer outside the room, so please don't leave."

Anna nodded. Erica just cried. I couldn't blame her for that. I left the room and hurried toward the dispatcher's conference room. Lee Hernandez was inside, leaning on the counter and talking to Jason Zuckerburg, but he agreed to babysit my suspects for a few minutes while I searched their vehicle.

Since I didn't know what Anna and Erica had driven that morning, I walked around the parking lot and streets around my station for about five minutes, hitting the panic button on their key fob until an alarm went off on a black Chevy Malibu. I turned off the alarm, popped the trunk, and peeled back the carpet, just as she said.

Anna wasn't kidding about the drugs. She had two gallon-sized Ziploc bags full of pills in psychedelic colors. There must have been thousands of them. A star adorned each pill. I carried the bags to the conference room with our dispatcher's station, where I filled out evidence tags so I could process things. Then I called Sheriff Delgado to explain what I had found. He agreed to come in and put together a search warrant affidavit for the Kelley house.

Meanwhile, I left the drugs in Zuckerburg's custody, went by my office to pick up some handcuffs, and returned to the interview room. Lee stood outside and nodded hello.

"Did you find what you needed?" he asked.

"Oh, yeah. Stick around for a minute longer. I'm making an arrest," I said, reaching for the doorknob. Lee followed me inside. I looked to the two women before focusing on Anna. "Anna Kelley, please stand up. I'm placing you under arrest for trafficking in a schedule I substance."

Anna stood and stroked her daughter's hair while Erica cried.

"It's okay, honey," she whispered. "You're okay."

"Do I need to handcuff you, or will you cooperate?" I asked.

"I'll cooperate."

"Good," I said, looking to Lee. "Take her downstairs for processing. She'll be our guest for a while."

Lee nodded and put a hand on Anna's elbow to lead her outside. I looked to Erica.

"You know where your fiancé is tonight?"

"At my house," she said. "With the baby."

"Great," I said. "There will be somebody there when our search team arrives."

"What about me?"

I looked at her and drew in a breath.

"Officially, I don't have enough evidence to charge you with a crime," I said. "Off the record, we both know you're up to your eyeballs in shit. No way your mom and boyfriend went into business together without your knowledge, but you've got a sick baby. If I push hard and arrest you, that sick baby goes to foster care. Maybe they'd place him with a great family that would love and take care of him, but maybe they wouldn't. I'm not willing to take that risk.

"So that's where we're at. You walk because I'm worried about your kid. Good luck."

I turned to leave, but Erica cleared her throat.

"What about Emma Hannity?"

I stopped and looked at her.

"Emma, Jasmine, and your son are the only innocent

people in this mess. I'll be releasing her without charges. If she's smart, she'll keep studying and go to college. If she's not, she'll stick around with you. I can't make that decision for her, but I can tell you one thing: next time I see you in an interrogation room, you won't walk out a free woman. For your own sake, don't screw up again."

I left her there and walked back to my office. Most times, I felt like going out for a drink to celebrate when I closed a tough case. This time, I needed a drink to forget. I may have put some bad guys in jail, but nobody won tonight. Sometimes justice sucked.

39

I filled out paperwork until almost two in the morning. Sheriff Delgado and a search team found a glass carboy containing nine pounds of a substance Joseph Stone— Erica's boyfriend—identified as safrole. He said it was enough safrole to make thirty-five or forty thousand ecstasy tablets. At five to six bucks a pill, that'd be worth two hundred thousand dollars or more on the street.

Besides the safrole, Delgado found lab equipment and almost forty thousand dollars cash. According to Joseph Stone, they made their drugs in the shed in the backyard and sold them to students at various high schools and colleges around the region. After hearing that their drugs had already killed several people, Stone gave up the names of the dealers who worked for them so we could make some arrests before they distributed more pills. According to Delgado, Stone seemed contrite, but contrition only went so far with multiple bodies on the ground. He'd still spend the rest of his life in prison.

Before driving home, I texted Dr. Sheridan to let him know we had found the source of the NBOMe-tainted ecstasy and had made multiple arrests. He wouldn't see my text until morning, but I thought he'd appreciate knowing.

Roy met me by the back door as soon as I made it home. He wagged his tail and licked my hand as I knelt to pet him.

"Hey, buddy," I said. "You missed me, huh?"

As if to answer, he put a paw on my knee so I wouldn't go anywhere. Even as tired as I was, I couldn't help but smile. I petted him and made sure he had water before going to my bedroom to change into pajamas. Muscles all over my body ached with exhaustion, which made my mattress feel even more wonderful than usual. As my head hit the pillow, Roy climbed onto the bed and lay down at my feet. I was glad to have him home.

I slept for about four hours until Roy woke me up. More than any other dog I had met, Roy liked mornings. In his perfect world, the day would start at 5 a.m. and end at noon. Since I couldn't live like that, I gave him some breakfast and let him outside so he could go to the bathroom. Then I went back to bed.

By the time I woke next, most of my aches and pains had left, but I still didn't know how to feel about what had happened with the Kelley family. I had arrested a guilty woman, but I didn't know whether I had done the right thing. Maybe I should have arrested Erica, too. Maybe I shouldn't have taken Anna's confession at face value.

When I'd sworn my oath of office and become a police officer after college, I had seen the world in black and white. People broke the law, or they didn't. If they broke the law, they were bad, and if they didn't, they were good. Since putting on my detective's badge, though, I'd noticed a lot of gray I hadn't seen before. Occasionally, I'd run into a human monster, and my decision would be clear: put him in prison for as long as possible so he couldn't hurt anyone else. Other times, though, there was no right choice. I just ended up picking the least shit-covered stick in the yard and hoping for the best.

Those were thoughts for another time, though. I had work to do, so I made some toast in my kitchen, dressed, and got ready for my day before tossing a tennis ball to Roy in the backyard. He retrieved it three times, which was good for him. Afterwards, he found a rubber chew toy in the dog run and went to town on that. He seemed content, and he had plenty of water. He'd be fine.

"See you later, bud," I said. He looked up and seemed to nod before turning his attention to his toy again. I drove to work and parked on the street about half a block from my building. If I had been up earlier, I would have seen frost on the grass, but now it was comfortable in a jacket.

Inside my station, I stopped by Trisha's desk. She smiled.

"Hey, hon," she said. "Big night last night, huh?"

I nodded. "Closed my investigation into Jasmine Kelley's death."

"And got a lot of dangerous drugs off the street. It's good work. You should be proud of yourself," she said, moving some papers around on her desk until she came to a handwritten note. "Dr. Sheridan called. He also wanted me to congratulate you and tell you that you've saved a lot of lives."

I nodded and sighed. "I had a lot of help."

"None of us work alone, but we wouldn't have two thousand tainted ecstasy tablets in our vault if not for you.

Learn to take a compliment, Joe."

She winked, and I smiled.

"Any movement on Sheppard Altman or Mickey Lyons?"

"Both are in the wind," she said. "Your story ran, though. Or Shane's story, I guess. The world thinks we've got several million dollars cash in the basement."

"I've heard," I said. "If anything changes, let me know. I've got interview notes to transcribe, after-action reports to write, and a lot of other stuff."

"I will, Joe," she said. "Good luck."

I thanked her and walked to my office. It had been a rough couple of days, but already I felt the weight on my shoulders ease. Paperwork sometimes did that to me. It felt weird to acknowledge that, but it was true. Paperwork was almost cathartic. It let me unwind a little and process what I had done and why. More than that, though, it'd help me guarantee that all my hard work would be worthwhile.

The criminal justice system ran on paperwork. As a cop, I had the power to make arrests, search homes and businesses, and examine the most intimate parts of people's lives. Paperwork was a check on that power. By documenting everything I had done in painstaking detail, I showed the world that I had played by the rules. It meant the evidence I collected would be admitted to court and that the men and women I put in jail deserved to be there. That mattered to me.

For the next three hours, I sat at my desk, drank

coffee, and typed at my computer. Then at noon, Trisha and I went out to lunch. She was a friend, and I hadn't spent a lot of time with her in the past few weeks. It was nice. At a little before one, we came back, and she went to the dispatcher's station in our conference room, while I returned to my paperwork. It felt good to close a case.

Then, at about 4:30, I was transcribing interview notes from a recording on my cell phone when Trisha popped her head into my office. She seemed almost breathless.

"Hey," I said, glancing up. "Give me just a moment."

"No time," she said. "Get down to the evidence vault. Mark's hit the panic button."

I furrowed my brow as my brain processed the comment. Then I pushed back from my desk and shot to my feet, spilling a cup of coffee on the carpet. I didn't care.

"Mickey Lyons is here?"

"Somebody is," said Trisha. "And he's in the basement now. I'm mobilizing everybody on the floor."

I checked my firearm and ran past her. Outside my office, Officers Gary Faulk and Katie Martelle sprinted down the hallway toward the stairwell. I ran after them. My feet pounded against the carpet. Trisha was a few steps behind me. When we reached the steps, I slowed. We had at least two officers heading toward the evidence room. If Lyons was still there, they should be able to subdue him with ease.

Trisha almost ran into me, but she caught herself and

slowed.

"What's wrong?" she asked.

"Nothing," I said. "We've got plenty of guys going to the evidence room. Go to the side door in case Lyons runs out. If you see him, be ready to protect yourself. I'm going to the front."

She paused just a split second and then nodded.

"Will do."

When we reached the first-floor landing, Trisha darted down the hallway toward the side entrance we used as our building's main entrance during construction. I turned the other way and stepped through a break in the plastic sheathing that separated our station from the construction zone. The work crews were cleaning up for the day, but there were piles of steel structural studs on the ground and exposed wiring in the drop ceiling.

A man in a white hard hat walked toward me.

"Can I help you?" he called.

I hurried toward him. "Are you the foreman?"

"Yeah, and you should be wearing a hard hat in this area, miss," he said. "We're finishing up for the day, so we've got guys carrying beams and pipes. If one hits you in the head, you could get really hurt."

"No time," I said. "We're looking for a guy named Mickey Lyons. He's six feet, medium build, brown hair. He's a cop from Chicago. Real dangerous. Have you seen anybody unfamiliar around here?"

He looked around. "I've got crews from two different HVAC companies and three electrical contractors. Half the people here are unfamiliar. Sorry."

"No problem," I said, looking around. The job site was dusty but organized. Men in hard hats of various colors were walking around and throwing bits of wire, wood, and insulation into trash cans, while other men stacked metal and wood studs into neat piles. Everybody had a job and a purpose. It was a cavernous space, and I could see from one side of the building to the other.

My eyes locked on a guy in a brown hard hat near what would become the main entrance. I pointed toward him.

"Who's that?" I asked. "He's not doing anything."

The foreman looked and squinted.

"Brown hard hat is a welder, but I shouldn't have any welders on site today."

I unholstered my firearm and stepped forward. Several of the workers near me backed off and put their hands in the air, but I couldn't focus on them. The toes of my feet dug into the concrete, and I sprinted forward. Lyons must have seen me move because he stopped midstep and looked at me. Our eyes locked. Lyons wore dark jeans and a black hoodie sweatshirt. He fit in well with the construction crews. It was no wonder no one had stopped him.

"Mickey Lyons, hands in the air. Now!"

As soon as the words left my mouth, Lyons ran. I was in good shape, but he was taller and faster than me. He hit the main entrance at a dead sprint and threw it open with his shoulder.

"He's going out the front door!"

I didn't know whether Trisha or any St. Augustine officers heard me, but I ran toward the front door and hit it with my shoulder just as it closed. Only, instead of throwing it open like Mickey Lyons had, pain ripped through my arm and side. I'd have bruises on my ribs and arm, but I could deal with that. I dug my feet into the ground and pushed hard. The door opened slowly but with increasing resistance with every inch.

By the time it was open enough for me to squeeze through, I could barely move it. Then I saw why it had started resisting me: Lyons had wedged an angled piece of lumber into the gap at the bottom of the door, creating a stop. I kicked it out of the way and threw the door totally open so my colleagues could follow.

Outside, the construction crews had erected a portable chain-link fence with a green mesh privacy screen to separate the construction zone from the surrounding streets. I couldn't find Lyons anywhere.

"He ran through the front doors!" I shouted. "He's outside somewhere."

Officer Gary Faulk came running around the side of the building.

"He's not in the parking lot!" he shouted.

"Then go around," I said, pointing to the west and running toward the chain-link fence. Gary ran behind me, and I put my hands on top of the fence and pulled hard so I could see over it. There was a brown hard hat on the ground.

"He went over the fence!" I screamed as I scrambled to climb over. Once my right leg cleared the top of the fence, I pushed off and jumped down on the other side. I couldn't see Lyons, but I ran toward his helmet, figuring he must have run in that direction. I made it about forty feet before I heard the roar of an engine.

A big forest green SUV pulled away from the curb. It was, maybe, fifty feet from me, and it was barreling toward me. I didn't have time to think. I raised my weapon and squeezed the trigger until the magazine ran dry. Each round slammed into the front window, peppering the safety glass with cracks. Then I dove to my right between a pair of pickup trucks that had parked alongside the road. The SUV slammed into the side of the trucks with a wrenching sound of metal on metal and then careened in the other direction to slam into a red four-door car. The heavy SUV pushed the sedan onto the sidewalk before momentum carried it into a metal utility pole.

Then, the SUV stopped.

I blinked a few times in the sudden quiet. Then I heard shouting. I dumped the magazine from my pistol and replaced it with another before scrambling across the road toward the SUV. The driver's door opened, and a man in a yellow safety vest tumbled out and onto the sidewalk. He had abrasions across his hands, face, and chest, but he clutched his neck. Blood ran through his fingers and poured out of his mouth.

For a moment, his eyes went wide as his life poured onto the sidewalk. There wasn't anything I could do, but I ran toward him, anyway.

"I need some help!" I screamed.

Mickey tried to say something, but no sound left his lips. He had a firearm in his right hand. He tried to lift it toward me, but I kicked it away. His weapon clattered to the ground, and he dropped his arm to the pavement. Footsteps pounded around me as I knelt down to him.

"You're dying. Anything you want me to tell your loved ones?" I asked.

Again, his lips moved, but he couldn't speak. I think he was trying to tell me to fuck off, though, so I stood. He died within about thirty seconds in a puddle of his own blood.

I hadn't known how to feel about Anna and Erica Kelley, but here, I had done what I had to do. I would have preferred to arrest Mickey Lyons and send him to prison, but I'd sleep fine knowing I had put him down for good. Mickey had been a sociopath willing to murder and torture strangers to get what he wanted. He would have killed me if he could. The world had enough problems without men like him in it.

I stepped away from his body and looked to Marcus Washington and Trisha, both of whom stood near me, trying to catch their breath.

"The suspect is down," I said. "Let's close the street and bring in Dr. Sheridan and a forensics team. Someone will need to call Sheriff Delgado, too. We'll need a supervisory officer. I'm punching out for the day."

40

My evening was long, but it wasn't stressful. Sheriff Delgado called in investigators from the Highway Patrol to look into Mickey Lyons's death. They interviewed me, every officer at the station at the time of the shooting, and every construction worker in the building. Gary Faulk had seen what happened, and he corroborated my story. The construction workers even confirmed that I had ordered Mickey to surrender inside. Someone from the Missouri Attorney General's Office would have to sign off on the investigation, but that didn't worry me.

I drove home at a little after nine that night and called my mom to let her know what had happened. She was glad I was okay and reminded me that my station kept a trauma therapist on retainer. Mom had never shot anybody, but she had been a cop. She understood the job. She and my dad offered to come down, but I just needed some quiet time to myself. Before hanging up, I told her I loved her. She told me the same. It was always nice to hear.

After talking to Mom, I took a sleeping pill and went to bed. I had nightmares, but every time I started talking or thrashing, Roy would get up and lick my hand or arm until I woke up. His breath wasn't pleasant, but his presence was comforting.

I had planned to take two or three days off, but my boss called me the next day after my morning run through

363

the woods.

"Hey, Joe," he said. "You doing okay? You sound out of breath."

"I was exercising. What's up?"

"You need to come to the station," he said. "I won't keep you too long, but I've got some video you need to see."

I hesitated. "Everything okay?"

"We'll talk when you get here."

I agreed, so he thanked me and hung up. I looked to the dog.

"Looks like I've got to go out today," I said. "Sorry, dude."

Roy yawned, which he did when I had confused him. I rubbed one of his ears before walking to my room to get dressed. It was cool, but I left Roy in the dog run out back anyway. He would have preferred to stay inside, but his coat would be thick enough to keep him warm during the day, and I didn't know how long this would take.

When I reached my station, I found an armored truck and two black Dodge Chargers parked in the fire lane. That was unusual. Since Delgado had called me, I walked straight to his office and found him along with two men inside. The sheriff nodded to me.

"Joe, thanks for coming," he said. He looked to the two men with him. "Detective Court, this is Special Agents Ellison and Gonzalez with the DEA."

"Hi, guys," I said, holding out my hand to shake. The two agents shook my hand and nodded hello. "What's going on?"

"We're here to pick up some cash and heroin one of your officers found during a traffic stop," said Ellison. "We've run into a snag."

"I'd say so," I said, nodding. "Somebody from the DOJ already came by and picked everything up."

Delgado shook his head and turned a monitor toward me.

"That's where we've got a problem," he said. I glanced at the two DEA agents. Both crossed their arms but said nothing. I looked at Delgado's monitor. He had spooled up surveillance video from our evidence room. On it, Mark Bozwell and Sheriff Delgado spoke to two men in black suits. One had dark skin and black hair. The other had lighter skin and was bald, but he had a thick, gray mustache. My gut plummeted into my feet. I closed my eyes and swore under my breath.

"The man with dark skin is Rajendra Gavani," I said. "He's a guidance counselor at our high school. The lighter-skinned man is Sheppard Altman. He's shaved his head and put on a fake mustache. When the news first ran a story about Tessa Armstrong's death, Mr. Gavani brought Altman into our station for an interview. They lived near each other and said they were friends."

"I'd say they're more than friends," said Gonzalez. "Why did you give two civilians three million dollars cash and seventy kilograms of heroin?"

"They came in a damn armored truck," said Delgado. "And they had paperwork from the DOJ. We expected them. Before the story ran, I called the US Attorney's Office in St. Louis. They said they'd send a team down to pick up the stuff."

"When you got here, did you even bother to call anybody to verify their paperwork and story?" asked Ellison.

"I did," said Delgado. "The Indian guy gave me the number of his supervisor. I called and spoke to Scott McClure in the US Attorney's Office in Kansas City. That's where these guys were from."

"There is no Scott McClure in the US Attorney's Office in Kansas City," said Agent Gonzalez. "What'd the armored truck look like?"

Delgado closed his eyes and shrugged. "It was an armored truck."

"Did it have the DOJ's logo painted on the side?" asked Gonzalez.

Delgado shook his head. "No. It was from a private company. It said something about security services on the side."

I covered my mouth and almost smiled. Then I shook my head in disbelief.

"We got played, boss," I said. "Altman and Gavani have balls."

"Forgive me for saying this, but I don't think there's anything funny about this situation, Detective," said Ellison.

"You're right," I said, looking at him and holding my hands in front of me. "So, what do we do now? Do we contact them and offer them asylum, or do we just let them die out there?"

"Don't do anything," said Gonzalez. "This is a federal case, so we'll find them. Just stay out of our way."

"Sure," said Delgado, his voice low. "Seems like you gentlemen have heard what you need to hear. Good luck."

Both men shook their heads and left. Delgado sighed and then crossed his arms as he looked at me.

"What was that asylum crack about?"

I blinked and then tilted my head to the side.

"I don't know a lot about drug cartels, but as best I can tell, Gavani and Altman have three million dollars and seventy kilograms of cartel heroin. Once this story hits the news, there will be a manhunt, and the DEA won't be the only hunters in the field."

Delgado processed that before nodding. Then he chuckled a little.

"Well, I guess it's a bad day to be a conman."

"I'd say so," I said. "You need me for anything else?"

"No, and sorry for calling you in today. If you need anything, let me know."

I nodded and thanked him. I should have driven home, but I had something on my mind. We had arrested a lot of people who sold Tessa Armstrong opioids, and we had shut down an entire drug-smuggling operation in St. Augustine, but we hadn't found out who killed her yet. Tessa may have made mistakes in life, but her death wiped the slate clean.

I walked to my office and called up her case file to

reread everything. Someone murdered her at the Wayfair Motel between 9:36 p.m. and 9:42 p.m. Her murderer drove Carl Armstrong's Range Rover, but it wasn't Carl. It wasn't her brother or her boyfriend, either, because they were both elsewhere, too. Our killer then placed a soda can with Carl Armstrong's fingerprints on it in the trash can. The killer then stashed the murder weapon inside Carl Armstrong's office.

I grabbed my notepad with notes from Tessa Armstrong's case and scribbled down a few things. My suspect pool wasn't large, but I knew little about most of the people in it. Then I flipped through pages of notes until I found those I had taken while searching Armstrong's mansion in Ladue. His estate manager was named Joel Sanderson. I didn't know what an estate manager did, but if anyone knew the staff, he would.

I called his cell phone and waited for him to pick up.

"Mr. Sanderson, this is Detective Joe Court. I'm investigating the death of Tessa Armstrong. We spoke several days ago while my team searched your employer's home."

"I remember," said Sanderson. "What can I help you with, ma'am?"

"We can start with a list of your employees and anyone else who would have had access to Mr. Armstrong's home. I'd also like to sit down with you for an interview. My investigation into Mrs. Armstrong's death has taken some peculiar turns, so your cooperation would be very helpful."

"I see," he said. "Do you have a court order compelling my cooperation?"

I grimaced.

"Mrs. Armstrong's dead. If you refuse to cooperate, it reflects poorly on you."

"I see," he said, his voice as even as if I had just told him it was cold out today. "Is there anything else?"

"To clarify, you're refusing to cooperate without a court order?"

He didn't hesitate before answering.

"Yes. I'm doing my job. Can I help you with anything else?"

I sighed. "I guess not."

"Once you secure your court order, I'll be glad to help."

"I'm sure you will," I said. I hung up. With the information I had, I could get a court order, but Armstrong's attorneys would contest it. I needed information now, not in a month after multiple hearings. I spun around in my chair for a few minutes, but inspiration didn't strike.

Truthfully, I didn't know a lot about Tessa Armstrong. She may not have been the target of this murder. It may have been someone just trying to get back at her husband. Even if this was about Carl, though, Tessa's killers chose her for a reason. Something about her made her an appealing target.

I stood and walked to Trisha's conference room to tell her I was going to St. Louis. Then I signed out an unmarked cruiser and drove north. Tessa's condo was still locked tight, so I picked the deadbolt and let myself in. With Tessa dead, Carl Armstrong would eventually take possession of the property, but for now, it was a piece of evidence.

I walked into the living room and then to the master bedroom, processing the scene in my mind. Tessa was artistic, and she had both wonderful taste and the means to buy beautiful clothes. My sister—a woman who loved clothes the way some people loved their children—might have killed for some of Tessa's dresses. Tessa hadn't died for her things, though. Despite her role in the drug trade, she hadn't died for drugs, either.

I walked to her front door and checked out her mail table. Her brother had gone through some of her mail before he died, so many of the envelopes were open. I hadn't given them much thought before, but I stopped now and picked things up. She had a lot of mail from banks. On my first visit, I had dismissed those as credit card statements or the typical junk mail a wealthy woman might have received, but now I looked closer.

Aside from multiple credit card offers, she had sales contracts and investment prospectuses from investment banks and brokerage houses in New York, Europe, and elsewhere. I started organizing the mail into piles on the island in her kitchen. One pile was junk, but the others looked promising. Then I stopped and held my breath when I saw the record of a bank transfer that Carl Armstrong, Tessa Armstrong, and their investment advisor—Sheppard Zimmerman—had signed. Zimmerman was Sheppard Altman's real name, the one he had used in Chicago when he worked for an investment bank.

A quick search turned up several more documents signed by the trio. The three of them moved money from one bank to another often, but they also purchased things. I didn't know what this meant, but I needed to find out.

I stacked all the mail I could find and bundled it with a rubber band from Tessa's junk drawer. Then I left the apartment, locked it behind me, and bagged and tagged it as evidence in my car. From there, I drove to St. Augustine to the offices of Darius Adams, CPA. Darius was in his late forties to early fifties, and he rented the basement of a building downtown. He had very dark skin and black hair. I had only met him a handful of times, but he smiled often and bragged on his kids or wife at every opportunity. I liked that a lot.

Though it was late in the day, Darius answered my knock.

"Detective Court," he said, his voice high with surprise. He stepped back and swept his arm out to let me inside. "Come in. Come in."

I thanked him and stepped inside the office. Darius had been a forensic accountant with the IRS before he and his wife had moved to St. Augustine. He was a good accountant and had helped us with cases before.

"How have you been?" he asked, stepping toward his desk and gesturing toward an empty seat across from him.

"I'm good, thank you," I said. "Unfortunately, this isn't a social call."

I showed him the documents I had taken from Tessa Armstrong's house and explained to him why I had taken them and who the major players in my investigation were.

"What do you need me to do?"

"Help me figure out what's going on," I said. "Sheppard Altman was a con artist and a thief. I think he and Tessa were ripping off Carl. As sophisticated an investor as Carl was, though, this is way beyond me. I need you to read through everything and see whether there's something fishy."

"I can do that. You want me to send a bill to the station?"

I nodded. "Yeah. Please do."

He nodded, and I stood.

"I'll get right on it and tell you what I think."

I thanked him, and he led me out of the office. My job was done. Now, I just had to wait.

41

It took almost a week, but with the help of Darius Adams, several subpoenas for bank records, and a little luck, we found what we were looking for. We knew who killed Tessa Armstrong and why. After putting together an arrest warrant, Sheriff Delgado and I drove to Ladue to update Carl Armstrong's family. Not long after we had released him, the FBI arrested Carl for his involvement with an illegal scheme to recruit and pay athletes to play at his former university, so his ex-wife Daphne Armstrong had moved into Carl's mansion to take care of their kids.

Sheriff Delgado looked over at me as soon as he parked the car.

"You ready?" he asked.

I nodded and opened my door.

"Yeah. Let's go."

Joel Sanderson, Carl Armstrong's estate manager, met us at the front door before we could knock. He wore an impeccably tailored black suit and smiled when he saw us.

"Please come in," he said. "Mrs. Armstrong and her children are in the solarium."

Delgado and I nodded and followed him into the house.

"So, Mr. Evans, do you work for Daphne Armstrong now, or do you just stay with the house?"

He cocked his head at me and smiled.

"I work for the Armstrong family, as I always have."

"I see," I said, nodding. He led us down a short hallway to a sunroom at the rear of the house. It was a modern, clean room with slate tile on the floor. Glass panels formed the walls and ceiling. There was seating for ten, but only four people waited for us: Daphne Armstrong and her children—Tyler, Hannah, and Ethan —who were sixteen, eighteen, and twenty, respectively. I smiled at them when I entered the room.

"Okay, everyone," I said. "Thanks for hosting us. I'm Detective Joe Court with the St. Augustine County Sheriff's Department. With me is Sheriff George Delgado. We've been investigating the death of Tessa Armstrong, and we're here to make our final update on the case."

"Let's get this over with," said Hannah. She was eighteen, and she had her father's nose and chin but her mother's green eyes. "Tessa was our dad's mistake. Not ours."

"I see," I said, nodding. "You all want the expedited version, then?"

Most of them nodded. Tyler, the youngest, was staring at his phone and not paying the least bit of attention to us. That would change soon.

"Okay," I said, looking to Daphne, their mom. "Daphne Armstrong, you're under arrest for the murder of Tessa Armstrong. You have the right to remain silent. If you talk to me, I can use anything you tell me against you in court. You have the right to an attorney who can give you advice before, after, and during interviews or interrogations. If you can't afford one, the court can provide one to you free of charge. Do you understand those rights?"

Tyler looked up from his phone. Hannah gasped. Ethan crossed his arms and shook his head.

"No way," said Ethan. "My mom wouldn't kill that bitch. Dad, maybe, but not Mom."

"Your dad didn't kill anybody," I said. "He was occupied at the time of Tessa's death. There were multiple witnesses."

"Hookers, you mean," said Hannah. "My dad was sleeping with hookers. Our lawyer told us. Mom didn't do it, either, though. Why would she? It's not like she wanted Dad back."

"Yes, Detective," said Daphne. "Why would I kill my ex-husband's little friend?"

"Wife," I said. "You may not have liked her, but Tessa was your ex-husband's current wife. You killed her. The least you can do is show her some respect."

"Fine. Why do you think I killed Tessa?"

"That's a good question," I said, starting to pace as I got into a rhythm. "First, we knew Carl didn't kill her. He had ample motive, but he didn't do it. Somebody tried to make it look like Carl did, though. The killer drove to St. Augustine in Carl's Range Rover, she used Carl's gun, she hid that gun in Carl's home office, and then she left a soda can in Tessa's hotel room with Carl's fingerprints on it. It was a good frame. I'm as cynical as they come, but I bought it. I figured Carl killed Tessa for stepping out on him and to save some money. A lot of men would get jealous if they learned their wives were having an affair."

"That doesn't mean Mom killed anybody," said Hannah.

"No, but it tells me Tessa's murderer had access to this house and your father's possessions."

"It could have been the help," said Hannah, looking to Mr. Sanderson. "They're jealous of our success."

"You're eighteen. You've done nothing with your life. Your father's a success, but you're a spoiled kid," I said. "That's beside the point, though. The household staff didn't kill Tessa."

Daphne crossed her arms.

"Why would I kill my ex-husband's current wife?"

I looked to Hannah and then her brothers.

"Money. Carl had a lot of it. Tessa and her boyfriend wanted it, but your dad refused to grant her a divorce. He said it would cost him too much. Instead, he gave Tessa a very large allowance, he paid for her car, and he paid for her condo. In exchange, she could do whatever she wanted with whomever she wanted as long as she lived within her considerable means and stayed out of the newspaper."

"They had a fucked-up marriage," said Ethan. "So what?"

"I don't care about their marriage except for what it told me about their lives. Tessa had a boyfriend named Sheppard Altman. She loved him, and he loved her. Mr. Altman was a confidence man. He convinced people to trust him, and then he stole from them. Your father was the perfect mark. Altman had an MBA with a specialty in finance from Northwestern, and he knew how to hide money from the IRS. Your dad had a lot of money to hide. I'm sure your dad jumped at the opportunity to save a few million dollars on his taxes."

Daphne's expression was measured, but the kids gave me dumbfounded looks.

"Why would my father hire his wife's lover to manage his money?" asked Hannah. "That's stupid."

"Your dad didn't know who Mr. Altman was. Mr. Altman gave your father his original name. He lived under a different name in St. Augustine," I said. "Now, I don't know whose idea the scheme was, but Altman was a master at moving money—even more so than your father. Your dad thought that by allowing Mr. Altman to invest his money, he'd avoid paying taxes. He didn't realize that Mr. Altman was moving your father's money to accounts he controlled all over the world.

"At the time of Tessa's death, she and her lover had stolen almost nine million dollars from your father. We've frozen most of those accounts."

"Jesus," said Ethan. "She deserved to die, then."

"Careful what you say, son," said Delgado.

"I'm not your son," said Ethan.

Delgado held up his hands and took a step back as he shook his head. Ethan focused on me, then.

"Tell me you arrested Altman," he said.

"No," I said. "He's gone, but people are looking for

him. I wouldn't be too concerned about him."

The room went quiet. Daphne gave me a bemused smile.

"Okay," she said, nodding. "So, your theory, Detective, is that I learned of Mr. Altman's subterfuge. Instead of murdering *him*, though, I killed Tessa and framed my ex."

"That's about right," I said. She laughed and then looked down.

"I don't know who killed that poor, stupid girl, but it wasn't me," she said. "I was in St. Charles antique shopping with Hannah the entire day. We stayed overnight in an Airbnb. My daughter will testify to that, I'm sure."

"I will," she said.

I looked at Hannah.

"If I were you, I'd stay quiet right now. You're eighteen. If you make a mistake today, I will charge you as an adult and send you to prison."

She raised her eyebrows.

"I'm not making a mistake. I was with my mother."

Delgado shook his head and looked down. I tried to keep my disappointed reaction from showing.

"Remember that I tried to give you a way out," I said, looking to Daphne. "We found your prints in the Range Rover and all over your husband's desk. We also found them on the firearm."

"Where did you even get my fingerprints?" she asked.

I tilted my head to the side.

"That was easy. You were a lawyer once, so you gave

the Missouri Bar Association permission to run a background check on you as part of its testing to ensure you had the character and fitness to practice law in the state of Missouri. They fingerprinted you as part of that test."

She gave me a sardonic look.

"I thought they destroyed those fingerprints."

"Nope."

She sighed and shook her head.

"The Range Rover was my ex-husband's car. I've borrowed it from Carl on multiple occasions, most recently to drive Ethan to college. And as far as my fingerprints on his desk…that sounds more like a concern to bring up with the housekeeping staff than to hang your hat on in court. I used to live here."

The look she gave me was pure smug.

"That's all true," I said. "But I know you were in St. Augustine."

"I was in St. Charles with my daughter," she said. "It's seventy-five miles away. I paid for everything with my credit card, so I can even get you a receipt."

"I don't doubt that your credit card was in St. Charles," I said, looking to Sheriff Delgado. He handed me a manila folder. I opened it and showed her the surveillance picture inside. "But you were in St. Augustine. This photograph is from a camera on the intersection of First Avenue and Bardstock Road in St. Augustine County. You were careful and obeyed all the traffic laws, but you couldn't control everyone around you. The guy in front of you ran a red light, and the camera caught you as well. This was a block from the Wayfair Motel. It's the easiest way to get to the interstate."

Daphne crossed her arms and tilted her head to the side.

"So what?" she asked, her voice softer than it had been earlier. "I've been to St. Augustine. Is that a crime?"

"Not at all, and we appreciate your tourist dollars," I said. "But the camera snapped the picture four minutes after the Range Rover left the Wayfair Motel. Tessa was alive when this car arrived at the Wayfair Motel, and she was dead when it left. You murdered Tessa because she and her boyfriend were robbing Carl blind, and he didn't even seem to care."

"Mom?" asked Ethan. Tyler walked toward his mother and put a hand on her shoulder while looking at me. Hannah looked at the floor and started to cry. I gave them all a minute to process what I had said. Daphne brought a hand to her face, but she didn't cry just yet. After about a minute, she brought her hands up.

"What the hell was I supposed to do?" she asked. "I told Carl that little tart was a problem, but he didn't believe me. I have one kid in college, and two who will go when their time comes. That bitch cleaned out their entire college fund. I couldn't pay Ethan's tuition. When I asked Carl about it, he said someone made a mistake."

"Did you confront Tessa?"

"No," she said. "I hired an accountant. She looked at Carl's transactions and told me what Tessa was doing. My accountant and I tried to tell Carl, but he told us that Tessa wasn't smart enough to rob from him. He was such a fucking idiot."

"You killed her and blamed him," I said.

"Mom," said Ethan, "don't say anything."

"It doesn't matter what I say now, honey," she said, touching her son's shoulder before looking at me. "I did it for my family. I preserved their legacy while they still had one. Because of me, my children will go to college, they'll have careers, and they'll raise families of their own. That was my job. I protected them. Sometimes protecting the ones we love means eliminating those who threaten them."

I would have told her that her kids could have gone to college and had wonderful careers even without trust funds, but she wouldn't have listened. Besides, I already had what I needed.

"Daphne Armstrong, as I said earlier, you're under arrest for the murder of Tessa Armstrong. We've got an hourlong drive to my station ahead of us. Will you cooperate and sit nicely, or do I need to handcuff you?"

"I did the right thing," she said. "A jury will see that. And you don't need handcuffs. I'm not a violent person."

The facts would seem to belie that statement, but I said nothing. I had spoken enough for the day. Delgado and I led her to our SUV and drove south to St. Augustine. It had been a tough few weeks. I'd closed cases and put bad guys in jail, but I'd also seen a lot of innocent people get hurt. Not only that, we hadn't solved everything yet. We'd shut down Mickey Lyons and his partners in St. Augustine, but we hadn't touched their organization's hierarchy. The Chicago Police Department wouldn't even return Sheriff Delgado's calls for information. In addition to that, Sheppard Altman and Rajendra Gavani were still out there. Maybe they were alive, or maybe they were dead. We didn't know.

My only certainty was that I needed a break. When we got back to town and processed Daphne Armstrong, I took the rest of the day off. In hot weather, I ran in the very early mornings so I wouldn't overheat. At this time of year, though, with gray clouds stretching across the horizon and the temperatures dipping into the forties on cool days, the world was my oyster.

I drove home, changed into some comfortable clothes, and grabbed a piece of beef jerky so Roy would get some exercise. Within half an hour of booking Daphne Armstrong for her ex-husband's murder and closing my case, my dog and I were stretching our legs on the trails behind my house. It felt wonderful.

The deeper Roy and I ran into those woods, the more I felt the rest of the world disappear. I didn't have to think about murder or drugs or overdoses. I could relax. Muscles all over my body released their pent-up tension. My chest felt light and good. About fifteen minutes into our run, Roy stopped. Even with beef jerky in my pocket, Roy wasn't big on exercise, so I knew he'd stop eventually. Usually he kept going until I gave him a treat, though.

I turned. Roy was sniffing and looking around. He

had a paw in the air as if he were pointing, and whenever the wind shifted, he'd pan his head around to follow the breeze.

"What do you smell, dude?"

The landscape in this part of my woods sloped downward toward a dry creek bed. Roy took a zigzagging path for about twenty or thirty feet, following a scent I couldn't detect. Then, he sat down in the dirt and looked at me. He looked so proud of himself I couldn't help but smile. And then, as I realized what he was doing and why he seemed proud of himself, the smile slipped from my face.

Roy flunked out of the program for being lazy, but he was a trained cadaver dog. He had just found a grave.

I ran my hands through my hair and looked around. There was a fallen silver maple tree to the east of Roy's position and a deer trail to the west. During the spring, water flowed down that trail to the creek like a miniature river. I didn't run here often because that creek became a mosquito breeding ground every time it rained. My gut started churning, and suddenly my legs trembled.

"Come here, Roy," I said.

The dog stood, exposing soft, broken dirt. My heart thudded against my rib cage but not because of the exercise. Peter Brunelle, the serial murderer in Terre Haute, had described a place just like this where he'd buried something he described as special. This wasn't right, though. He couldn't have been here.

I led Roy home and put him in the dog run before

going to the shed for a garden trowel and a tarp. When I reached the bare, broken spot in the woods where Roy had sat down, I laid out my tarp and began digging in the soil with my trowel. About a foot down, I found a thick, black trash bag. The plastic still felt smooth. Time had yet to rip a single hole in it. This was new.

My fingers trembled, but I kept digging until I found a seam I could pull open. I put my trowel down and slipped a finger into the joint, exposing the interior. Then I closed my eyes and held my breath so I wouldn't vomit.

Cold seeped through my body and into my bones. I stood but then fell backwards onto my ass. Then I scrambled to my feet again and leaned against a tree until my strength returned. I hurried to the house. Roy whined when he saw me and then dove into a play bow, so I opened the dog run's gate. He bounded out and followed me inside, where I took a couple more breaths and picked up my phone to call Special Agent Bryan Costa with the FBI.

"Hey, Joe," he said, his voice bright. "What can I do for you?"

I ran a trembling hand through my hair and cleared my throat so my voice wouldn't crack.

"I found Peter Brunelle's body dump," I said. "The one he told me about on the phone. It has the fallen tree, the creek, the mosquitos, all that."

Costa paused.

"Are you okay? You sound shaken."

"I am shaken," I said. "My dog just found a trash bag

full of goddamn heads in my backyard. And Bryan, they're fresh. They've still got skin and muscle and hair. This is new. The victims are all men, too."

"Brunelle's been in prison for over a decade. What do you mean they're fresh?"

"These heads aren't ten years old, and neither was the grave. It wasn't there two weeks ago, or Roy would have found it. Brunelle has a partner, and that partner knows where I live. I warned you about this. I told you he was working an angle."

Costa paused. "I'm on my way. I'll be there as soon as I can."

"Hurry," I said. I hung up the phone and went from room to room locking my windows and doors. Then I went to my bedroom, changed into some jeans and a clean shirt, and took my service pistol from the lockbox in my closet. Roy had good ears and a bark that carried long and far. He had flunked out of the cadaver dog program, but he was a great watchdog. He would have heard someone approach my house long before I did, and he didn't seem concerned. Still, I couldn't help but feel like someone was watching me from afar.

As I'd learn only weeks later, I had every reason in the world to worry.

Did you like *The Woman Who Wore Roses*? Then you're going to love The Man in the Park!

Detective Mary Joe Court returns in a twisted story of murder and lost identity in the sixth novel of New York Times' bestselling author Chris Culver's Joe Court series.

Joe was on a date when she got the call. A man's body was found beside the picnic tables in a local park. He has abrasions on his knuckles and several cuts on his palms and forearms. The victim defended himself, but his opponent brought a gun to a fistfight.

At first, it looks like a simple case, but as Joe quickly discovers, it's not.

The victim lives almost a thousand miles away. His wife says he's in town to fish and camp, but he didn't bring fishing tackle or a tent.

He came for an altogether different purpose.

As Joe investigates, she finds herself drawn into a dangerous world steeped in lies and deception. With every insight she gains and every clue she finds, she comes closer to solving her case. But with every second that passes, the people she's hunting draw closer to their prey.

It's a race with innocent victims as the prize. If Joe wins, she saves the day. If she loses, many will die…

Chris Culver

including her.

Paperbacks will be available on December 5, 2019!

Enjoy this book? You can make a big difference in my career

Reviews are the lifeblood of an author's career. I'm not exaggerating when I say they're the single best way I can get attention for my books. I'm not famous, I don't have the money for extravagant advertising campaigns, and I no longer have a major publisher behind me.

I do have something major publishers don't have, something they would kill to get:

Committed, loyal readers.

With millions of books in the world, your honest reviews and recommendations help other readers find me.

If you enjoyed the book you just read, I would be extraordinarily grateful if you could spend five minutes to leave a review on Amazon, Barnes and Noble, Goodreads, or anywhere else you review books. A review can be as long or as short as you'd like it to be, so please don't feel that you have to write something long.

Thank you so much!

Stay in touch with Chris

As much as I enjoy writing, I like hearing from readers even more. If you want to keep up with my world, there are a couple of ways you can do that.

First and easiest, I've got a mailing list. If you join, you'll receive an email whenever I have a new novel out or when I run sales. You can join that by going to this address:

http://www.indiecrime.com/mailinglist.html

If my mailing list doesn't appeal to you, you can also connect with me on Facebook here:

http://www.facebook.com/ChrisCulverbooks

And you can always email me at chris@indiecrime.com. I love receiving email!

About the Author

Chris Culver is the *New York Times* bestselling author of the Ash Rashid series and other novels. After graduate school, Chris taught courses in ethics and comparative religion at a small liberal arts university in southern Arkansas. While there and when he really should have been grading exams, he wrote *The Abbey*, which spent sixteen weeks on the *New York Times* bestsellers list and introduced the world to Detective Ash Rashid.

Chris has been a storyteller since he was a kid, but he decided to write crime fiction after picking up a dog-eared, coffee-stained paperback copy of Mickey Spillane's *I, the Jury* in a library book sale. Many years later, his wife, despite considerable effort, still can't stop him from bringing more orphan books home. He lives with his family near St. Louis.

Made in the USA
Coppell, TX
10 April 2021

53505473R00229